Han adjusted his position so he was lying on the floor like Duff. "They call you Fat Sherlock on the streets, you know."

"I've heard better nicknames. My friends call me Thor."

"No, we don't," said Abe.

"They used to call me Viper."

"Never did that, either," said Abe.

Han propped his head up on his hand. "You know what they call me?"

"Is it Zeppo? I feel like it's Zeppo."

Sean Patrick Little

BRING THE HEAT

An Abe & Duff Mystery

SPILLED INC. PRESS

Published by Spilled Inc. Press, Sun Prairie, Wis.
Printed and bound in the United States of America.

Lyrics to "Summer in the City" by The Lovin' Spoonful used with permission from John Sebastian.

ISBN: 979-8-218-68602-4

Fiction - Mystery - detective - soft-boiled

For everyone who keeps reading.
I couldn't do this without you.

BRING THE HEAT

1

CLIVE STAPLES DUFFY was bored. He stared into the middle distance in a vain attempt to force his mind to go blank, but it wasn't working. He had never been able to meditate. He didn't understand how someone could empty their mind. In his head, thirty different trains of thought careened down his mental tracks at any given moment. All fought for dominance. All were important. It had been that way his entire life. He envied people with no internal monologue because he had never had a moment's rest from his, not even while he slept.

Duff stood on the roof of an apartment building. The rattle and hum of Chicago's busy streets played out ten floors below him. It was an unholy sweatbox of a summer night. The temperatures were still near eighty degrees even after sunset. No breeze, just thick, damp humidity lying over the metro like a wet blanket. July was pounding the Midwest with the kind of heat that made most of the region's denizens long for the gentle caress of a negative-ten wind chill.

As a larger-than-factory-standard guy, even wearing a t-shirt and jeans made Duff uncomfortably warm in this weather. He considered stripping down to his skivvies but decided against it in case he needed to vacate the roof in a hurry. He would ride the night out with a layer of sweat over his body and a graduated case of swamp-ass.

As if the heat wasn't torture enough, Duff was saddled with an earworm that would not leave him alone. He hated the Lovin' Spoonful, just as he hated most popular music, but John Sebastian's lyrics were stuck on endless repeat in his brain, and he could not help but hum the melody while mumbling the words in his flat, atonal way.

Hot town, summer in the city…

It angered him to an irrational level that the song was stuck in his head, but it fit the moment, and it somehow decided to loop itself endlessly through his brain.

Back of my neck gettin' dirty and gritty…

Duff was on a stakeout. It was a low-stakes stakeout, but a stakeout nonetheless. Earlier in the week, a woman had come to the spartan office of Allard & Duffy Investigations and asked them to procure proof of her husband's extramarital affair.

Vicky Bloch's husband, Robert, hired a new secretary two months ago. He had been promoted in his company at the beginning of the year and treated himself to a twenty-something, blonde, former bikini model as a personal assistant. His wife instantly went on high alert.

According to Vicky Bloch, their marriage was already strained, and they were drifting apart. If Abe and Duff could bring her proof of her husband's infidelity, she would be able to destroy him in divorce court.

It wasn't Duff's favorite sort of case, but it paid well, and it was low-risk. It was the sort of low-fuss case that often paid the rent on their office, which was also Duff's home, so they took it.

Been down, isn't it a pity…

Abe and Duff tailed the guy for a few days, and earlier that afternoon, the mark went into a nice, but not overly nice, hotel and secured a room. Duff watched him leave the lobby with a plastic card key.

It took $200 cash slipped to the college kid working the front desk to learn the room number. It took another five minutes of triangulating the room and figuring out the easiest way to look into the room's windows. A building across the street from the hotel had a rooftop practically on the same level.

Doesn't seem to be a shadow in the city…

Duff slipped the building superintendent a pair of crisp Benjamins for one night's loan of a key to the rooftop door. The guy couldn't have cared less and probably would've given him the key for nothing, but a little profit keeps people from asking too many questions.

Duff went back to the apartment and dug out his camera from the mess in his closet, an expensive Leica digital DSLR with a beast of a telephoto lens, the same sort of gear NFL photographers use to capture the most exciting moments. The lens was a few thousand dollars, the Leica was almost eight grand on sale. Duff's business partner, Abe Allard, had blanched at purchasing it at first, but Duff argued it would eventually pay for itself. It made them money over the years, and it was still a good camera, so Duff won that debate.

After nightfall, Duff made his way to the rooftop across the street from the hotel with the camera, a two-liter bottle of Diet Coke, and a Jimmy John's Hunter's Club sub for a late-night snack.

All around, people lookin' half-dead…

Then, it was just like any other stakeout. Watch the room. Try not to nod off. Get the pictures. Go home.

The problem with any stakeout was a lack of a solid time frame. Stakeouts took as long as they took. There was no way to hurry them along. Was the guy even coming back to the room? If so, when? There were a lot of variables in play.

Many times over the years, Abe and Duff had done a stakeout only to spend twelve or fourteen hours doing diddly-squat and come up snake-eyes with nothing to show for their efforts.

Duff was on the roof for more than three hours. It was after midnight, and his cell phone battery was already down to thirty percent. He had been reading Wikipedia articles for fun and distraction. It wasn't quite as satisfying as reading an actual book, but now he knew a lot more about Chief Crazy Horse, Spetznas, and the wreck of the *Andrea Doria* than he had earlier that day, so the night wasn't a total waste.

The song continued to linger in his brain.

Walkin' on the sidewalk…

The hotel room flooded with light. The pop of the white-yellow glow in the previously dark windows roused Duff's interest. He brought the camera to his eye and peered through the viewfinder. The hotel room was brought into sudden clarity, as if it were within arm's reach. Duff adjusted the telephoto lens and trained it on the room beyond the glass window. There was no action for a moment, but Duff saw a shadow moving along the wall near the door. After another second, a man emerged into the light.

It was Robert Bloch. However, he was alone. That was unexpected. Where was the blonde?

The husband was dressed in a black business suit, tie hanging loosely, and a bottle of something in his right hand. Duff zoomed in on it. Cheap whiskey, looked like Evan Williams. The bottle was half-empty. The man walked to the floor-to-ceiling window and leaned against it, his head resting on his left forearm as he peered to the street far below. His posture revealed sadness and utter defeat.

Duff felt the hackles on the back of his neck rise. Something was wrong. Nothing about this man's demeanor was of someone planning on having wild hotel sex with a former bikini model. Nothing about his bearing showed confidence. This was not a guy who was cheating on his wife. Duff started taking pictures. Was the dude going to jump? Something in Duff's gut told him Bloch might jump.

Duff held down the shutter button, and the automatic Leica clicked picture after picture as if he were shooting an animated sequence on film.

...hotter than a match head.

The window splintered; one entire eight-foot-by-eight-foot glass pane spider-webbed. A millisecond after that, Duff heard the telltale crack of a high-powered gun, a sniper or hunting rifle, something long-range, long-barreled. Behind the shattered glass, Bloch took two steps backward. Duff saw a crimson bloom spreading across the man's chest from a gunshot wound to the heart. The poor guy barely had time to register what happened before he collapsed. Duff knew the shooter had done his job well. The target was dead before he hit the floor.

Duff looked up from the viewfinder of the camera and searched the area around him. He spun in a slow circle. Everything was shadows and darkness. He had no idea where the shot originated. Given the height of the shot, he didn't know if it would even register on the city's Shotspotter alert system. The report of the rifle caromed off nearby buildings, obscuring the direction of its origin. The constant drone of the city night swallowed up any echo.

Duff continued to rock in a slow circle. He thumbed his phone and called 911 to report the murder. He hung up before the operator could ask too many questions. He texted Abe to meet him at the hotel on the double. Then he called another number on his phone, police detective Malcolm Betts, a police liaison and sometimes foil of Abe and Duff. They'd worked together many, many times before.

Betts answered on the fourth ring.

Duff didn't wait for a hello. "Good morning, sunshine. I have a murder for you."

But at night, it's a different world...

2

TALLER AND MUCH thinner than Duff, Aberforth Allard stood by the hotel's front doors watching the steady stream of activity as a cadre of Chicago's Finest prepared the crime scene. There was a constant in-and-out flow of police through the lobby.

Duff sat on a low rock wall next to Abe. He kicked his feet out and let the heels of his unlaced Nike high-tops bounce off the wall like dulcimer hammers while he mumbled the lyrics to the same Lovin' Spoonful song plaguing him all night. He began to fear he'd never get it out of his head. *"Go out and find a girl…come on, come on, and dance all night…"*

"If you don't stop singing that song, I'm going to shoot you in the knee."

Duff stopped singing long enough to point out the fact that his partner was not carrying a gun. Neither was he. Being unarmed was typical for both of them. There were not really gun guys.

Abe nodded toward the swirl of blue uniforms. "I'll borrow one. Do you think there's a cop on the Chicago PD who wouldn't love to watch you catch a bullet?"

"That seems harsh."

"But true."

"But true," Duff conceded.

A black, unmarked Chevy Tahoe pulled to the curb, a single spinning cherry on the dash and emergency flashers below the bumper. Police Detective Malcolm Betts was out of the driver's side door quickly. He was dressed in a black blazer over a black t-shirt paired with jeans. Normally, he was a coat-and-tie guy, slacks, not denim. He'd recently shaved the bushy mustache he'd worn for more than a year, so the sight of a bare upper lip on

Betts was still unsettling. Betts was a creature of refined habit, so any change was automatically disturbing.

Diana Gates, Betts's partner for the last year, slid out of the passenger side. She was a tough, no-nonsense Latina with long, straight, black hair and dark, but fiery eyes. She wore jeans as well, but she had managed to find a button-up shirt. She wore Nike cross-trainers instead of flats.

Getting a late-night call rousting you from a warm bed was always tough. Professionalism was difficult if you'd only been asleep for two hours. Both Betts and Gates were carrying paper cups of Dunkin' coffee the size of pony kegs.

Betts launched straight into the standard verbal volley when he saw the two PIs waiting for them. "How do you twits manage to find yourselves in these sorts of messes?"

"It's a gift." Duff tilted his head toward the cup in Betts's hand. "You stopped for coffee and didn't bring donut holes? Seems rude, Malcolm."

"Donut holes are for good little boys who don't wake me up after midnight."

"Do you want a good murder case or not? You should be honored that you're the first person I thought of when I saw it happen."

Malcolm blew into the top of his cup to cool down the lava-hot brew inside. "Fine. Tell me everything."

"Well, my parents met in 1972 at a little country bar outside of Waukesha, Wisconsin—"

Betts cut Duff off before he could elaborate. "I meant about the shooting, dumbass."

"You didn't specify when you told me to tell you everything. I thought we were having a moment."

"We're not. We never will, either. No moments for us, ever."

Duff turned to Gates and started to open his mouth, but she held up a finger to stop him cold. "You and I will *never* have a moment, fat man. Don't even pretend to ask."

"Your mouth says *no*, but your eyes say *hell no*."

"Got that right." Gates sipped her coffee. "Now spill it."

Duff raised a hand like a nervous student. "Before I start with the murder, can I ask about the new woman you're seeing Uncle Malky?"

This stopped Gates in her tracks. She spun on her partner. "You're seeing someone?"

Betts scowled at Duff. "What the fuck makes you say that?"

Duff listed reasons on his fingers. "You shaved your 1970's gay porn mustache, and your formerly salt-and-pepper temples are now all pepper, which means you've been combing Just For Men through your hair every morning. I'm going to assume this new lady was not a fan of mustache rides, and the hair dye is so you can look younger. This means she's younger, probably, what, early-to-mid-thirties? She's at least ten years younger than you, probably more. You are wearing a new t-shirt that's a little tighter than the shirts you normally favor, so that means you're trying to show off a little more. You also smell faintly of lavender, which means you either switched detergents—which I highly doubt because you're a Tide man through and through—or you've been seeing a woman who favors that scent. In fact, I'd be willing to wager that when I called you, you had probably been asleep in her bed because you were both all tuckered out from making the humpy-bumpy mattress beast. I'd put money on the notion that earlier tonight, you fully nuded up and went for gold in the undressed olympics. Probably got a six-point-five from the Russian judge, though."

Gates's mouth dropped open. All thoughts of the murder were temporarily put on hold. Malcolm Betts seeing someone who wasn't just a gun bunny he picked up from a bar was big news. "You *are* seeing someone. Spill it. Who is she?"

Betts tried to deflect. "Let's focus, people. A man was just murdered."

Duff said, "Statistically speaking, two people get murdered in Chicago every day, but you getting laid is an anomaly of the highest order."

Betts wheeled on the portly detective. He jabbed a finger in Duff's face. "Fuck off, Chubs. I hate it when you pull that Sherlock Holmes bullshit on me."

"Just tell us her name, and we'll move to the murder."

Betts heaved a heavy sigh and rubbed at his eyes. "Her name is Hannah, and I just met her a couple of weeks ago."

"Hannah. I love it!" Gates seemed more excited for her partner than he did. "It's about time you found someone. Dry spell over."

"Shut the hell up, all of you. Let's get to the murder, please." Betts turned to Abe because he knew he could count on Abe to get to the facts. "What do you know, Aberforth?"

Abe cleared his throat. "The victim is Robert Bloch. He's forty-one, married, and was recently promoted at his job. He is an accountant for Hanley, Dodge, and Briscoe."

"Why were you following him?"

"His wife thought he was boinking his secretary." Duff circled his forefinger and thumb and jabbed his other forefinger through the loop in the familiar playground gesture.

"Was he?"

Duff shrugged. "Not to my knowledge. We were operating on the notion that he was going to boink the secretary tonight, but instead he caught a bullet."

"Was she in the room?"

"He was alone. Didn't look like he was expecting company, either."

Betts frowned, a series of wrinkles creasing his brow heavily. "I can already tell this one is going to be a headache."

Duff pushed himself off his seat on the rock wall. He wiggled his fingers. "Do I get to wear the purple gloves this time?"

Betts opened the door to the hotel and held it for the others. "No, you get to stand by the doorway and touch nothing."

"What if there's a bunny in there? Would you expect me not to touch a fuzzy bunny? Because let me tell you something, mister—if there's a bunny in there, I'm goddamn touching it."

"Fine, if there's a bunny, you can hold it. Just don't go all *Of Mice and Men* on me."

Abe and Duff followed the cops into the hotel lobby. Duff leaned into Abe and looked up at him with a simpleton's puppy-eyed stare. "Tell me about the rabbits, George."

ALL HOTELS SMELL the same. Abe was no connoisseur of hotel scents by any stretch, but every hotel he'd ever been in smelled identical, and Hotel Afton was no exception. Abe had a sensitive nose, and he could always pick out the underlying scent of old cigarettes in hotels that were more than thirty years old. No amount of cleaning removed the decades of nicotine caked into the walls from the before-time when cigarettes were ubiquitous. Piled on top of that was the reek of cleaning chemicals. It was as if all hotels bought supplies from the same wholesaler. If the hotel had a pool, there was usually a tinge of chlorine, but the Afton lacked in that regard, so there were only old cigarettes, cleansers, and the deeply pervasive funk of time.

The Afton was once a high-end hotel in the days of the Rat Pack and even into the early 1980s. It was one of the hippest places to stay for touring musical acts and visiting celebrities. Now, it passed as a *nice* hotel, the kind people only frequented because of the history, or because they thought it had an old-fashioned sense of character that modern establishments lacked. The hotel was bordering on being shady and sketchy, but it remained serviceable, not yet cascading into the realm of low-end establishments where rent-by-the-hour was on the service menu. It wasn't Abe's normal sort of hotel because he favored basic, lower-end chain hotels, the sort typically found at interstate highway exits, but Abe liked it, aside from the odor.

The quartet took an elevator to the ninth floor. They walked a long hallway decorated with a deep red industrial carpet worn thin in the center from the shoes of thousands of customers. A pair of uniformed officers stood on either side of the door to the room. They stepped aside without a word when Betts flashed his badge. The police detective gestured at Abe and Duff with his thumb. "They're with me."

The room Robert Bloch rented was painfully standard, as far as hotel rooms went. Plain, light gray, patterned carpet on the floor. The walls were a cool greige color, something from the lighter end of the Sherwin-Williams gray charts. A generic, mass-produced art print in a cheap frame was anchored to the wall over the king-sized bed. A standard bathroom was close to the entryway. A flat-screen TV hung on the wall at the foot of the bed over a long, low credenza. A black, faux leather wing chair with a small, circular wooden table was in the corner. A wall-mounted air conditioner was next to the window. It was the sort of room people booked for overnight business stays or illicit sexual escapades. It was a practical, no-nonsense room for people who wanted something fancier than a Holiday Inn, but less expensive than a DoubleTree.

Duff wrinkled his nose at the digs. "Not really the sort of room I'd splurge on if I was trying to impress a bikini model."

"Would you ever try to impress a bikini model?" asked Abe.

"Only if she was really into seeing how many California burritos a dude can house in a single sitting."

A medical examiner knelt by the body. He was young-ish, but still on the job long enough to have the grizzled expression of someone who had seen this sort of thing too many times already. The medical examiner wore a coat and tie, no Tyvek body cover. A hotel room was a terrible place for crime scene evidence because who knows how many hair fibers, skin cells, and god-knows-what other sorts of genetic markers could be found due to the innumerable masses staying in the room before the crime. Plus, given the nature of the crime and the fact that Duff caught it on film while it happened, scrubbing the room for DNA or fingerprints was irrelevant and a waste of time.

The late Robert Bloch was flat on his back in a modified starfish pose, arms angled downward instead of straight out to the sides. His legs were splayed. His head was in a neutral position with eyes closed and mouth open in a slack, resting manner. If not for the large red stain in the center of his chest, he would have looked as if he had passed out from drinking.

The bottle of whiskey he'd been holding was on its side near his feet; a considerable amount had emptied onto the carpet. It was currently perfuming the air with fragrant hints of Kentucky's favorite export.

The ME looked up as Betts and Gates approached. He nodded a greeting. "Pretty clear-cut here. Looks like it was right in the heart. Death was almost instantaneous. I won't know the type of gun that killed him until I do the autopsy and remove the bullet, but I'd guess that it was a good-sized long-distance weapon, given what the fat guy told me before I came up to the room."

Duff pretended to be insulted. "The fat guy has a name, you know."

"But he still answers to fat guy." Betts took a knee next to the ME. He pulled on a pair of purple nitrile gloves. He pointed at the two private detectives for the ME's benefit. "Gary, this is Abe Allard, and the fat guy is Duff. Boys, this is Gary Schuck, one of our newest medical examiners."

Schuck nodded a greeting. "Just Duff? Only one name like Cher?"

Duff nodded back at the ME. "It seemed fitting because I also believe in life after love."

"No, you don't," said Gates.

"That's true. I'm not much of a fan of life or love."

Betts leaned over the body and searched the man's pockets. "Abe and Duff were tailing the victim because they're private investigators. As you said, the fat one saw the murder happen."

"Long-range rifle. Had to be. Quick and clean," said Duff.

The ME glanced at the spider-webbed window. A dime-sized hole in the glass whistled as air sucked through it. "I thought all these tall buildings would have ballistic glass."

"Not even close. Too expensive." At one point in his undergrad years, Abe had briefly considered becoming an architect, but a lack of creativity hampered him. He wasn't a big dreamer who could think up grand designs. That fact had not stopped him from reading several books about the field. "Most hotels have heat-strengthened glass, and some might even have armored glass, but ballistic glass is extremely expensive and not part of code for any building at this point."

The ME was impressed. "You're hanging out with a higher quality of people lately, Malcolm. I approve."

"Gary, if you think these idiots are high quality, you need to get out more." Betts searched the dead man's pockets. He produced a small money clip with a modest stash of twenties, nothing extravagant or alarming. He found a key fob with a couple of keys. He found a pen, just a cheap one, the type stocked in every office in America. He rolled the body slightly and pulled Bloch's wallet from the back pocket of the man's slacks.

Betts flipped through the wallet. "Nothing out of the ordinary." He tossed the wallet over his shoulder to Duff. "Do your little party trick now and solve this thing by looking around the room."

Duff gave the room another cursory glance. He gave the body a once-over. "He went to Northwestern, was left-handed, and has been thinking about divorce for a long time."

"How? How'd you figure that out from a dead body?" Gates hated Duff's ability to read people. "It's because you've been following him, right?"

"Nope. Gathered those three details just now."

"How?" The junior police detective put her hands on her hips and waited for an explanation.

"His cuff links are purple and have the NU seal on them. His left hand has ink on his wrist and the meaty part of the hand below his little finger. That means he was writing and dragging his hand across the page like southpaws are prone to do. Also, if you look at his left hand, he isn't wearing a wedding band. He hasn't worn one in so long that you can no longer see the lighter band of skin around the finger that comes from wearing rings. Now, that could be because he doesn't like rings, but since his wife came to us about possibly starting divorce proceedings against him, I'm betting he stopped wearing the ring months ago when the marriage hit the big rocks, and his wife just never noticed because couples on the edge of divorce stop looking at each other."

"But nothing about who shot him?" said Betts. "Big help you are."

Duff snorted. "Betts, it's a hotel room, and the dude got punked by a sniper. What do you expect me to do?"

"I figured you'd have some sort of silly magic tricks up your sleeve where you look at how he combs his hair, and from that you figure out he's a Russian spy or something."

"I'm good, but I can't invent things that aren't there." Duff started flipping through Bloch's wallet. He pulled out the credit cards, the driver's license, and a few stray bills. Combined with the money clip, Bloch was far from rolling large. "He was carrying less than a hundred bucks."

"What does that mean?" asked Gates.

"It means a short night at a strip club." Duff tossed the wallet back to Betts. "Nothing in here means anything to me. Give me a pair of your silly little gloves."

Betts hesitated. "Why don't you just tell me what you want to look at, and I'll do it."

"Take his shoes off."

"Why?"

"I put money in my shoes sometimes. It's a good hiding place."

Betts pulled the man's shoes. They were black Florsheim Oxfords, not necessarily cheap shoes, but they weren't the sort of high-end product that breaks the bank, either. The police detective looked inside them. "Nothing."

"Pull the insole," said Duff.

Betts did as asked and came up with nothing. He threw Bloch's left shoe to Duff.

Duff caught it, glanced it over, and tossed it back. "What about his jacket pockets?"

"Cell phone. That's all." Gary held up the cell phone. It had escaped unscathed from the bullet.

"Can I look at it?"

"It's screen-locked." Gary pushed the power button, and a password screen appeared.

"See if he has a biometric lock."

"And how do I do that? Just use a dead man's finger to open his phone? Is that even legal?" The ME looked to the two police detectives for confirmation.

Betts shrugged. "Legal enough. It's not like we're going to be charging him with any crimes at this point."

The ME picked up Bloch's lifeless hand and touched the index finger to the small, circular indent on the back of the phone. Nothing happened. "Swipe pattern or nothing, looks like. We got tech guys who can get past this stuff, if necessary."

"Give the fat guy the phone." Gates took a step back from the body and leaned against the wall near the TV. "He's a little hinky when it comes to things like that."

Shuck tossed the phone to Duff, who caught it out of the air, bobbled it, nearly dropped it, but managed to secure it after a series of awkward near-grabs.

Betts bit back a condescending chuckle. "For a guy who wears a baseball cap all the time, you suck at catching."

"I'm a stats guy, not an athlete." Duff moved to the desk lamp on the little circular table in the corner. He angled the phone into the light. "A lot of times, if it's not cleaned regularly, the gorilla glass on these cell phones can get stained by the oils on our fingers, and it leaves a pretty easy path to follow." Duff stared at the glass for a few more seconds and then began trying a series of zig-zag swipes across the phone. After a few seconds, he held up the unlocked phone screen in triumph. "Easy-peasy."

Betts snatched the phone from Duff's hand. "A grown man shouldn't say easy-peasy."

"You just did."

"Only to point out how stupid it sounds when a grown man says it."

Abe and Duff moved behind Betts to watch as he cycled through the various apps looking for information or clues. Gates crowded next to him. "Duff was right; you do smell like lavender."

"Hush your face." Betts looked through the texts on Bloch's phone and found them mundane. "Nothing but a few boring business texts and a couple of texts from his wife, basic and terse exchanges about what to have for dinner and weekend plans. I'm going to assume they don't have kids."

"They do not." Abe knew firsthand that if the Blochs did have kids, the text chain between them would have a lot more back-and-forth about the children and not just dinner. His text chain with his ex-wife, Katherine, consisted solely of exchanges concerning their teenage daughter, Matilda.

Betts checked the email app. It was nothing but a secondary access point for his business emails. Betts glanced through the first few. They looked mundane at first blush, as well.

"Check the trash folder." Duff tried to reach over Betts's shoulder to tap the icon, only to get his hand slapped.

Betts tapped the trash folder and found only more mundane emails. "This guy must have been one of the most boring humans on the planet." He clicked into Bloch's camera folders and found nothing but boring photos of Bloch, his wife Vicky, and their escapades to various restaurants, wine tastings, and hiking trails around the area. No kids. No pets. No hobbies.

Duff was unimpressed. "No nude photos. No salacious texts from the bikini model. No emails other than things concerning work. Nothing fun at all. Maybe this dude paid someone to shoot him just to get him out of his boring-ass life."

"Is that how you plan to go?" asked Betts.

Duff feigned an indignant reaction. "I plan to have a massive coronary due to obesity and an unhealthy lifestyle like a real American."

"Tomorrow?"

"If I'm lucky." Duff reached out and tried to touch another app, but Betts slapped his hand again.

"You look with your eyes, not your fingers. Just tell me what you want to see."

"There's a notes function in Google's office suite. Go there."

Betts found the app and opened it. There was a single note, and that note contained a single name. "Who is Jennifer Rose Carthage?"

Duff pulled out his phone and typed the name. Google returned a slew of pictures of a slim, stacked strawberry blonde in sexy, but not lewd, poses in various bikinis across various tropical locales. Duff showed the phone to the group. "I think we found our bikini model-turned-secretary."

Gates gave a low whistle. "I don't even swing that way, but I would have hired her, too. That's a ridiculous body."

"Her body is perfect. Duff's is ridiculous," said Betts.

Duff smoothed his t-shirt over his stomach. "At Golden Corral, I'm considered quite svelte, thank you."

Betts opened a few more apps on the phone but found nothing noteworthy. He looked at the contacts menu. There were almost thirty names in it. "It'll take a while to go through these and clear them as suspects."

Gates moved toward the window and looked with one eye through the small hole where the bullet pierced the glass. "Shot could have come from just about any of those buildings out there."

Duff pointed out where he'd been on the roof across the street. "It came from either left or right of that building."

"That narrows it down slightly."

Gates looked at the entry hole in the victim's chest and took an educated guess. "I figure our victim got hit with something domestic and easy to attain, probably a thirty-ought-six or something similar."

"That's the sort of gun owned by every deer hunter in the Midwest." Abe was not a hunter, but he had a decent working knowledge of guns; it was a byproduct of being in his line of work.

Gates said, "Given the method of murder, I would lean toward considering this to be something professional."

"A mob hit?" Duff scoffed at the premise. It didn't make sense. "Mob guys like to get up close and personal. They like their targets to feel some fear first. It sends a message to others who might try to cross them. They like to strap the victim to a chair and tenderize them for a while before killing them and dumping their body somewhere public as a warning. If this is professional, it's murder-for-hire, but those are extremely rare. Even rarer than mob hits. Let's face it, organized crime ain't what it used to be."

"Who profits from this man's death?" Abe knew the two main reasons for murder were passion and money. Something like this almost always came down to money. Figuring out who stood to gain the most from Bloch's death was the best way to find suspects.

"The wife," said Betts. "It's always the wife. She'll be the beneficiary of any of his life insurance policies, I'm sure. Big ol' payout if the hubby snuffs it."

"Vicky Bloch would have gotten more in a divorce settlement over time, I think. Bloch just received a healthy promotion. She would need a massive life insurance policy to make it worth risking her freedom to kill this guy before a divorce settlement," said Abe.

"We'll look into it." Betts gave up on the phone, relinquishing further information. He handed it to Gary Shuck to be bagged. "But usually with a murder-for-hire, we find the spouse put up a brand new life insurance policy with a big payout a few weeks ago. It's a dead giveaway."

"What about his car?" Duff pointed to the pile of items Betts had gotten from Bloch's pockets. The key fob for a Toyota was lying next to the wallet. "Might be something in his car."

Betts grabbed the fob. "Let's check it out."

THE PARKING GARAGE beneath the Hotel Afton was only two levels deep. It was not a huge space, but the majority of people using the hotel were taking cabs or Uber, not driving.

Betts led the group out of the elevator. He clicked the lock button on the fob, and somewhere in the garage, a car bleated a short, shrill honk. They walked deeper into the ramp with Betts intermittently hitting the fob buttons until they saw the lights blink on a black Toyota Highlander.

The SUV was the sort of vehicle Duff called *typical Yuppie trash*. Overpriced, but reliable. No one in Chicago truly *needed* an SUV, no matter how bad the snow was, but it was a status symbol. It was cooler than a sedan or minivan and more practical than a pickup truck for commuting. A guy making a certain amount of money needed a distinguished black vehicle to show he was rolling large. Maybe the Highlander wasn't quite Land Rover status, but Bloch had only recently gotten his big promotion. Perhaps an upgrade would have happened in the future.

Betts popped the locks on the Toyota, and everyone took a door, with Betts in the driver's position. They scoured through the car with practiced efficiency. Duff rooted through the glove compartment and found only the owner's manual and the paperwork from the dealership of the car's purchase. Gates and Abe took the backseat, and both came up empty-handed. Betts found nothing of worth in the driver's door or the center console. The entire cabin of the SUV was devoid of character. Betts even checked the radio and found Bloch had only programmed two channels: WBEZ and WFMT, Chicago's home for NPR and classical music, respectively.

Duff gave a low whistle. "This guy might be even more boring than Abe."

"Hey, you're boring, too." Abe could not deny Duff had a point, though. Robert Bloch seemed like a video game NPC. He had no character, no wit, and no *joie de vivre*.

Abe had flashbacks of how he, himself, behaved toward the end of his marriage when he and Katherine were walking on eggshells around each other, both too afraid to admit what was happening between them. Abe stopped doing things at home because he did not want to make Katherine angry. She had become snippy and unreasonable with him. He worked longer hours to stay away from the house. When he was there, he spent his time helping Matilda with schoolwork at the kitchen table because Katherine was holed up in the bedroom upstairs with the door locked. Abe had taken to sleeping on the couch because he knew he was no longer welcome in the bed he once shared with his wife. All the pieces of his marriage finally crumbled when Katherine finally accepted who she was and announced her long-denied sexuality. After that, she relaxed, Abe relaxed, and they were able to come to an amicable, even friendly, détente between them.

Duff walked to the back of the SUV and popped the rear hatch. "Got a briefcase back here."

Abe had a gut feeling based on what he sensed in Bloch's situation and behavior. "Check it for divorce paperwork."

Duff unsnapped the latches of the black leather Samsonite case. Inside were a half-dozen manila folders with stacks of spreadsheets in them, and beneath the folders, bound with an alligator clip, was a thick pile of papers for formal divorce proceedings filled out by a lawyer. Duff was impressed. "Nicely done, partner. I might make a detective of you, yet."

Gates snagged the stack of papers from Duff. "I get how fat boy does the Sherlock Holmes tricks, but how'd you know what was in there?"

Abe felt himself blushing. "I just felt a kinship with the guy. I know the signs of a man heading for a breakup."

"Life experience, right?" Gates flipped through the sheaf of divorce papers. "Looks like boilerplate stuff. Division of assets was going to be fifty-fifty. No alimony or child support. It looks like Robert Bloch wanted a quick, clean, no-fuss divorce."

"Which puts the wife back up to suspect numero uno." Betts closed two doors on the driver's side of the SUV and walked to the back. He skimmed the divorce papers over Gates's shoulder. "If she wanted to get paid, but knew he was going to come out with a no-fault, simple separation, she might have grounds to pop him before he could file, then she gets everything, insurance or not."

Abe pieced together everything he knew of Vicky Bloch, which was not much. She did not appear unhinged or violent. She was upset at her husband's recent emotional distance from her, and she assumed his distance had something to do with an affair. She mentioned specifically that she did not want to divorce her husband, but she also said if he was having an affair, she wanted to destroy him in the divorce.

Abe also knew people have killed other people over dumber things than money.

Duff pulled up the carpet in the trunk. He exposed the access panel for the tire kit. Underneath, he found the donut spare, the jack, and the tire iron. Not finding anything of worth, Duff opened the storage compartment on the right side of the rear. A matte black Ruger nine-millimeter rolled out of the space and thumped loudly on the spare tire.

Duff took a step back, hands raising as if someone was pointing the gun at him. "Get your purple gloves, Detective. Something tells me that gun is up to no good."

"How'd you know there was a gun in there?" Gates fumbled in her back pocket for a pair of latex gloves.

Duff continued holding his hands at surrender. "Honestly, that was pure luck. I didn't figure I'd find anything. I was just being Curious George."

Betts looked into the little storage recess in the Highlander. "Why did he have a gun in such a difficult-to-access spot? If I'm carrying a weapon for protection, I'm sure as hell not hiding it in the trunk."

Gates hefted the gun with her gloves on, ejected the magazine, and made certain the chamber was empty before she set it back on the trunk's floor. "I got two answers: one, he didn't know it was in there because someone else put it there."

"Seems unlikely," said Betts.

"Two, he either did something bad with this and hadn't found an opportunity to have gotten rid of it, or he was going to do something bad with it, and he just hadn't had a chance to do it."

Betts radioed for a uniform to bring an evidence bag to the garage. "You know, I could be waking up in an hour or two and having a lovely breakfast with Hannah. Instead, I'm in a garage with a new case that's probably unsolvable with Shemp and Gummo. This is not how I wanted to start my Saturday morning."

"If it helps, you can buy me a lovely breakfast, Malcolm." Duff gave the police detective his sweetest smile. "I know a place with a wonderful country-style eggs Benedict."

"Duff, try not to take this the wrong way, but if I ever find myself in a spot where you're my only option for a breakfast date, I'm going to eat a bullet, instead."

The radio at Diana Gates's hip crackled with static. A female uniformed officer's voice came through the fuzz with a clipped announcement. "Found the shooter's nest."

Betts saw a pair of young uniformed officers get off the elevator with evidence kits and gloves. "Bag the gun. Bag the divorce papers. Give the car a once-over and see if there's anything I missed." To Abe and Duff, he said, "C'mon, geniuses. Let's see if you can find anything before I tell you to get out of my sight."

3

WHEN A SHOOTING occurs, it falls on the rank and file police officers to spread out, ask questions, get statements, and search the perimeter while the detectives and supervisors get the glory work of securing the immediate crime scene and processing evidence.

It's thankless work. Most of the people from whom the uniforms have to take statements never saw the shooting, but they like the attention nonetheless, so they embellish their accounts or straight-up lie to be involved in the action. The rest of the witnesses, those who aren't excited to be interviewed, are mostly either indifferent or hostile. They give one-word answers, argue about things they don't need to argue about, make bizarre statements about their Constitutional rights, and have a tendency to view the police as the enemy. This shooting, having happened many stories above the street, was light on eyewitnesses.

Because there was no one to interview directly, this meant the uniforms had the task of going to all the nearby buildings that could have harbored the shooter's nesting site, finding the building supervisor to gain access to otherwise locked rooms and roofs, and searching all possible places where the shooter might have been hiding. Sometimes, no matter how hard they search, the uniforms don't find anything. It can be morale-destroying.

Finding a sniper's nest was a major win for a patrol officer. It meant moving up in the eyes of supervisors. It meant a possible naming in the write-up of the investigation. Most importantly, it meant going home feeling like what they did that night contributed to the investigation, instead of giving the lonely crazies a willing ear to listen to them expound about a crime they never saw.

The shooter's nest was discovered by patrol officer Jo Dunbar. She had been on the force just long enough to still be thought of as *new*, but was no longer considered a rookie. Dunbar was late to the police game, not deciding to go after a shield until she was in her early thirties, after earning a sociology degree from DePaul, and after spending a little time in the county system as a social worker trying to help the less fortunate.

She and her partner, Keith Schrader, were combing the buildings based on the intel Duff gave the CPD of the shooter's potential locations. The building to Duff's right had been just barely too short to give the shooter a decent look into Bloch's room, but Dunbar figured out the building one street back would have had a perfect rooftop to angle down and see the entirety of the victim's window.

While Schrader spoke to the building super, Dunbar reconnoitered the high-rise tenement and rode the elevator to the top floor. She located the roof access door and found someone had crowbarred the lock from the door. She knew she was in the right place. In a matter of moments, she found a spot where the fine, white pea gravel on the roof had been disturbed, a place where the shooter had hunkered down with binoculars to wait for his target. The rooftop ledge had a perfect view of Bloch's hotel room.

Betts introduced Dunbar to Abe and Duff. She made no fuss when Duff didn't accept her proffered palm, and he looked past her as though she were transparent; his reputation preceded him. She offered a hand to Abe. "I've heard a lot about you."

Abe froze. He was too old and pragmatic to believe in clichés like feeling his heart skip a beat or hearing a choir of angels, but both of those things were close to what he felt when he locked eyes with Jo Dunbar.

She was pretty. Very pretty.

And he was lonely. Very lonely.

Abe had been divorced for over a year, but never adjusted to the isolation. Sharing an office with Duff didn't count. After so many years together, most days they barely spoke because everything they ever needed to say to each other had already been said.

Abe knew Dunbar was out of his league, and she was probably too young for him. He tried not to show any interest in her.

And then failed miserably.

"I'm Abe." Abe smiled as best he could. He had sad eyes, a hangdog face, and a weak chin. In some aspects, he looked like a turtle. He was not someone with a natural, easy-going smile, and any positive expression looked a little out of place on him. Duff once said Abe possessed a gargoyle's scowl even in his happiest moments.

"I know. Detective Betts said that."

"Yeah. I'm sorry. I just. Abe Allard. Did he say my last name?"

Dunbar's hand was smooth and cool in Abe's grip despite the heat. He was suddenly very aware of how hot it was outside, and he was aware of the thin sheen of sweat on his high forehead and closely-cropped, balding pate. Neither Abe nor Duff had much hair to speak of, but Duff almost always wore a baseball cap, so no one noticed. Abe preferred to let his head be exposed to the elements, possibly because he looked even taller and more Frankenstein-like in a hat. Abe was suddenly aware of how much he was sweating and tried to wipe the layer of misty dampness from his face with his free hand.

"You guys are sort of mythic heroes in the department. Some people are really impressed by you, and others…not so much."

Abe was still holding Dunbar's hand. He knew it had been an awkwardly long handshake, but part of him did not want to let go. He forced himself to break the grasp. "That's kind of you to say."

"Who are these people who aren't impressed with me?" Duff wanted names.

"Most of the CPD."

"Especially me," said Betts.

"Really, Betts? Give me back the friendship bracelet I made for you."

Abe pushed Duff aside. "Please ignore anything he says. It's the easiest way to deal with him."

Betts walked to the sniper's nest. He kicked some of the gravel around with the tip of his shoe. "Come here and do your magic eye thing and solve this case, Chubs."

Duff did not move toward Betts, but he looked around the roof for a long moment. His strange observation skills were taking in every detail and piecing together the killer's actions.

Abe could not stop feeling Dunbar's presence next to him. He detected a faint scent of vanilla body spray. Abe forced himself to push thoughts of Dunbar out of his head. It wasn't working. He kept picturing her with her hair down instead of in a tight bun on the back of her head. Abe made himself breathe through his nose, a deep, cleansing breath. He needed to focus on the matters at hand. He didn't need impractical schoolboy fantasies.

Duff walked to the edge of the roof where the shot was taken and looked down at the street below and the roofs of the nearby buildings. He found the spot where he, himself, hunkered with a camera that evening. "Shooter could have put one in the back of my head if he'd wanted to."

"Maybe he'll try harder next time."

Duff ignored Betts and soldiered on with his assessment. "Single shot. Took the weapon with him. Picked up his brass. At first glance, this looks like a professional hit, or at the very least, the shooter knew what he was doing."

"Told you it was a hit." Betts rubbed at the bridge of his nose like a migraine was starting. Professional jobs were hard to break, if not impossible, because the killer typically has no connection to the victim. The crime had to be pieced together through a go-between of some kind, and if both the hitter and the employer were smart, it would be impossible to make the link. Most murder-for-hire cases broke because the hitter would get copped for something else down the line and then use what they knew for a plea deal to get off on a lighter charge with far less jail time. "We're likely never going to solve it, then. Chicago gangsters hide their hitters."

"*You* might never solve it because *you* give up too easily." Duff did not hide his disdain. He believed the police were too focused on easy cases due to budgetary constraints and a need for positive public relations fodder. The difficult cases were the fun ones, the ones that actually meant something.

"We got a lot of cases."

"If you were willing to pay us more often, we might solve some of them for you."

"Talk to the city council about the budget."

Duff knelt by the edge of the roof. The cement barrier around the rooftop was too high for a kneeling shot. Duff stood. He was taller than your average man, but not by much. The roof's safety ledge was too short for him to take a standing shot unless he was holding the rifle in both hands, which most pro hitters did not like to do unless they had to; a stationary barrel propped on something solid was better for an accurate shot over distance. It made for fewer variables to worry about when squeezing the trigger. The smaller the chance for error, the better.

"Unless he had a tripod on the barrel, I'm betting he stood and took the shot." Duff mimed holding a rifle and sighting it. He shuffled his feet until he was a few inches back from the edge of the roof. He still had a good shot with no change in angle or view. "Probably did it from back here so he would be better hidden in the shadows. A standing shot like this says it probably wasn't a professional job at this distance, but the shooter still knew his stuff."

"Ex-military, you think?" asked Abe.

"Either that or an avid hunter with a lot of time at the range, maybe both. Distance shooting is a use-it-or-lose-it skill. If you haven't done it in a while, you're probably not making this shot with one bullet. I'm willing to bet whoever pulled the trigger spent a lot of time on the practice range recently."

Gates scribbled in her notebook. "We'll check the ranges, maybe see if we can find a name that rings some bells."

"Most of those ranges won't want to give you information like that. It might be a lost cause." Duff knew most of the men who owned shooting ranges liked to fly the *Back the Blue* flags because they knew their clientele ate up overt shows of authoritarian solidarity, but those same men also knew their Constitutional rights and wouldn't willingly give out information they didn't have to give without a warrant. Or cash. They loved Constitutional rights, but they loved capitalism more.

"Never know. Might get lucky," said Gates.

Abe was trying to think of the logistics of the situation. He wasn't as fast as piecing together the practicals as Duff, and he didn't have Duff's eye for finding nearly insignificant details, but he did have a mind for planning, which Duff lacked. As the man who kept their shared detective business running on the day-to-day side, Abe was the one who kept the bills paid, the budget balanced, and made sure they had enough mundane work to keep them afloat between bigger, better-paying cases. Abe knew his role in their partnership well. It didn't mean he didn't have a mind for crime, though.

Abe glanced around the rooftop and tried to picture how the shooter brought a long gun into the building without being seen. And more importantly, how did the shooter leave with a long gun without being seen?

The first thought was that the shooter had a gun capable of being broken down into a briefcase or duffel bag. That would make it much more insignificant to passersby. However, those guns were not always accurate with the first shot after being reassembled. Often, they required two or three test shots to make sure the scope was sighted correctly. An assembled weapon was probably not the killing weapon.

The second thought was that the shooter lived in the building. This was statistically highly unlikely. The shooter with a grudge against Robert Bloch just *happened* to live in the complex where a good shooting angle would magically present itself on a random Friday night. Not likely. If the shooter lived in the building, then he did not know Robert Bloch, and this was a very random killing. Those sorts of murders did happen, but they were rare.

Random killings were always terrible and difficult to solve, if not impossible. The likelihood of solving a completely random shooting was infinitesimal. Most of the time, a completely random killing would only get solved if the shooter bragged about it, which, strangely enough, they often did.

The third thought Abe had was a long jacket. An overcoat could hide a long gun, but overcoats were winter wear. There was no such thing as a summer overcoat, especially not in the upper Midwest. Any man wearing a London Fog topcoat would instantly stand out in a summer crowd. On a day when the temperatures flirted with triple digits, even the homeless drug addicts shed their layers. A long coat would have been a major red flag and easy to spot.

The last thought was that the shooter brought the gun up and down in a manner that would have disguised it to people on the street or in the building. The shooter needed a costume for the weapon. This was the only thing that made sense to Abe, but where was the proof of a hidden weapon? How did the killer bring it to the roof without being spotted, and how did he leave with it?

"Duff, where's the gun?" Abe interrupted his partner's train of thought. "How'd he get the gun up here?"

Duff arched an eyebrow. Abe watched his partner go through all the thoughts he had just considered. Duff's eyes darted left and right as he stitched together the various possibilities as Abe had done. He came to the same conclusion. "Unless he had a drone that could have flown the gun up here in the dark, he had to have some sort of covering for it."

"How many people are using drones to fly sniper rifles to rooftops where the killer had to break a lock off a door to access it?" Betts asked.

"Probably none," said Duff. "This guy had a long gun and a crowbar, and he took an elevator up ten stories. Someone had to have seen him."

"Unless he looked like a janitor." Abe thought the only thing that made sense to him was a classic janitor's cart disguise. The long gun hides in the waste receptacle part. The upright mop and brooms keep people from seeing the barrel sticking out. No one expects a janitor to be carrying a sniper rifle.

Duff jabbed a finger into the air. "To the basement!"

They packed into an elevator, Jo Dunbar and Keith Schrader included. Betts hit the button, and the doors closed. Dunbar said, "Does anyone else smell lavender?"

Duff said, "Did you know there was a study done that found people who give off the scent of lavender are typically deeply closeted perverts with dark desires best left unspoken?"

"Duff, I'm going to shoot you in the face and make it look like a suicide," said Betts.

"That's a really weird dark desire, you deeply closeted pervert."

They rode down to the lowest level of the building.

JUST AS DUFF predicted, a heavy-duty Rubbermaid janitor's cart was abandoned in the below-ground parking ramp of the building. It was near the visitors' spaces as though someone had taken it down the elevator to a waiting car, removed the weapon and the crowbar, and driven away as though nothing had happened.

"Simple enough to figure it out, right?" Duff pointed around at three visible security cameras. "Gotta be more than just those. Just look for the car that drove away a few minutes after the shooting."

"On it." Dunbar headed for the main office of the building to access the security tapes.

"We might get a picture of the shooter's face, but I doubt we'll be that lucky." Duff eyeballed the cart for a moment and saw nothing of importance.

"Is it worth it to dust this thing for prints?" asked Schrader.

Betts shook his head. "If the shooter was professional enough to not spit or piss on the roof and take his brass with him, then he wore gloves throughout the process. He wouldn't be dumb enough to leave a print."

"Besides," said Abe. "How many people do you think have touched this cart? Plus, it's porous plastic. Very tough to get a decent print from it. Might get partials, but they'll never stand up in court."

The building was mostly residential. The garage was for the people who lived in the building. A handful of visitor stalls were near the top of the ramp leading to the street. The choking scent of exhaust was permanently fused into the concrete. It was a simple garage with an open design and supported by thick columns extending into the bedrock. Concrete covered every surface. Every noise echoed with fury.

"Not much activity late at night down here. No one saw the shooter use the elevator, and if they had, they would have only seen a janitor." Duff already knew the score. This was as clean a professional job as a person could possibly do. They knew where the target was. They got in and out with minimal fuss. On a Friday night, people were either in for the evening or out until bar time. A van parked in the visitor parking space would not have been noted by anyone as long as it wasn't there too long. The level of professionalism made Duff lean toward this being a paid hit on Robert Bloch. The question then was not so much who pulled the trigger, but who paid to have the trigger pulled.

Dunbar's voice sparked on the police radio. "Got minimal footage, if you want to come see."

The cadre walked out of the parking garage and to the main office. A bored-looking African American kid in his early twenties sat at a desk with a couple of small black-and-white monitors on it. He wore jeans and a t-shirt advertising a metal band. Abe was not up on his underground Norwegian death metal, so the band's spiky logo was indiscernible. Dunbar introduced the kid. "This is Max. His dad is the building super."

"Where's your dad, Max?" asked Betts.

"Out. It's Friday. Pops don't work on Friday night. There's beer to be drunk and darts to be thrown, man." Max's tone was churlish.

The angles of the security cameras were bad. The footage revealed little. What they saw was a clean shot of the elevators. The doors opened, and someone pushed the janitor's cart off the elevator. The shooter knew the camera was there and kept their head down behind the wall of mop and broom heads extending from their respective holders. It looked like the cart was pushing itself, the shooter barely more than a lumbering mass crouching low behind it. The shooter pushed the cart out of view of the camera. It was as if they knew exactly where the camera's view ended.

A moment later, another camera showed a plain, white cargo van roaring out of the parking lot at a healthy clip. The driver held a flashlight in front of their face as they passed the security camera at the exit. The camera only caught a sunburst glare from the front window. The driver had covered the front and rear license plates with cardboard placards to hide the numbers. It would be a simple matter of getting down the road a few blocks, pulling over, and yanking the placards to escape into the night with no one the wiser.

"That's as professional as it gets." Duff gave a low whistle. "Dude was a hired hitter, or else he was just really, really good."

"Unless we got that van on traffic cameras somewhere, game's over," said Gates.

They walked out of the ramp and looked up and down the street. The nearest traffic lights were two blocks north. The van had to have turned south, then. If someone was professional enough to avoid the cameras in the building, they were professional enough to get down the street away from the camera before pulling the cardboard.

To the south, it was almost six blocks before there were traffic lights. There were alleys and side streets without cameras everywhere. And even if there were cameras, the streetlights were notoriously dim.

Betts ran a hand through his hair in frustration. "Well, that was fun while it lasted. Might as well slap this one in the unsolvable file and give it to Cold Cases right now. You know, Duff—next time you witness a pro hit, don't call me."

"But I can still call you when I find a sale on those Hello Kitty bikini briefs you like to wear, right?"

Betts said, "Give it to me straight: what are the odds we solve a pro hit like this?"

Duff considered the facts. He did the math in his head, a finger dancing in the air in front of him as if to record the factoring in case he was asked to show his work. "Slim."

"What do we know about hits like this?"

Abe knew the facts and data. It wasn't promising. "Statistically, the most likely purchaser of a professional hit is a spouse. The second most likely purchaser is a business associate."

"So, if the wife didn't do it, then someone he worked with did it."

"But don't forget about the Ruger in his vehicle," said Duff. "If you're going to carry a gun for personal protection, you carry it on your person, or at the very least you carry it in your glove box so you can get to it quickly. Bloch had it hidden in his trunk where it would be highly inconvenient to retrieve at a moment's notice. That tells me that gun wasn't there for personal protection, but something a little darker."

"You're saying the vic was into some shit," said Betts.

"That's exactly what I'm saying. How much and how deep, that remains to be seen."

"So, we got a vic who was heading for divorce, had a hot bikini model secretary, and just got a new job that paid him a lot more money. He was into something shady somewhere in his life, hence the Ruger in his vehicle, and someone paid a pro to pop him. Are we all on the same level, here?" Betts looked at the gathered group on the sidewalk.

"Sounds right," said Abe.

"At least, it was probably a pro. Might have been someone who was good with a gun and had a beef against Bloch," said Duff.

"Could it be random?" asked Dunbar.

"No," said Duff. "The killer knew where they were shooting. They found a spot where they could hide, take the shot, and get away cleanly. If they knew where they were shooting, why Bloch? There were other open windows in the building. Why wait for that one guy?"

"Murder clearance rates in Chicago are less than fifty percent," said Abe. "I fear this one might slot into the larger side of that divide."

"Is it really that tough to solve a hit like this?" asked Dunbar.

Abe could only nod. "It can be done, but it often requires a lucky break. Usually, something this cold and calculated is hard to trace."

Betts checked his watch. It was after four in the morning, heading fast toward five. "I'm thinking we might have to go wrap up the statements and call this a night. You guys want to come with me to tell the widow?"

"Hard pass." Duff's face wrinkled in disgust. "Weeping and emotions? No, thanks. Not a fan."

"You can tell her Duff saw it happen, but we don't have much to go on other than what we found here tonight," said Abe.

"I'll tell her she can call you if she has further questions." Betts turned on his heel and headed toward the Hotel Afton.

Diana Gates followed him. "Thanks for the help tonight, fellas."

Duff gave a lazy tip of his Brewers cap. Abe waved. "Anytime."

Schrader bid his farewell to the two private detectives and hustled after the police detectives. Jo Dunbar stuck out a hand to Abe. "It was nice meeting you."

Abe shook her hand again. It was no less thrilling than it had been the first time. "Mice to neet you, as well. I mean, nice. Nice to meet. Meeting you was good."

Duff slapped a hand to his forehead. "Jesus, that was as smooth as untreated herpes."

Dunbar smiled at Abe and followed her partner.

Abe and Duff watched her jog away into the darkness. Duff clapped a hand onto his partner's shoulder. "Well done. You almost successfully talked to a woman. You know, I can't tell if the fact that you have a child is a modern miracle, or if Kathrine just had a bar that low."

"Why not both?"

"That's the other acceptable answer. Are you certain Matilda is your kid?"

"You know she is."

"Have you even touched a boob since you broke up with Kathrine?"

Abe wouldn't even deign to answer a question like that. He started walking back to the public ramp where he'd parked the battered Toyota Sienna Duff called *The Bad-Luck Charm*, the vehicle that served as their main transportation around the city.

"What are the odds Vicky Bloch calls us to figure out who killed her husband?"

Duff considered it for a moment. "Better than average."

"What are the odds we can figure out who killed her husband?"

"Below-average, but still better than if she waited for the CPD to do it." Duff pulled his phone out of his pocket. The battery was down to a single-digit percentage. "It'll be five by the time we get back to the office. Want to grab breakfast?"

"I'd rather go back to bed, considering it's Saturday and some of us enjoy not going into the office once in a while."

"So, let's celebrate the weekend by grabbing some breakfast. Then you can go back to bed."

"I'm pretty tired."

"Dude, listen to the tone in my voice: we are getting breakfast."

Abe stopped walking and turned to look at his partner. "Why?"

"Because it's the most important meal of the day. Stop asking stupid questions and just do what I tell you to do."

"I always do what you tell me to do. That's how I got into this mess in the first place."

"And you wouldn't have it any other way." Duff walked past Abe and grabbed the hem of his sweat-dampened t-shirt, fluffing it away from his body several times to act like a makeshift fan. "Hotter than a politician on the witness stand today."

4

ABE DROVE FROM the Hotel Afton to their office, which also doubled as Duff's home. When they neared the vicinity, Duff told Abe to take a turn he usually wouldn't have taken. This led them down a side street toward Abe's old house, where his ex-wife still resided with his daughter. When Abe turned to Duff with a questioning eyebrow arched, Duff said nothing. He gave another command to take another turn and then told Abe to find parking. Abe did as bidden.

When they bought it, *The Bad-Luck Charm* was a decade-old minivan that had high mileage but at least looked like it was in good shape. After a year of Abe's ownership, the van had become a pockmarked monument to unfortunate circumstances. For whatever reason, the Sienna acquired scars like Duff's bedroom accumulated empty cans of Coke Zero. It was missing the passenger-side mirror. Three of the four hubcaps were gone. The right rear window was cracked. There were a half-dozen dents and scrapes along the body panels, war wounds from parking on Chicago streets. The most recent injustice it suffered came at the hands of one of the youth gangs in the neighborhood of Abe's bachelor apartment building. Some kid had thoughtfully written *NARC* across the back of the Sienna's dented trunk gate with neon-orange street-marking paint. No amount of scrubbing on Abe's part had managed to dent the spray-on sheen. It was now a permanent part of *The Bad-Luck Charm's* quirky allure.

They left the van curbside on an empty street only four blocks from Abe's old house. At five o'clock in the morning, only the barest minimum of people were up and about on a steamy Chicago Saturday morning. They were the people who *had* to be out for service jobs that made everyone else's life a little easier on such a day. Baristas, newspaper delivery trucks, bread delivery, fruit and veggie delivery trucks heading to restaurants—no rest for the wicked or the weary. Chicago was a starving beast and demanded constant feeding.

Abe's old neighborhood had always been family-oriented, but recently, one of the streets near him started a rebirth. It was becoming gentrified, and a couple of new restaurants had been installed—higher-end, fancier places with menus meant to lure childless young couples with disposable income to feast on specialty breads, upscale meals, and craft cocktails mixed by people with $150 haircuts, tattoo sleeves, and nose piercings.

Duff led Abe to a storefront splashed with bright yellow paint and illuminated in the early dawn light with several kitschy neon signs. A bright pink whirl of neon tubes declared the diner's name: Molly Ginger's Morning Spot.

"Who's Molly Ginger?" If Duff was playing a joke on him, Abe wasn't getting it. This looked like the type of place Duff spent his entire life raging against. Duff hated places that looked like they were going out of their way to be splashy and quirky. He hated pretentiousness and people who sought out fancy things. Duff was a die-hard dive-bar and fast-food guy. He ate most of his meals from street vendors. He didn't fully trust food that didn't come wrapped in foil or wax paper.

"I've heard good things." Duff opened the door. The faint sound of 1940s jazz wafted out of the doorway, a medley of soft horns accompanied by a rhythmic Epiphone electric hollow body.

"About a place with a cutesy name that plays jazz?" Abe put a hand on his friend's forehead. "Are you sick? Did you finally have that mental breakdown I've been predicting for years?"

"Just go find a table, dumbass."

A perky brunette with turquoise horn-rimmed glasses and a curve-hugging sundress welcomed the detectives with a smile. "Good morning! Welcome to Molly Ginger's!" Her voice had more perk than an entire pot of Folger's crystals. It made Duff visibly wince. "Just the two of you?"

Duff pulled a crumpled five-dollar bill out of his pocket and held it out for her. "Yes, and if you don't speak again, you can have this."

The hostess smiled and took Duff's money. She led them to a table wordlessly and sat them, handing them each a menu.

The restaurant was nearly empty. It had only been open for fifteen minutes when Abe and Duff arrived. The only other patron was an elderly woman at a table near the window. She was drinking coffee out of a comically oversized mug and scanning the first section of that day's *Chicago Tribune*. She also paused occasionally to wave a Chinese paper fan at herself.

The restaurant had air conditioning, but it hadn't been running overnight and was now struggling to overcome the pervasive heat.

The restaurant's decor looked like a modern twenty-year-old's idea of what the 1950s looked like. It was all kitsch and glamor, with loud fabric prints as tablecloths and old, tin Coca-Cola ad placards on the wall. Abe eyed the place dubiously. He leaned across the table to hiss at his partner. "You *hate* places like this."

"This one is growing on me." Duff looked at the menu. The cutesy names of some of the listed options made him scowl involuntarily. They were, no doubt, good plates of food, but Abe could not even fathom hearing Duff order the *Betsy's Best Biscuit Platter.*

A waitress materialized from around the corner and set a hot latte in a silly, oversized mug in front of Abe and a Diet Coke in a tall plastic glass in front of Duff. It must have been a mistake. Abe raised a finger. "We didn't order—"

"And yet, I knew this is what you'd be ordering."

The waitress's voice made Abe freeze in his seat. He turned to see his sixteen-year-old daughter standing next to him in a bright yellow, 1950s-style waitress skirt and gauzy white lap apron. A name tag clipped to her left shoulder read *Tilda.* Her blouse matched her skirt and had puffy shoulders to hone the kitschy retro look.

Tilda leaned down and kissed the top of her father's bald head. "Good morning, Daddy."

"You got a job?" Abe was stunned. Tilda hadn't mentioned it, and Katherine hadn't said anything, either.

"I got a job. Surprise!" Tilda's face lit up like the approaching dawn. "Can you believe it? Mom knows a lady who was an investor in this place, and she got me an interview. I just started on Monday, so this is really the first day where they're giving me my own section."

"That's...amazing." Abe was at a loss for words. He kicked Duff under the table. "You knew about this?"

"Not until last night. The kid texted me and told me about it. She said I should get you here early for breakfast if I could."

"A job, though?" As much as Abe hated to admit it, he still saw Tilda as the toddler who used to cling to his leg and demand he walk so she could ride along. When he looked at her in her uniform, it suddenly struck him how much she'd grown in the last few months. She was getting her height from her father and heading toward being six feet tall. The growth spurt had sapped any remnants of her prepubescent baby fat from her cheeks and turned her into a tall, slim, beautiful girl who could easily pass for twenty-one with the right makeup. Her normally bushy red hair was pulled back in a sleek ponytail, and even with light makeup, no one would have mistaken her for a teenager in that little restaurant. Abe didn't like it. It made him feel old, and it made him miss the little girl she had been. She was a baby only yesterday. When did she become an adult?

"I figured I needed to get a job as soon as I could if you and Mom still want me to go to Northwestern."

"I want you to go to college wherever you want to go, even if it's out of state." Abe hoped he sounded convincing. Matilda was all he had in the world. He wanted to keep her as close as possible for as long as possible. Since he and Katherine were former Wildcats, Northwestern seemed like the best place to keep Tilda nearby for a little while, at least.

"You liking waiting tables so far?" asked Duff.

"It's all right. The people who come in here tip pretty well. I've made a few bucks. It's nice. I'm not a fan of getting up at four in the morning to get here, though. Still, I can't complain. It could be worse." Matilda started to gather up the menus.

Abe protested. "I haven't even had a chance to look at it yet."

Matilda gave Abe her best haughty, hawkeyed look, like Holmes about to crack the case. "Sir, I'm the daughter of a world-famous detective. I already know what you both want."

"Prove it," said Duff.

"Duff, you want whatever has the most grease and carbs, specifically anything with biscuits and sausage involved. Bonus points if it has a Tex-Mex slant. Sadly, this one won't, but you'll still love it. Dad, you will typically order something that claims to be healthy, like the spinach-and-mushroom omelet. However, you *really* want something decadent and fun because it reminds you of being a kid, but you're too much of a stick-in-the-mud to let yourself order it, so I'm just going to surprise you with something I know you'll love, even if it isn't healthy."

Abe held up his hands in defeat. "Your powers of deduction amaze."

"I might not know what everyone wants, but I know what you two want." Tilda flashed her million-dollar smile. She had recently had her braces removed. Her teeth were perfect and white, worth every penny Abe had paid for the alignment.

More people began to trickle in, so Tilda busied herself with other tables.

Abe looked across the table at his partner. Duff looked tired, his forehead covered with a light sheen of sweat. The band of his navy blue Brewers hat was stained dark.

"She got a job." Abe was still astounded at the surprise of seeing his daughter in full uniform.

"She's a great kid. You and Katie did pretty good."

"You had a hand in raising her, too."

"Yeah, here and there. It doesn't count. You did all the hard stuff. All I did was teach her to look at wristwatches and shoes because those usually reveal someone's real income."

Abe watched his daughter glide around the restaurant. Her natural charm was evident as she flashed big smiles and joked with the customers. Neither Abe nor Katherine was gifted with overt charm. Duff was the antithesis of charm. Where Tilda picked up hers was a truly unanswerable mystery.

"So, Jo Dunbar." Duff deftly changed the subject before Abe could start to get watery eyes over his daughter's impending adulthood.

The name of the pretty CPD officer snapped Abe out of his reverie. "Say what now?"

"You had it so bad for her. C'mon, man. I haven't seen you lose yourself like that in a while, not since that art history professor, the one who went west."

"Officer Dunbar was attractive, but no. I didn't lose it. She's too young. I'm too old. She can do better."

"They can all do better. That's not the point."

"I don't want to talk about Jo Dunbar." Abe sipped the latte Matilda brought him. She knew him well enough to know he drank coffee only because he believed men should drink coffee, not because he enjoyed it. The latte was spiked with French vanilla cream and cinnamon sugar. It was more like a dessert than a drink. He loved it.

"I know you well enough to know you'd be better off not being single." Duff sipped his own drink. Duff only drank diet sodas and the occasional beer. Abe couldn't even remember Duff drinking water voluntarily unless it was the only thing offered to him.

"Maybe someday, but Officer Dunbar will not be that someday. Half your age plus seven, that's the rule, right?"

"Not if you're rich or famous."

"I'm not rich or famous."

"Your daughter just said you were a world-famous detective. How is that not famous?"

Abe held his latte with two hands. The cup was so large that it required a dual grip. "She was pretty, wasn't she?"

"Tilda? Absolutely."

"No, Officer Dunbar."

"Her? Sure. Why not? Let's say she was."

"So, she's pretty. She's educated. She's got a good job. In what world would someone like that want anything to do with a forty-something train wreck like me?"

"I dunno, man. Sometimes, people do weird things. And by weird things, I mean you. Frankly, you need to be done, my man. She might do you."

"And you might go on a diet."

Duff slumped back in the booth. "Yeah, you're right. I don't know what I was thinking."

Matilda appeared from the kitchen with a serving tray hoisted to her shoulder. She walked to the table and slid plates in front of Abe and Duff. "For the discerning gentleman who eats like he's praying for a heart attack, we have Auntie Emily's Biscuit Bombs, two savory sausage-and-cheese biscuits with cherry jam and sawmill gravy. And for my father, who is still a child at heart, I have the Elvis Special: French toast stuffed with peanut butter, grape jelly, and banana, topped with powdered sugar and authentic Wisconsin maple syrup harvested from trees from deep within the exotic forests of the wintry lands of our neighbors to the north."

Abe had to admit she got his order exactly right. If he had ordered for himself, he would have gotten something labeled as *HeartSmart*, and he would have hated it but eaten it without complaint while wishing for something else the entire time. "Thank you, Tilda."

"Can I get you anything else?"

"Probably going to need a coronary bypass after this is over, but I'm good for now." Duff whetted the edge of his knife across the tines of his fork.

"I'll check on you in a bit." Tilda flashed another smile that lit up the room and skittered away to take food to other diners.

Abe took a bite of the Elvis Special, and his eyes rolled back. It was a heavenly concoction of something sinfully good. Rich and sweet, heavy in flavor and calories. He would have to add another mile or two to his daily run later, but it would be worth it. If nothing else, the full sensation he would get from that plate of food might help him sleep like a champion as soon as he got home.

Duff ate like a machine. He ate like a man who did not savor food, but instead merely shoveled it into his face to get the mild dopamine hits that good food could bring because it was the only way for him to get any serotonin into his brain. He did not eat because food was fuel; he ate because it brought him a thimbleful of joy.

Abe went the other route. He savored the bites. The cook at Molly Ginger's knew their stuff. This was ordinary diner food elevated to an elegant level. It was simple, but made complex with hints of flavors from orange zest and banana extract in the French toast custard.

The two men did not speak while they ate. The mark of a true friendship is the ability to enjoy the silence. Abe and Duff had been monitoring silences for years. Abe was not a talker by nature, and Duff usually only talked when it was part of a case. When they were alone in the office together, they did not natter or discuss the weather. It was mostly work talk between them, spliced occasionally with strange, out-of-the-blue non sequiturs from Duff.

"We should get a detective cat."

Abe almost choked on a mouthful of banana and peanut butter. "What?"

"A detective cat. We could go to the pound and find a cat that seems to be regarding us with a wise and oddly discerning stare as if it knows who we are and what we do. Then, he will start giving us clues to help us solve murders. Like, he'll knock a book off the shelf, and the author will have the same name as the murderer."

"I don't think that's how cats work."

"They do in the books I've been reading lately."

"You've been reading books?" Abe was shocked. Duff had been an avid reader in his childhood, but over the last two decades, he'd been self-medicating during his downtime with countless hours of video game baseball on his PlayStation. The activity on the screen kept him from thinking about other, darker things he'd rather not remember.

Duff pulled his phone out of his pocket and showed Abe a screen full of black-and-white text. "The kiddo over there showed me some app that lets me download digital books from the library onto my phone."

"I thought you declared the library as being dead to you when they banned you because you kept writing the names of the killers in the unsolved true crime books."

"Yeah, they're still dead to me, but now I can beat the system. I don't have to go to the library; the library is on my phone."

Abe set his fork down. "And you've been reading cozy mysteries?"

"That's why we should get a detective cat. There's this one cat in one of the books, he's got extra whiskers, and that's how he knows things beyond his owner's ken. The cat senses when someone in town gets murdered and always yowls when they do."

"Aren't you allergic to cats?"

Duff had already considered this. "There are hypoallergenic cats out there. We could get one of those hairless buggers that looks like Walter Matthau's ballsack."

"How about we don't?" Years ago, Katherine had a fellow teacher at her school who owned a hairless cat. She said when she picked it up, it was like holding someone's butt in her hands. Abe swore off hairless cats after that mental image.

Matilda slid up to the table. She had a sly smile on her lips and gave them a very formal, "Can I get you gentlemen anything else?"

Duff had already powered through his meal, but Abe still had a bit to go. "You could refill my Diet Coke, if you are so empowered."

Tilda grabbed his nearly empty glass and whisked it to the soda fountain behind the long diner counter near the door.

Duff's eyes followed her with a sad, wistful look. "She used to be tiny."

"So tiny."

"When did we get old?"

"We were always old. Now we just look like it."

Matilda returned with a full glass of soda, lightly foaming at the rim. She set it in front of her uncle-by-proxy and slipped the bill onto the table face down nearer to her father than Duff. "I'm assuming you're making Dad pay, of course."

"Your assumptions are correct." Duff sipped the refreshed diet soda. "Pay the lady, my good man. And don't be stingy with the tip."

Abe was used to this behavior. He didn't actually buy Duff's meals most of the time. Since Abe kept all the books for the business, he just took it out of the stipend Duff got weekly as his pay from the agency. Duff never noticed, and Abe was still able to pay his mortgage on time, which he wouldn't have been able to do if he had truly been footing the bill for his rotund friend.

Abe pulled his debit card from his wallet and handed it to Tilda. "Everything was amazing, Tildy. Tell the cook that this mess on my plate was perfect."

"I'll let him know." Tilda flashed her smile and disappeared to run the bill.

"Plans for the day?" asked Duff.

"Sleep. You?"

Duff pulled his phone from his pocket. The battery level light was flashing a warning. The act of checking the time drained the remaining power, and the phone went dark in his hand. "I'll be charging my phone and waiting for Vicky Bloch to call."

"You think she'll call?"

Duff's tone was certain. "She'll call around nine. She will be devastated by the news of her husband, of course. She will have to make a handful of terrible calls to his family. She will wait for a respectable time in the morning to soften the blow. No one wants to wake a family member out of a sound sleep to tell them their son is dead. After she makes those terrible calls, she will be completely out of tears and sadness. Anger will set in. When anger sets in, she will want to know who did this to her husband. I suspect that will happen around nine this morning."

"It's a Saturday."

"No later than nine-thirty."

"So be it. If she wants to come into the office, call me. I'll sleep in my clothes so I can be there in five minutes."

"A rumpled Aberforth is a busy Aberforth."

Matilda came back with the two slips of paper: a merchant copy and a customer copy. "Thanks for coming to see me. I'm really glad you were my first customers."

"Wouldn't have missed it, kiddo." Duff polished off his remaining cola.

"I've got to get back to work. I'll talk to you both later." With that, Matilda turned on her heel and made her way back to the pass-thru where a giant platter of food was waiting to feed a table of gentlemen with white hair and thick glasses having a Saturday morning bull session in the farthest corner of the place.

Abe signed the bill and looked into his wallet. He pulled out a twenty and set it on top of the bill. "My baby has a job."

"That she does." Duff stood and stretched. "It's been a day, amigo of mine. Let's go home."

Duff waited for Abe to extricate himself from the booth and lead the way out of the restaurant.

When he got to the door, Abe turned to use his shoulder to push open the door onto the steamy sidewalk. In doing so, out of the corner of his eye, he caught sight of the table they had just abandoned. He saw a crumpled bill sitting on top of his own twenty.

Duff, trying to hide his goodwill, had waited until Abe's back was turned before tossing a fifty onto the already extravagant tip. Even at a distance, Abe could see the unseemly visage of Ulysses S. Grant staring at him.

If Duff saw Abe catch sight of the extra-generous tip, he said nothing. Abe was content to let Duff think he got away with that one. Duff was a lot of things, and not all of them were good, but since her arrival into the world, Matilda had been his biggest weakness. It was that sort of kindness and giving which made Duff more family than business partner, but he would deny he possessed any kindness if Abe ever confronted him about it.

Abe checked his phone before he got into *The Bad-Luck Charm*. The weather bug on the home screen told him it was almost 6:00 AM, and the temperature was already 81 degrees. They were looking toward a high in the mid-90s with a massive dose of lakeside humidity to season the summer day. The heat index would be in the triple digits, and the National Weather Service had issued a UV exposure warning.

On the other side of the minivan, Duff flapped his shirt over his expansive girth for air once again. "Jesus Christ. Feels like my balls are turning into *dim sum* over here. Do you have a river of sweat running down your ass crack, or is it just me?"

5

ONE OF THE most difficult things about being divorced from the mother of his child was resisting the urge to call or text Katherine about every minor thing concerning Matilda. In his cramped, cheaply decorated apartment, in a complex specializing in renting to recently divorced men, even as tired as he was from being up all night, Abe's first instinct on arriving at his place was to text Katherine so they could share the milestone of their daughter's first job.

But Katherine already knew about the job. She helped Tilda get the job in the first place. Abe wanted to share in that moment, but he was the last to know about it. He had to endure his daughter's milestones alone. He wasn't angry at Katherine or Matilda for keeping it a secret; he knew why they did it, and it was a pleasant surprise after a long night, but he couldn't revel in the joy with anyone. He couldn't lean on someone who felt the same.

Instead, he sat on the edge of his bed and stared into the middle distance.

Abe slid under the covers and then immediately kicked them off. It was too hot for covers. He had abandoned the idea of sleeping in his clothes like he said he would for the plain fact that it was too damn hot. He wore a threadbare Pink Floyd t-shirt Matilda bought him years ago and a pair of cotton running shorts with the fabled Motion W logo of the University of Wisconsin. He never got any Wisconsin apparel during his grad school years, other than the free t-shirts the UW Law School foisted on him during welcome events. True to the dull nature of the legal system and those trained to conduct business within it, most of those shirts simply said *Wisconsin Law*, like a bad Dick Wolf TV pilot. Matilda insisted on buying him Wisconsin apparel as gifts for his birthday or Christmas every so often, but they weren't something he'd go out of his way to get.

A good Pink Floyd shirt, though—that was a different story.

Abe closed his eyes and tried to sleep. Without covers, he felt too exposed. He pulled the thin sheet over him, but it was still too hot. The apartment was in the upper-70s, and the little window AC unit, though it chugged along gamely, was not kicking out nearly enough juice to do battle with the swampy weather, especially as the temperatures steadily rose.

Abe left his bed and dug out a circular fan from the closet. He plugged it in, pointed it at the bed, and turned it on full. It helped channel cooler air from the main living space, but it was like spitting water on a forest fire. The heat was miserable.

Abe contemplated taking a sleeping pill. He didn't like to use drugs for sleep, but sometimes, it was a necessary evil. If Duff needed him later, as predicted, then Abe needed to be alert enough to get to the office. There would be no sleeping pills that morning. Instead, Abe lay in bed, the top sheet ruffling in the weak breeze from the fan, trying to remember what it was like to be cold.

Invariably, Jo Dunbar's face popped into his head multiple times, and he pushed it out of his mind each time. He didn't need that distraction, no matter how lovely it was.

Abe reached out to his phone. He went into the apps menu for the one app he wouldn't allow himself to put on one of the menu screens, a dating app that was supposed to be for Chicagoans over forty. Talk about hyper-specific marketing. Abe downloaded it in April after Katherine started formally dating a woman named Patty.

Abe liked Patty. Tilda liked Patty. Even Duff met her once and declared her to be *not the worst human on the planet*, which, for him, was akin to a major humanitarian award. Patty and Katherine were spending a lot of time together. Katherine seemed happy, and that pained Abe because he hadn't seen her like that since Tilda was small. She had always been kind, polite, and exceedingly civil in all their interactions, but she hadn't been *happy*. Now she was happy, and she was happy largely because Abe was mostly out of her life. It stung. He knew it wasn't personal, but it hurt more than he would ever admit.

Chi-Town Dates was supposed to help him find a way to move on and be happy, too. It wasn't working. After almost two-and-a-half months on the app, he had received zero messages. Not a single woman had swiped right on his profile. He knew it was because of his face. He was an unfortunate-looking specimen. This was not news.

Abe opened the app and scanned through a bevy of new listings. He swiped left on the ones he immediately knew were out of his league, which were most of them, and swiped right on the remaining few, a fresh batch of women who were now free to ignore him.

Abe envied Duff's ability to live an odd, pseudo-monastic lifestyle. He had his video games, bad TV, and occasional drinks with some of the neighborhood guys at a hole-in-the-wall bar that showed Brewers games—a rare animal deep in the realm of the Cubbies and ChiSox. No woman had ever shown interest in Duff, and he seemed to like it that way.

Well, no woman except his best friend from childhood. The murder of Becky Sigrud and her family had damaged Duff at a fundamental level. Abe believed that horrible event altered Duff's DNA. It changed him from a good student who preferred reading to sports or socializing into someone who focused so hard on a subject that he was often blind to everything else. The trajectory his life took after that moment broke him and warped him into whatever he was now. Nothing else mattered to him except putting the world right in Becky's honor since he couldn't bring her justice.

Abe thought he would grow old with Katherine. He thought they'd eventually retire and spend their days chasing grandchildren together. Life has a way of throwing curveballs, though. Abe could never hit curveballs. He couldn't hit fastballs, either.

Shit, he couldn't hit slow-pitch softballs. Whenever he was forced to participate in baseball or softball in gym class, the rest of the guys would mock him and call him *Easy Out* or *Captain K*. Abe didn't care. He swung at everything they threw—inside, outside, ball or strike, it didn't matter. He knew if he swung the bat three times, he'd get to sit down again. It was easier than trying to be good at a sport.

Abe closed his eyes and tried all the tricks to clear his mind. Nothing worked. He stared at the inside of his eyelids for a while and then rolled over and watched the sunrise through the small gap in the curtains of his bedroom window. He had to look over the empty side of the bed as he did.

DUFF DIDN'T ATTEMPT to sleep. He wandered around the one-bedroom apartment that served as his office and home. He took a cold shower. He ate a room-temperature Pop-Tart. He drank a Coke Zero while standing naked in front of the open refrigerator. The little window AC unit had long needed replacing, but as with most Chicago landlords, their appeals for a new unit were consistently ignored.

Normally, Duff being naked in the apartment outside of the shower or his room *with the door closed* was verboten in his partnership agreement with Abe. Let's face it: no one wants to walk into an office for the day and catch one of their coworkers freeballin'. And no one, male or female, wanted anything to do with any of Duff's brand of nude magic.

Not even Duff himself.

But Abe was gone for the day and wouldn't be back until Duff called him because Vicky Bloch was coming in to ask them to find out who killed her husband. Which wouldn't be until at least nine in the morning.

Duff checked the wall clock. It was almost seven. He had two hours to kill.

Duff dressed in a worn Milwaukee Braves throwback t-shirt he'd bought off a website several years ago and a pair of silver basketball shorts he'd bought at Walmart. Duff wore sports apparel because he liked the drama and statistics of sports, not because he had any natural athletic ability. Plus, they were comfortable. Most clothes weren't comfortable for big guys. Belts cut into the hips and waist. Suspenders chaffed the nipples. Duff liked soft elastic waistbands and oversized, loose-fitting shirts.

Some of the staff and fellow inmates of the boys' home where he was stowed at the age of fourteen had tried to teach him sports. He could throw a round ball pretty far, but with zero accuracy. Any footballs he threw wobbled like a dying duck and fell out of the sky after fifteen yards. He could take a punch like a prizefighter, but couldn't throw one. He ran like an angry hippo out of water, a ball of swaying lard with a comical grimace plastered to his face. Because Bensonhurst was in Canada, they tried to teach him to play hockey, but he skated on his ankles and disliked how the sport was basically an excuse for the other boys to hit him with sticks.

Much like his partner in crime-solving, it was best that Duff avoided sports altogether, especially now that he was in his mid-forties, and his body was falling apart faster than a '88 Yugo in a hailstorm.

Duff flopped on the beat-up recliner in his bedroom. It needed to be thrown out, but because replacing it was more trouble than simply using the old one until it fell apart beneath him, he would continue to use the old one no matter how frayed it became.

Duff had no bed. He had not had a bed since he left Bensonhurst, save for nights he slept in hotels while working somewhere other than the Chicago metro region. He preferred the recliner. It kept him upright and at a slight angle. It helped minimize his snoring. He slept better. Truth be told, his idea of sleeping was more like most people's naps. He slept lightly and in short bursts.

When he had first been remanded to Bensonhurst as a chubby, scared, confused adolescent, he quickly learned night was not a time to be caught sleeping. The other boys liked to launch their worst physical assaults when they could catch a boy asleep. They liked to have one guy land on the sleeping boy's head, shoving it hard into the mattress, because then the boy was at their mercy. If the head can't move, the body stays put. The other boys would run up and take free shots. Kidney punches if the boy was face down. If the boy was face up, then it was a lot of genital punches and fists to the soft area just below the sternum. They just wanted to cause as much damage as possible. It was funny to them when a boy cried and wailed while clutching his nuts and gasping for air. The more horrible and piteous the wailing, the better.

Duff learned to sleep in short bursts at Bensonhurst. When he slept in hotels with Abe in the other bed in the room, he let his guard down and would get a decent night's sleep. He trusted Abe to look out for him. The rest of the time, Duff preferred to play video games until exhaustion took him, and then he'd sleep just long enough to rid himself of the need to sleep any further.

Duff once read an article in a medical journal stating that people who get less than eight hours of sleep per night were taking time off their lifespan. If that article was accurate, Duff figured he probably dropped dead six years ago and still hadn't figured it out.

Duff booted up his PlayStation. He had a game paused. He continued where he left off, running a Milwaukee Brewers franchise in his favorite game, a baseball simulator called *MLB The Show*. The version he owned was already four years old at this point. He never upgraded to a newer version, despite some minor graphical enhancements, because the one he had was good enough. He was not a connoisseur of video games, nor did he consider himself a *gamer*, a term he disliked. He liked what he liked, and that was it.

Duff liked baseball because it was his escape in Bensonhurst. No matter how bad the nights were, the days started with checking scores and stat sheets in the *Toronto Star*. During his first year stuck in the wilds of Canada, he learned about AM radio and built a functional radio with a cardboard tube, a bunch of copper wire, a couple of transistors he salvaged out of a broken radio, and an earpiece he bought via mail order from Radio Shack. Once he made the radio, he learned that if he tuned it just right, provided the weather wasn't too bad, he could pick up 620 WTMJ-AM out of Milwaukee. It became a lifeline back to Wisconsin, to the life he used to know. Bob Uecker's voice would carry out of the darkness that had become his life for three hours a day, 162 days a year. It was all he had. On the extremely rare occasion a Brewers game was on TV in Canada, usually only when they played the Blue Jays at the Skydome, or when the Jays traveled to old County Stadium in Milwaukee, Duff always made sure to reserve the TV room so he could watch it.

Video game baseball wasn't as good as watching the real thing, but it filled in the gaps where live games weren't being played. It was a good placebo for him. He kept expecting to get tired of baseball, but if anything, the closer the Brewers got to making the postseason, the more it mattered to him.

Duff managed to finish the game he had paused and go a full nine innings in another game before the clock rolled around to nine. He paused his game once again and turned off the TV.

He went to his desk in the office and sat in the battered chair at his habitually messy desk. He stared at the phone. He knew it would ring soon enough.

Vicky Bloch called at 9:21 AM to ask if she could see them.

Duff said yes. Then, he called Abe.

ABE WAS SO tired he felt as if he was starting to see the code lines of the matrix. Everything felt just slightly out of phase with reality. There was a trembling, hazy edge around solid objects. He could shake it off if he blinked a couple of times and took a deep breath through his nose, but it returned quickly, washing over him like a rising tide. He was yawning uncontrollably and felt embarrassed, so he tried to stifle them as best he could. It made his face contort so he looked like Lon Chaney in the Phantom makeup. If Vicky Bloch noticed, she said nothing.

Vicky Bloch was an average Midwestern woman. She was a five-foot-six brunette. She wore plain glasses with dark tortoise-shell frames. Her hair was styled in an easy-to-care-for businesswoman's bob. She dressed well, but not fancy. She wore comfortable, white canvas sneakers, khaki Capri pants, and a blue linen blouse. She was sweating slightly, partly from the heat, but mostly from the stress of the morning. Her eyes were red from crying, but she had passed through the worst of her grief for the time being. She was still processing, still in the awful state of dark surreality ubiquitous with the sudden death of a loved one.

She sat in the chair opposite Abe's desk. Abe had given her a bottle of cold water from the refrigerator. She worked the cap with a trembling hand and sipped. "I'm sure you can forgive me if I'm a little shaken."

Abe sat behind his desk and tried to convey concern and empathy with his facial expression. "It had to be a traumatic morning for you."

Duff said nothing. He was watching Vicky intently.

Vicky sipped more water. "Traumatic is an understatement. After the initial shock, I went from sadness to fury and every emotion in between. I had to call my in-laws and tell them their son was dead. No one tells you about the heartbreak of making that call when you take your vows."

"In a perfect world, no child would ever die before his parents," said Abe.

"This world is far from perfect, isn't it?" Vicky's eyes were starting to get glassy again. She swiped away any tears and sniffed back her sob. She turned to Duff. "The detective who came to my house told me you witnessed Robert's murder."

Duff still had his feet on his desk, his fingers interlaced over his ample belly. "Saw the whole thing."

"Because you were working on my case?"

"I had no other reason to be tailing him."

"Was he cheating on me?"

Duff let the question hang in the air between them for a long moment. He inhaled sharply through his nose and said, "He was not."

Vicky slipped a damp tissue from a small purse she'd laid at her feet and dabbed at the corner of her eye. "Is that your official opinion?"

"Based on the facts and data at hand, yes. In no way, shape, or form did I find evidence to link Robert Bloch to any sort of extramarital affair. Not with his assistant, not with anyone. Hell, from what I saw, it seemed like he was on platonic terms with you, as well."

"So, why was he in the hotel, then?"

Duff shrugged. "If I were to hazard a guess, the simplest answer is that he might have felt a need to get away from you for the night."

Vicky looked down at her hands. Her fingers flexed nervously, and then she curled them into fists. "Robert and I started having problems a little more than a year ago. I don't know what happened. I thought we were happy. We were both successful at our jobs. We went on nice vacations. We enjoyed each other's company. And then one day, he came home and seemed distant. I thought maybe he had a bad day at work, but he was still distant the next day, and the day after that."

Vicky Bloch bit her lip for a moment, and a shudder ran through her as if she was fighting off the urge to cry again. "He stayed distant. And when he got his new promotion and hired that assistant of his, I guess I did the math and figured he was heading out of our marriage. Maybe I got old. Maybe I got fat. I don't know."

Abe leaned forward. "Maybe it had nothing to do with you. Maybe it was something entirely different, and he didn't tell you about it. Or couldn't tell you about it."

Vicky shot a glance at Abe, all regret and sadness. "I guess we'll never know now, will we?"

"What my bulldog-jowled compatriot was trying to tactfully breech is, what did you know about the handgun in his trunk?"

Vicky's head jerked back toward Duff with alarm. "What?" From the tone in her voice, it was clear she knew nothing about a gun.

"A Ruger nine-millimeter handgun. Found it behind one of the accessory panels in the trunk."

"A Ruger?"

"It's a type of gun." Abe tried to be helpful.

"I was in the Army for four years, I know what a Ruger is," said Vicky.

Abe was chastened. "Thank you for your service."

Vicky blew off his comment with a huff and rolled her eyes. "Please. My service was to be a secretary for a handsy lieutenant colonel. I didn't have to dodge bullets, just innuendo. I only did it for the GI Bill." She turned back to Duff. "I knew nothing about a Ruger. We have a Taurus 856 in the drawer of our bedside table for home defense, but that's all."

"No rifles?" asked Duff.

"No, neither of us hunts."

Duff and Abe exchanged a glance. Abe knew exactly what Duff was thinking. Vicky Bloch mentioned she was in the Army. In Basic Training, they teach recruits to shoot rifles and make them qualify on the range. That put her on Duff's suspect list even if she didn't know it.

"Did you ever confront him concerning your feelings about his distance?" Abe knew well that feeling of distance. Katherine figured out her sexuality somewhere around Matilda's fifth birthday. It took her almost ten more years to fully confront that fact, and the whole of those ten years were marked by increasing distance and friction between them.

"We were in counseling, if that's what you mean. Still, even the counselor said it felt like Robert was putting up walls between us. He would never give out more than he had to in counseling, so it was kind of a lost cause. It was like he was just going through the motions to make me happy. His heart wasn't in it."

Abe asked, "You automatically suspected adultery. Why?"

Vicky Bloch blinked at the question. "Isn't that what it always is? I mean, look at me, then look at his new assistant. She was a bikini model, for Christ's sake."

"Then you had reason to be worried, you're saying? Did Robert stray before? Did he have a wandering eye?"

Duff threw a crumpled ball of paper at Abe's head, but it missed and sailed past him. "Wandering eye? No one says wandering eye anymore. C'mon, Grandpa. Get with the times."

"You're older than I am by almost three months."

"But my eternal optimism keeps me youthful and hip."

Abe regrouped. Duff was a master of dragging things off course. "I'm sorry. Ignore him. Did Robert stray before?"

Vicky shook her head. "No, never. Before the distance started, he was always kind and responsive. I felt loved."

"What changed, and why did you assume it was the secretary?"

Vicky gestured at her torso with two hands. She was not without some attractive qualities, despite her plainness, but she was in a formless, loose top and had some of the middle-aged spread starting at her midsection. "I'm not a bikini model. She is."

"Bold of you to assume ol' Bobby could score a bikini model," said Duff. "Takes two to make that equation work. What makes you think she could be swayed by him?"

"He made good money. He was smart. He might not have been the most handsome man on the planet, but he had a way about him. He had many girlfriends before he met me."

"From what I gathered after tailing him most of this week, he not only wasn't cheating on you with a bikini model, he was sad, anxious, and alone."

Vicky looked to Abe for confirmation. "Is that what you saw, too?"

"Duff did most of the tailing on this case, but that's what he reported to me."

"Was Bob a drinker?" asked Duff.

"He'd have a glass of wine occasionally."

"Nothing harder?"

Vicky shook her head. "No, not really. He might have a glass of whiskey on the rocks at a business function, but most of the time, he sipped at it and never finished it. He didn't like whiskey all that much. Why do you ask?"

"He was almost three-quarters of the way through a bottle of Evan Walker last night."

Vicky's eyebrows shot up in surprise. "I've never even heard of Evan Walker."

"You've heard of Jack Daniels?"

"Of course."

"Evan Walker is like Jack's cousin who lives in a trailer park and has three cars on blocks on his lawn."

Vicky understood immediately. "Rot-gut whiskey?"

"Not quite that level. It's about ten bucks cheaper than basic Jack, though. I mean, Robert could have afforded far better stuff, I'm sure. He didn't, though. He went with lower-end, grocery-store booze."

"You hadn't noticed him drinking at home, though?" asked Abe.

"No, quite the opposite. We don't even have alcohol in the house."

"Did you argue before he left the house last night?" asked Duff.

"He never came home last night. He texted me and said he was going to a business dinner, and then back to the office to work on a new account. Told me it had to be done before two in the morning because he'd need to email it to some account in California before midnight on the coast."

"Did that kind of thing happen often?" asked Abe.

Vicky thought about it for a moment. "Often enough, I guess. Maybe once or twice a month. His company handled a lot of accounts around the country."

"And instead of working, he left the office and got a key for a hotel room." Duff began tapping his chin rhythmically, deep in thought. He kept a steady, slow beat with his index finger.

"Where did he go after he got the key?"

Duff shrugged. "Didn't follow him because we had no reason to follow him. We were looking for proof of infidelity at the time, nothing more. I knew he'd be back at the hotel at some point. I figured he'd be there with the bikini model eventually, so I went home to get my camera, and then I posted up in a spot to take photos."

"You saw him…get…" Vicky could not finish the sentence.

"I did."

"Did he suffer?"

"Not in the least. Death was instantaneous. I doubt he even had time to register pain."

Vicky dabbed at her eyes again. "That's a comfort, at least."

Abe leaned toward her. "Mrs. Bloch, you wanted to meet with us. Why? What are you hoping for here?"

Vicky took a moment to regain her composure. She folded the tissue and hid it in her fist. She swallowed hard. "I need you to find out who killed him."

"Easier said than done." Duff spun his chair away from her and turned up the AC unit at the window. The temperature was climbing in the stuffy apartment as the sun was fully hitting their windows.

"I've watched enough TV shows to know the police suspect the spouse first."

"Do you have any reason for them to suspect you?" asked Abe.

Vicky looked chastened. "They're going to find out about the life insurance, but it wasn't my idea. Robert did that on his own."

"Life insurance?" Duff spun his chair back toward her, suddenly interested.

"He increased his life insurance policy significantly when he got his promotion at the beginning of the year. The policy is less than six months old. It's going to look suspicious, I'm sure."

"So, you don't need to find the killer so much as you need to be cleared of the crime." Duff was inherently suspicious. It was part of growing up in a boys' home where everyone around him was stealing from him or waiting to beat him for no reason.

"I don't have an alibi. I was home alone last night. I watched a couple of hours of TV, and then I went to bed. That's it. No one saw me. When the police ask where I was last night, I'll tell them the truth, but no one can corroborate that fact."

Abe saw no signs of deception in her face. Her eyes did not shift. She made no discernible tics. She seemed nervous, but not nervous from guilt. Abe and Duff exchanged a glance. Duff gave Abe an almost imperceptible nod.

"We'll look into it for you, Mrs. Bloch." Abe pulled a contract form from his desk drawer and began to fill in the details. "Standard rates apply, of course."

"Thank you so much." Vicky took Abe's pen and signed the paper. "I was told you were the best in the city."

"I don't know about that," said Abe.

"I do." Duff kicked back in his chair and put his feet on his desk. "And you're right."

"How will you proceed?"

"We'll look at the facts and make inferences from those facts. We'll explore avenues of interest in connection with the case, and if those bear fruit, we will pursue further clues until we come to a concrete answer."

Vicky's face crinkled in confusion. "What do you already know? Who do you think killed my husband?"

Duff thought about it for a long moment. "Your husband was killed by a long gun from a good distance. This indicates someone who hunts regularly or is, or was, a trained sniper. The shot was long, but not overly difficult for someone who shoots regularly. It could have been done by an average guy, but the Ruger in Robert's trunk points toward him being involved in something sketchy, so we have to start with the assumption that this might have been a professional hit. If it was a pro job, then we have to assume that your husband crossed up the wrong guy."

"Or guys," said Abe.

"Or guys," Duff conceded.

"Are you saying the *mob* had him killed?" Vicky couldn't even pronounce the word aloud. She half-whispered it and put a hand to her mouth afterward as if uttering it could summon a bent-nose thug in a pinstripe suit to magically appear.

"Possibly," said Duff. "Which mob is the real question."

"My husband was boring. He was just a dull suburban guy. What kind of craziness could he have been involved with that someone would want to shoot him?"

"That's what you're paying us to find out," said Duff.

"Your husband might have been boring, but he was an accountant." Abe knew Bloch's company, Hanley, Dodge, and Briscoe, did the taxes for many different fiscal entities. "It's possible this might be related to his job. It's possible he was doing something on the side. You said he became distant about a year ago, correct?"

"Well, yes."

"That's before the bikini model became his assistant," said Duff.

"It's possible that's about the time he became involved with something shady." Abe was already trying to map out a rough timeline in his case notebook. "If he became distant a year ago, I imagine that's when whatever he was involved with started going south on him. That's usually how this stuff goes. Someone starts something they shouldn't be doing, and then it spirals out of control quickly."

"Did you notice any extra money coming in lately?"

"Not really," said Vicky.

Duff tapped his finger against his chin again. "Did you see him trying to hide anything from you? Like, did you catch him texting someone and hiding the screen from you?"

"No."

"Any weird phone calls at odd hours?"

"None."

"Did he sometimes have unexpected overnight trips that he blamed on business?"

"On occasion, but that's something he's been doing for years. His company has a lot of clients. Sometimes, they need a representative at the facility to help prep for an audit or clean up their books. It's common, but not frequent."

Abe asked, "Did the detectives tell you we found divorce papers in his briefcase?"

Vicky's face darkened. She shifted in her chair and swallowed hard. "Yes, sadly. I could feel it was heading in that direction, but I was unaware he'd moved to have them drawn up."

"That's another reason the police might suspect you, isn't it?" said Abe.

"I fear it might be, yes."

Duff took all this in. "Do you happen to know your husband's computer passwords?"

"Yes, I do. We always shared passwords in case of an emergen—" The word caught in Vicky's throat, and she sobbed into the tissue again. She fought hard to force the emotion back. "We shared passwords in case something like this happened. How ironic."

"Death isn't ironic," said Duff. "Something can't be ironic when it happens every three seconds somewhere in the world. You prepared for the worst-case scenario, and it happened. That's not ironic, just an outcome you hope never happens."

Vicky took another sip of water from the bottle Abe had given her earlier. She capped it and set it on the floor next to her chair. "I suppose you're right."

"I'm always right. It's a character flaw."

"Don't listen to him," said Abe. "What was that password?"

"It's my first and middle name with a dollar sign instead of an S and then three eights: *Vicky$ue888*. I don't know where he came up with the eight-eight-eight part."

"Pretty standard as far as passwords go. Capital, special character, and a number. Gotta have them all," said Duff. "Most people pick ones or zeros, and if the company makes him change frequently for security, then it's plausible he just went up or down to eights, depending on how many times he's changed it.

"I trust you gentlemen can work quickly?" Vicky picked up her purse. She was gathering herself to leave. "I have a very long weekend ahead of me. My family and Robert's parents will be here by noon to help me prepare Robert's funeral arrangements."

"We will work as quickly as we can," Abe assured her. "This might take time, though."

"If you have any other questions, feel free to call. If I don't answer, leave a message. I'll get back to you as soon as I can." Vicky stood to leave.

Abe stood as well, out of respect and tradition. Duff remained reclined with his feet on his desk.

"I thank you both."

"Money is really the best way to thank us," said Duff.

Abe escorted Vicky to the door. When she was gone, he locked the deadbolt and returned to his desk.

They shared a silence between them, partially out of habit, and partially because they were waiting to make sure Vicky Bloch had gone far enough away that she would not hear them murmuring to each other behind the hollow steel door of the apartment's main entry.

"She seemed a little off, yeah?"

Abe nodded. She was sad, yes. That was obvious. Abe read a half-dozen other emotions on her face and in gestures: scared, confused, worried—all the standard emotions present in someone after receiving surprising and tragic news. But there was more. There was something off-balance about her, like she was putting up a wall or hiding information. She was good at it, though. It was difficult to tell exactly what she was doing, if she was doing anything strange at all. As far as Abe knew, maybe this was just who she was.

Maybe this was her normal self, a little awkward and unsettled. He had no baseline reading of her actions beforehand. The day she had hired them had been straightforward, and she was seething with the barely contained fury of a woman who thought she was being replaced by a younger model. There was no need to ask a lot of questions. She wanted proof of an affair, and they had done that particularly distasteful mission dozens of times over the years. It was always the same: stalk, stakeout, snap. Trail the target, watch the target, take a picture when the target is in the throes of passion. The second you had good art, the case was over.

One of the first things Abe learned when studying psychology was that emotions were a broad spectrum and everyone experienced emotional stimuli differently. For some people, a spouse's death would be a sobbing, screaming, retching affair where they would lose motor function, collapsing into a heap and praying for their own death because they knew they would never find the strength to carry on without their partner. For others, a spouse's death was an obstacle to be endured. It was sad, yes, but that sadness was a weight they would carry. It was a personal issue, not something to burden others with, and not something they would use to seek attention. Everyone carried their own burdens, and for some, a tiny burden would break them in an instant, while others could gamely bear a thousand times the emotional weight of the broken person. It was hard to deduce who someone was until that weight was placed on their shoulders.

Abe yawned. It was an epic, jaw-cracking, involuntary, and impossible-to-stifle yawn. "I need to get some sleep. Did you sleep yet?"

Duff had not. "I think I'm catching my second wind."

"What say we start this case on Monday, then?"

"What about tomorrow?"

"Tomorrow's Sunday. Don't you like to take days off?"

Duff gestured at the piles of paper on his desk from their legal work cases. "I like to take days off from this nonsense. When we actually have something interesting, I'd rather work on it right away."

"Fine. You can start tomorrow. Call me if you find anything."

Abe exited the apartment and walked to the minivan on the street. It wasn't even eleven in the morning, and the heat was unbearable. Abe was sweating a small river. The smell of hot asphalt overpowered the usual familiar smells outside the building.

Abe waved hello at Cesar Salazar at El Muro, the taco stand on the first floor of their building. He was in no mood for a taco, but Cesar was a good guy. Cesar waved back.

Abe drove home, desperate to find some time alone with his pillow.

6

DUFF SAT MOTIONLESS at his desk for a long time after Abe left. He ran the facts of the events through his head. There were few.

Someone killed Robert Block with a long-range shot. Not super-sniper range, but far enough. The killer had to be good with a gun. The killer's lack of evidence at the scene and the careful steps he'd taken to obscure his face and license plates gave credence to the notion that he had done that sort of job before. This fact indicated that he was probably a professional. At the very least, he was an above-average thinker who knew the system and how to avoid getting caught in the usual dumb ways.

The Ruger in Bloch's trunk led Duff to believe the man was into something underhanded. Was the gun for offense or defense, though? Was Bloch the aggressor, or was he protecting himself? Duff doubted he was using the gun for protection because it was too far from the driver's position. The glove compartment or center console was the place for the weapon if it was for protection. Hiding a gun in the back of the car made Duff think it was an offensive, not defensive, weapon. If Bloch was the aggressor, who was his target?

And did the bikini model matter? If so, why? If not, why not?

Did Vicky Bloch's time in the Army mean anything, or was that just a coincidence and not circumstantial to the case?

There were more questions than answers, and Duff hated that.

Duff expected solutions to everything. If something happened, there had to be a reason for it. That was Physics 101. Something begat something else. A finger pulled a trigger, which released a hammer, which drove a firing pin into the primer of a shell casing packed with gunpowder, which ignited the gunpowder, which caused a controlled explosion, which launched the bullet from the barrel of a rifle at 2800 feet per second, which flew through the air, which hit a target, which shredded the skin, pectoralis major, and ribs before tearing through a heart and causing death. It was poetic, wasn't it? A bullet in motion caused a heart in motion to cease all motion.

Physics.

Duff looked at the pile of work on this desk. He wasn't going to touch it on a Saturday. Or a Sunday. That was all stuff for weekdays when Abe was there to make him do it and there was nothing better to do. It was busy work. Mind-numbing. Aggravating. Beneath him.

He glanced at the door to his bedroom. His PlayStation and recliner lay just beyond. He could go back to playing baseball until noon, and surely there would be a real baseball game on TV by that time. He could spend the afternoon in front of a roaring three-speed fan trying to forget about how much he was sweating.

Wheels's Bar was just down the street. Wheels and the rest of the rummies he called friends would be there. They would all be picking on Sally Salazar, unless Sally picked up Saturday hours. Then they might be picking on Earl because he was old and always told them to shut up or he'd kick their asses so hard they'd get shoe polish on their tongues. Wheels would also have at least two different sports on the TVs.

That is, unless the guys were watching *Under a Tuscan Sun* again. No one could get enough Diane Lane in that bar, and Duff couldn't blame them. He would have rather watched *Indian Summer* because it had Alan Arkin in it, but he never turned off *Under a Tuscan Sun* if it happened to be on when he was flipping channels. At least the guys at the bar were no longer on their *Rumble Fish* kick, because Duff had grown very tired of Matt Dillon.

It was hot. The lakefront beaches would be packed. He could take the bus out to Gurney Mills and go to Six Flags, but that place would be packed, too. Besides, at his size, most of the rides were off-limits to him. He would only be going to eat half his body weight in deep-fried carnival food.

Maybe he would spend a day at the theater watching movies he would not care about, simply to take advantage of the theater's golden air conditioning. He could swill popcorn coating in that artificial butter-oil and slug back Diet Pepsi until his liver decided to quit.

Or, he could do what he was best at and find answers to some of his questions.

Duff glanced at his phone. It was almost noon. A bus headed downtown would be along soon. He dressed quickly, slipped his feet into his worn Nikes, and grabbed his wallet and keys.

THE PETERSBURG BUILDING was one of the nondescript skyscrapers cluttering Chicago's downtown business district. It was gray. It was tall. It had a lot of windows. It was one of those forgettable structures where different corporations would inhabit different floors, sometimes taking up four or five of them, depending on their size. There was a front desk manned by security guards during the day. There were freight elevators, passenger elevators, and lots of stairs. The Petersburg was only sixty-one stories, so it never made the lists of the pantheon of great Chicago high-rises like the John Hancock Tower or the Willis Tower, even though to Duff and most everyone else in the world, that particular building would forever be the Sears Tower. The Petersburg was a grand column of architecture and human ingenuity, a monument to iron workers, architects, and engineers.

It also housed the prestigious accounting firm of Hanley, Dodge & Briscoe.

Duff exited a bus not far from the Hotel Afton and walked seven blocks to the Petersburg on the shadowy side of the street, even though the early afternoon shadows were slight and close to the buildings. He wore jeans and a white Brewers t-shirt with the Barrelman swinging for the fences in blue rubber paint on the front. He also wore a Brewers cap, dark blue with the wheat-M logo. The hat band of the cap was damp with sweat, but he kept it on. It helped keep the top of his head from catching a burn when he wasn't bathed in shade. As someone who did not frequently do outdoorsy things, Duff was exceedingly pale and burned easily.

Duff walked to the Petersburg and strolled around the entire city block it encompassed. He made note of the main entrance and watched the coming and going from the front door. There were roughly forty different businesses inside the Petersburg. They ranged from finance to accounting to engineering firms. They were all high-dollar, white-collar businesses, and true to the grind mentality of those they employed, none of them seemed to comprehend the meaning of weekends. The Petersburg was busy constantly. Even late at night, food deliveries would arrive for the peons forced to work after normal business hours so their seven-figure-earning bosses could be home with their families in their luxury apartments or Gold Coast mansions, or perhaps at their weekend villas on one of the many lakes just over the border in Wisconsin.

Duff waited in the sun and tried not to think about the temperature. It was becoming more uncomfortable as the heat gathered strength in the afternoon. A flashing sign down the street proclaimed the temperature to be 93 degrees, which was far too hot for a summer day in the Midwest. It was still early, too. It would easily gather up another five or six degrees before the heat would break around five that afternoon, when the sun would finally start to relent during its descent in the western sky.

Duff watched the sidewalks in front of the building without looking like he was watching them. This was a practiced skill he'd picked up over the years. He knew enough not to stare at the doors, and he knew how to glance around occasionally without looking too suspicious. He knew exactly what he was looking for. The only question was, when would they show up? The most likely arrival time for second-shift workers would be around two-thirty in the afternoon. He just needed to find the right group of guys.

A steady stream of people in weekend casual attire walked in and out of the building. Occasionally, someone in a more formal business suit would pull up in a cab and head into the building. Sometimes, someone in a business suit would leave the building and get into a cab. Duff always wondered what people who had to wear suits did on the weekends. Duff owned three neckties, but he prided himself on having only worn each of them once in the last twenty years. When he was at Bensonhurst and his therapist asked him what he wanted to do with his life, he'd said, *Anything that doesn't require a uniform, a name tag, or a tie.* So far, he'd been able to hold to that promise. However, the irony of dressing in the same style of clothes every day since he was sixteen, thus making it an ersatz uniform, was entirely lost on Duff.

After an hour of patient waiting, a pair of Latino men approached the Petersburg. One carried a black steel lunch box, the other carried a small Igloo cooler. They were wearing shorts and flip-flops in the heat, but each carried practical work boots in their other hand. Duff caught sight of socks sticking out of the tops of the boots and knew he'd found his guys.

When the two men walked up the small flight of steps toward the lobby, Duff moved quickly to trail them. He stayed a few paces behind them, not close enough to rouse suspicion, but close enough that he looked like he might belong with them. He was clearly not Mexican, but Duff found his lack of redeeming quality features made him forgettable to most people. Other than his girth, which wasn't all that uncommon in the Midwest, he was entirely unimpressive and unremarkable physically. Just another pasty white guy with bland, doughy features. He might catch someone's eye for a moment, but it would be a glance, nothing more. The second he was past them, their brain would erase his existence from their mind like an Etch-a-Sketch.

Duff trailed the Mexicans as they walked into the lobby. One of them nodded toward a security guard at the desk. He nodded back. Nothing more.

The Mexicans turned hard left toward a door marked *Authorized Access Only*. One of them pulled a laminated card from his pocket and touched it to a square reader next to the door. The door buzzed and unlocked. The first guy opened the door and held it for his friend. Duff nodded at the guy and walked through the door as well. He kept walking. Neither of them said anything. They all traipsed down two flights of steps and exited in a basement hallway the general public was never meant to see. It was built in floor-to-ceiling cement blocks. The narrow passageway was poorly lit and smelled of cleansers, industrial boiler oil, and dust, with a faint hint of black mold for a little respiratory razzle-dazzle.

The two Latinos ducked into the third door on the left. It was a large, unmarked locker room without keycard access. This was where the building's maintenance and custodial staff changed and showered. Duff followed them into the locker room like he was meant to be there. The two Mexicans did not give him a second glance.

Duff rambled to a long line of toilet stalls and entered the furthest one down. He took a seat on the commode and waited. He wanted the locker room to be empty, or at the very least, he wanted the two custodians he'd entered with to leave.

Duff knew from experience that walking into a place as busy as the Petersburg building was just a matter of confidence and looking like you knew what you were doing. The turnover rate for the bottom-level Joe jobs at a building like this was always high. The security guards would have stopped and checked him if he'd wandered in and looked around the lobby like it was his first time indoors, but because he kept his head down and followed the guys the security guards already knew, they just figured he was part of the team.

The two guys took their time getting ready, chattering at each other in Spanish. Eventually, they slammed their lockers and left the room. Duff heard their voices fading away as they walked down the hall on their way to work.

Duff's Spanish was only good enough to order at a restaurant or to find out where the library was. Anything beyond that was Greek to him. Given his intelligence and ability to learn, it sometimes bothered him that he didn't turn his significant mental abilities toward languages. He was never bothered by that fact for long, though. He had other things begging for space in his already crowded brain.

Duff exited the stall. The locker room was silent, but he knew anyone could enter any second. Duff glanced up and down the corridor of lockers and saw a bunch of dark gray custodial jumpsuits hanging on a rack at the far end of the room. He grabbed the biggest one he could find, only an XXL, and stuffed himself into it.

It wasn't a pretty sight.

Even lying down on his back and attempting to exhale all his oxygen while sucking in his gut like he was trying to fool people into thinking he wasn't one of the larger land mammals in North America, the zipper fought him every step of the way, and when he finally got it zipped to his mid-chest, the zipper threatened to give up the fight and slide back down with every motion. Duff found a safety pin on one of the desks in the custodian's break room and managed to secure the zipper to the fabric to prevent it from backsliding.

Duff checked himself out in a mirror. He looked like six pounds of bratwurst in a five-pound casing. He'd looked worse, though. Maybe it wasn't the best costume he'd ever worn—that honor went to the old Ben Cooper Inc. Buck Rogers vinyl costume and plastic mask he'd worn for Halloween when he was five—but it would do.

Duff opened the door and checked the hallway corridor. It was still empty and quiet. Duff went down the lockers and tried the handles. Every locker room had at least one guy who didn't keep anything of value in his locker, so he didn't care if whatever he kept in his locker got stolen. Those guys always had something worth taking. Luckily, Duff found several of those sorts of guys.

In one locker he opened, he found a ring of keys on a clip-on retractable pull-chain. On the ring was a custodian's all-access keycard emblazoned with a photo ID and the name *Orlando Monces*. Orlando was a chubby, bald Filipino man. If someone only gave the card a quick glance, Duff might be able to pass for Orlando Monces if anyone stopped him and demanded to see his ID. He doubted they would stop him, though. The important part of the card was having one. No one was out there comparing faces and ID badges on the fly.

Duff clipped the ring to his belt and clipped the ID card to the overalls pocket on his chest. He left the locker room, walked down the hall to a supply room, and grabbed a janitor's cart. Then, with his disguise complete, Duff pushed the cart to the freight elevator and hit the call button.

Duff already knew where the Hanley, Dodge & Briscoe offices were, thanks to tailing Robert Bloch earlier in the week. He also had a general idea of where Bloch's office was. Nameplates would be on the doors for anyone important, so Duff did not worry about having difficulty finding it.

The elevator doors opened on the fifteenth story of the Petersburg Building. Duff was greeted by a plain, white access hall where custodial staff could access the offices without passing the front desk. Even though it was Saturday, and it was highly unlikely for someone to be working the front desk on a weekend, Duff preferred to use the side entrance like a janitor would. The less disruption he made, the better.

He pushed the cart through the office and did not make eye contact with the few people working at their desks. If they noticed him, they said nothing. After all, he was just one of the serfs, one of the small cogs that made the big machine run. He carried out their trash. He wouldn't be interested in whatever was on their Excel spreadsheets; thus, they had no common ground.

The office was arranged in a large square, with cubicles for the lowest-ranking members of the firm in the center and offices with doors on them around the edges for the higher-ranking members. The cubicles were lit by sickly fluorescent lights, which were dimmed for the weekend. There were two executive hallways shooting off from the main square with bigger, better offices on the outside edge of the offices, so they would have windows to give them a sparkling view of the city beyond the glass. There were meeting rooms and break rooms in the central space. No pristine fifteenth-floor views for people in meetings, and the break rooms were visible from the senior partner offices, so people couldn't even enjoy their state-mandated fifteen-minute respites in peace. No, the vulture eyes of the old men who owned the company would be there to make sure you were nervous while you took their money with your lollygagging.

The office depressed Duff so much that he briefly considered chucking himself out the nearest window. He would not have been good in such an environment. He could barely function in an office where he was a half-owner. He couldn't believe people lived like this. It was a stifling den of boredom and rigor, a suffocating hell of conformity and toadying for a paycheck. There was no joy in that office. Not until you made the big bucks, at least. Then, the only joy came from no longer being a minion.

Duff pushed the cart down the executive hallway, reading the nameplates as he did. The names read as lily white as a minivan in the suburbs. Gerald Rich. Ronald McGuire. Amy Franke. David Prince. Mark van der Boom. He found Robert Bloch's name in the middle of the hallway on the right. The lights in the office were dark. Duff used Orlando Monces's keycard to access the room.

Like all the executive offices, there were two rooms: the first room was a small waiting room with an administrative assistant's desk in the corner opposite the door. The assistant's desk was just far enough back to allow the door to swing open fully. There were two industrial waiting room chairs to the left. The main door to Bloch's office was in the center of the left wall of the waiting room.

Duff closed the door behind him, and the electronic lock clicked into place. The keycard gave him access to Bloch's office. He moved to the floor-to-ceiling windows and closed the Venetian blinds so no one could see him from the hall. Then, without prying eyes, Duff sat at Bloch's desk. He relaxed in the comfortable executive chair. It was plush and had all the bells and whistles a man would want. Heat, a silent massage feature, orthopedic lumbar support, silent wheels. It was a thousand-dollar chair. Bloch had it good.

He did not have a window, though. The office was dark without the sickly yellow light from the hallway.

Duff touched the space bar of the expensive computer on Bloch's desk. It was one of those with a hidden hard drive, so the desk consisted of two huge flat-screen monitors, a keyboard, and a mouse. That was all that cluttered his workspace. No photos. No coffee mug. No pencil cup. Just the computer.

The screens blazed to life after a second and lit the office like daylight. Duff knew it would happen, but he was unprepared for exactly how bright it would be. Duff used the dimmer command on the keyboard to take the brightness down as much as he could, but there was still plenty of light glowing around the edges of the blinds in the windows facing the hallway. If anyone walked past, they'd know someone was in Bloch's office.

Duff cursed silently and got to work as fast as he could. The security login screen popped up. Bloch's login name was in the first box, which was helpful. Duff only needed to type the password. He tried *Vicky$ue888* and was immediately rejected. He tried *Vicky$ue999*. No dice. He tried *Vicky$ue777*, and then he tried *Vicky$ue0000*, assuming that the company required people to change passwords frequently enough that Bloch had lapped the three-digit numbers and was now on four-digit numbers. Still, no joy in Mudville.

After the fourth attempt, a warning screen popped up telling him he had tried too many passwords. Another failed attempt would lock the computer and force him to call IT to unlock it.

Duff laced his fingers and cracked them outward like every computer hacker in every movie and TV show ever. He pondered his next move. It would be worth trying one more password. But what password?

Bloch was a man facing a divorce. He wouldn't be using his soon-to-be ex-wife's name anymore, would he? What was the only other name Duff knew to associate with him? The name that was so important he'd put it in his notes tab on his phone: the bikini model secretary. Her middle name had an S in it, so Duff assumed Bloch would use his dollar-sign trick again. The only questions were, what numbers would he use, and where was he in the company's security policies?

Duff had to assume he would start over with *111* as a final tag. The company forced him to change passwords. He'd need the numbers. He couldn't go straight to *888*, Duff reasoned. Also, the bikini model had not been working for him for too long. If the security protocol forced him to change passwords every six months, he'd still be on the first trio of numbers.

"Fuck it; here goes nothing." Duff poised his fingers over the keys and typed slowly, making sure a typo did not derail his final chance to crack the security page. He typed *JenniferRo$e111*.

Duff poised his index finger over the return key. He felt a tightness in his stomach. His brain started to second-guess. He shoved all doubts aside. Worst-case scenario, this wouldn't work, and he'd only have wasted his afternoon on nothing. That had happened many times before. Detective work was far more strikeouts than home runs. If you kept your average above .200, you were doing fine.

Duff clicked the return key. The computer spun for a second, and then the home screen loaded.

Duff breathed a sigh of relief. Social engineering didn't work all the time, but it worked *most* of the time, and that's why everyone should demand two-step verification on anything that requires a password.

This brought up a whole new set of questions about the bikini model, though.

The desktop home screen looked foreign to Duff. He was not great with computers, but he could get by. He looked like the sort of guy who would be a pro on a computer, but Bensonhurst never had them in the mid-90s, so Duff's teenage years were lost. He did not use a computer until he and Abe founded their agency. He had to play a lot of catch-up. Abe was the computer nerd. He'd used them throughout all his schooling in college and grad school. Duff was out of his depth when it came to anything beyond the basics, although he could fake it when necessary.

The home page of Bloch's computer was an artwork of files, forms, and program icons. Duff kept his own omputer desktop very neat because he didn't require a ton of files. For someone like Bloch, who was doing a thousand different tasks every day, a cluttered desktop was the outcome of how busy he was.

Duff opened a couple of files and found financial charts, data sheets, and spreadsheets aplenty. It was all the sort of highbrow money stuff any man would expect to find on an accountant's computer. Duff was not an accountant. He was not good with money. While he had a rough education in finance, what was on those computer files was like cuneiform to him.

Duff searched Bloch's desk and found a small flash drive in the upper right drawer. It wasn't hidden, just lying in the open. He found the small, square computer in the drawer opposite. He popped the little thumb drive into the USB port. It was mostly empty, only a couple of PowerPoint presentations for training purposes. Duff deleted those. Then, he dragged all the files on the desktop onto the thumb drive for Abe to look at later.

Duff dug further into Bloch's files. He went into the Documents folder and found hundreds of folders. He also saw two different levels of folders:

the local files on Bloch's computer and the cloud-based files for company use. Duff knew he could ignore the cloud-based files. If Bloch was doing anything sketchy enough that it would result in him catching a bullet, it would be in the local files only. He wouldn't want the company to know what he was getting into on their dime. The local folders were awash in the same sort of technical accounting files as the desktop, so Duff dragged them onto the thumb drive, too.

Duff opened the email folder but found only the inane back-and-forth company emails, all written with that faux-polite business-speak that made him want to poke out his own eyes. Duff checked the emails sent to Jennifer Rose Carthage from Bloch's computer, hoping he might find something salacious in them, but found them only to be formal and professional, even exceedingly polite and supportive. Anything involving the bikini model felt like a dead-end, but then why would Bloch use her name as a password?

Duff kept searching through the files, scanning several levels deep into many of the folders. He then looked in other, less likely spots. He did not spot anything that raised his Spidey senses. Everything looked to be on the level. It stuck in his craw. Duff felt like the guy had to be dirty somehow, otherwise, he wouldn't have been targeted. He started to wonder if the assassination might not have been work-related. Duff's mind kept wandering back to the hidden Ruger. Why a gun, and why hide it in the trunk?

Out of desperation, Duff pulled up the Google browser and typed *how to hide files on a computer* into the search bar. It was a simplistic, elementary idea, but if he was a regular forty-something guy with a regular job like an accountant, that accountant probably wasn't a government-level hacker, so this would be the route a regular guy might take.

The first website he clicked suggested turning folders into protected operating system files and then checking the *hide operating system files* box in the folder options menu.

It couldn't be that simple, could it?

Duff opened the folder options menu and found the *hide operating system* folder checked. He unchecked it and then dove back into the system files menu.

A slew of files magically appeared. Most were protected, true operating system files. However, there were three unprotected. When Duff opened them, he found a slew of records and spreadsheets with large amounts of money indicated. Immediately, the hairs on Duff's neck started to rise. He was not sure what he was looking at, but he knew it was suspect. He dragged the folders to the thumb drive, gave them their own folder to keep them separate from the rest of the files, and closed all the menus.

Duff pocketed the drive and closed the computer. Abe would have to sort out what he'd found later. Duff retrieved a dust cloth and some cleaning spray from the custodial cart in the outer office. He used the spray on the cloth and wiped down the desk, keyboard, and door handles. He wasn't worried about the cops dusting for prints in Bloch's office, but better safe than sorry.

Duff was about to leave the office, but paused. Out of curiosity, he searched the desk of Jennifer Rose Carthage. He found nothing of value or interest. Her desk was sparsely stocked, but professional. No knick-knacks or personal photos. No clutter. She seemed to be an adequate secretary, at worst. This profoundly disappointed Duff.

Duff cracked the door to Bloch's office and scanned the hall. A few underlings were busy in the bullpen, but no one had noticed him. Duff pulled the cart out of the office, wiped his fingerprints from the door handle, and moved further down the corridor.

As long as he was in the office, he let his curiosity override his common sense. He moved to the first office with a bigwig's name on it: *Michael Hanley*. He slipped into the secretary's outer office area and found Hanley's assistant's space to be almost twice what Jennifer Rose Carthage's little office was. Executive Assistant privilege, he supposed. Hanley's secretary also had a window near her desk. The sweltering Chicago sun beat against the glass relentlessly. Despite the building's high-quality air conditioning, the outer office was at least five degrees warmer than the sunless hallway.

Duff didn't have a password for Hanley's computer, nor did he spot enough things around the office to even bother with trying any of his social engineering tricks. Instead, he perused the large bookcase behind the man's desk and scanned the books, trinkets, and photos Michael Hanley kept in the office.

Everything was mundane and raised no alarms in Duff's head. College diplomas. A picture of a very fancy Chris-Craft motorboat docked on a lake. An expensive scale model of a '65 Corvette, black with white accents. Nothing important or pertinent.

Duff moved to the next man's office, finding the name *Walter Briscoe* on the door. He slipped inside the door and found a nearly empty office. Briscoe looked to be in the process of retiring from the company, or he wasn't into decorating, because his shelves were empty, as were his desk drawers. One of the few pictures on the man's shelf showed an elderly man accepting an award at a gathering. Duff assumed the man receiving the award was Walter Briscoe. If this was the correct assumption, Briscoe probably should have retired long ago. With a rough estimate of age based on his appearance, Briscoe was easily in his eighties in the photo, and the photo looked at least five or ten years old. Briscoe could be well into his nineties now.

Duff moved to a third office. The nameplate on the door read *H. Arlo Dodge*. It made Duff pause. Arlo Dodge and Walter Briscoe sounded like names for cowboys. Hell, Walter Briscoe looked like he was born before the automobile, so maybe it was fitting.

Dodge's office was well-stocked with many items of personal history, most notably several plaques and framed medals from his time in the military. Dodge appeared to have joined the Army as an enlisted man and then used his GI Bill to fund his college education to become an accountant. There were no medals for accountancy in the military Duff knew of offhand, but Dodge had been a man of action in his youth, serving at Fort Benning in the Cavalry Brigade.

Benning no longer existed, per se, having been subjected to a name change when the military purged the names of assets relating to the Confederacy. It was now Fort Moore. Benning/Moore was a well-known Army base, though.

There were no photos of Dodge himself. Whether that was by accident or on purpose, Duff did not know. He mentally crossed Walter Briscoe off his list of potential shooters, but now wondered about Dodge. What exactly did Dodge do in the military as an enlisted man?

Duff pulled out his phone and checked the Wikipedia page for Fort Moore. The summary said it had an Army Infantry School, but nothing else that made Duff's senses alert—until he saw the garrison information panel.

Fort Moore housed an Army Marksmanship Unit. Snipers.

Duff's Spidey senses went on full alert. Was Arlo Dodge a trained sniper? And if so, might he have been the guy to pull the trigger? Duff needed to get out of the office and alert Abe to this newfound information. They also needed to do a full background search on Arlo Dodge.

Duff opened the door to the outer office and pushed the cart into the hall. He almost ran into a young woman hurrying through the corridor. She was mousy and frazzled in khaki Capri pants and a blue-and-white striped top from the Gap's business casual collection. The girl reacted with surprise as the sudden appearance of a janitor's cart almost knocked her over.

"Whoop, sorry there." Duff buried his usual accent, which was mostly general American neutral with some hints of Milwaukee and a skosh of northern Canada. He put on a heavy Chicago accent as if he were auditioning to be a new regular in a reboot of the old Saturday Night Live *Bill Swerski's Superfans* sketches. "Ope, didn't see ya, dere."

"You're not Miguel." The woman looked at Duff quizzically.

"Nope. Name's Arthur. Call me Art." He chose a random man's name. He'd been told he looked like an Arthur once before, so he hoped it fit him.

"Where's Miguel?"

Duff shrugged and started moving toward the exit. "I dunno, lady. Da boss, he told me to come up to sixteen and clean da offices, so's I comes up to sixteen and cleans da offices. I just do what I'm told."

"This is fifteen. Hanley, Dodge and Briscoe." The woman gave him a quizzical look.

"Is it?" Duff feigned surprise. He looked around in shock. "Well, hell. I'm kinda new here. Does this building got a thirteenth floor? Some o' dem don't, ya know. Superstitions and the like."

"I don't know. I haven't looked."

"Well, shoot. I guess I'm in da wrong place. Does Miguel clean on sixteen, too?" Duff pushed the cart toward the door.

"I don't know."

"Well, I'll call him and find out. If he doesn't, maybe he'll be up here soon." Duff was nearly out of the executive hallway. "If he does show up, let him know I got these first three done for him." Duff pushed his cart past the bullpen cubicles. The secret was to take his time. He ambled like a man who was being paid by the hour. He was in no particular hurry to get to sixteen, as far as she knew.

The woman was following him. "What was your name again?" She pulled a pen from her pocket and found a Post-It lying on a desk.

"Art. Art van Leeuwenhouk." Duff used his keycard to open the door to the hidden maintenance corridor.

"How do you spell that?" The woman was scribbling on the pad as she walked.

"With a shit-ton of E's and a K at the end, just like the famous microbiologist." Duff started a smooth, prattling rant like someone who had been asked how to spell his name many times. He knew that if he could keep talking, she probably wouldn't interrupt him until he was done, and he might be fully out of the office by that point. "My mom did our family gene stuff a few years back, and she tells me dat me and him was related. Can you believe dat? He was called da Father of Microbiology. I'm more like da father of picking up trashy broads and getting screwed on child support, if ya get me. But, hey—dat's probably my own fault, right? Gotta use a rubber, and I'm too stupid to do dat sometimes." Duff was almost through the door.

The woman changed her tone to apologetic. "We just have to have a record of everyone who comes into the office."

"Lady, I'm on the maintenance crew. Just ask Orlando about me. He knows me. Trained me in last week." Duff was closing the door behind him.

The woman waved off the suggestion. "I'm sure it won't be necessary. I just have to put it in a file in case something comes up. That's why we usually just have Miguel clean the office."

Duff gave her a good *aw, shucks* move. "He's a good kid, dat one."

"He's sixty-four."

Shit. Duff covered as quickly as he could. "I know. A lot of the guys in custodial call him *kid* like how da guys call me *Slim* or *Tiny,* you get me? We're all just bustin' balls out here. It's all in fun. Makes the days a little faster if you have some fun."

"Oh, of course." The woman gave him a polite smile. "Well, have a good night."

"You, too. Don't work too hard. It might be hot out, but it's a weekend. Get out and live a little." The door to the maintenance hall closed. Duff was free.

He pushed the cart to the elevator and rode to the locker rooms. He ditched the cart, ditched the Cintas jumpsuit, and tossed Orlando's keycard back into the unlocked locker. Then, he followed the signs pointing to the delivery loading dock and exited through the least-watched door in the place. Security never got too giddy about the loading dock, especially on the weekends when all the deliveries were scheduled, not random like they were during the week. No one said boo to Duff.

He walked back into the blast furnace of a blistering Chicago summer day and immediately burst into a waterpark's worth of sweat. Most fat guys didn't like the heat. Duff never minded the heat, but he could live without the sweat.

THERE WAS A knock at the office door at 6:00 PM. Duff had just turned off his PlayStation and was preparing to wander down the street to Wheels's place, where he planned to have a bottle of cold domestic and watch the Brewers game, maybe order a pizza to be delivered there.

Duff checked his phone for messages he might have missed when he was engrossed in the play-by-play of his video games. He glanced at the office answering machine. No flashing light to indicate a missed call.

Duff was intrigued. No one came to visit him socially, especially not on a Saturday night. It might have been the kid coming over to check on him, because she did that sometimes, usually after she baked a treat she knew he would like. Tilda was good like that.

Duff unlocked the door and opened it. A tall, slim African American woman in a dark blue blazer, charcoal slacks, and black pumps stood in the hall. Her hair was pulled back from her face in a tight chignon on the top of her head. Duff recognized her instantly. "Mindy. Long time, no see."

Mindy Jefferson's real name was Minerva, but she had the same distaste for her first name that Duff had for his. She had hired Abe and Duff a year prior to find out why someone was trying to kill her. After solving the case, they had not heard from her since.

Mindy walked into the office and looked around. Her nose wrinkled. "Why does it smell so funky in here?"

"Because the AC doesn't work for shit. I'm basically cooking low and slow like pork ribs. Stick around, maybe you can baste me."

"I'd sooner jump out that window." Mindy sat in the chair opposite Abe's desk. "Where's Slim?"

"Well, it's Saturday, so I imagine he's home staring blankly at the wall or sifting through his record collection. He's getting back into vinyl. Can you believe that?" Duff sat at his desk. He turned his chair to face Mindy.

"All the cool people collect vinyl nowadays."

"Yeah, hence why I'm shocked as hell Abe bought a turntable. Those things aren't cheap anymore. He dropped like three-hundo on it, plus another hundo for a receiver. He cheaped out on speakers, though. He's got some dinky-ass pair of Bluetoothed JBLs, but then again, he really can't crank the Pink Floyd too loudly; his apartment walls are basically shoji paper."

"What about you? What's new with you?" Mindy studied him with a raised eyebrow.

Nothing ever changed with Duff, so he had nothing to hide. "Not a damn thing. I hear people like consistency."

Mindy inclined her forehead toward him. "You're wearing cargo shorts. I didn't see you as a cargo shorts kind of guy."

"I'm not, normally. But it's balls hot out there, and my basketball shorts won't stay up with my wallet and phone in the pockets. If they made basketball shorts with belt loops, I'd switch back."

She gestured to his t-shirt. "Still haven't given up on the Brewers?"

"What? Give up on a team who never had a pitcher throw a perfect game, and only had one pitcher in their history throw a complete game no-hitter? One of only five teams to never win a World Series? Never. I'm not going to bandwagon to some team with actual success. Leave me alone in the basement with the Brew Crew. We're a match made in heaven."

Duff gave her a half-smile as he finished his rant. "Look, I'd happily shoot the shit about baseball with you all night, if that's what you're here for. Hell, we can go down to Wheels's place, and I'll buy you a beer while we watch the Brewers-Rockies game."

"You know I didn't come to talk baseball. Besides, I'm an O's fan."

"I figured." Duff sat back in his chair. "Too bad. If I'd walked into that bar with a woman as pretty as you, the rest of the fellas would have anointed me as their new god."

"Not a king?"

"Pretty as you? No, I'd be their god. They'd build me a shrine and everything. Probably start writing gospels about me." Duff gave her an appraising look. "Why are you here, then?"

"I'm not going to just give you that information. Do your party trick, smart guy. Tell me why I'm here."

Mindy had not given Duff much to work with, but he didn't need much. He looked her up and down and took a deep breath. "Your outfit tells me you're here on business, not pleasure. You're working. That means you got a new job. You're not with the CIA anymore, but you're still fairly young, and you have a lot of contacts in the greater Washington, DC area, especially since the news of your brother went public. I'm betting some of those fancy DC types knew what kind of clout your brother's unwitting adoptive father carried, and one or two of them probably called you up to throw you a bone. You're dressed formally on a stupidly hot Chicago night, so I'm guessing you didn't fly into town on assignment. You live here now, and I'm not talking about that crappy temp apartment you had when we met. You got a real place somewhere. Northside, I bet. That means you also work here. I guess you decided to move here after the dust settled so you could be closer to your brother and maybe get to know him better, seeing as he's your only living family. Plus, you needed a change of scenery."

Mindy could not hide her amused smile. "You're on fire, Mr. Duffy."

"Just Duff." Duff leaned forward and appraised her some more. "If you're working a federal job in Chicago, it's probably one of the three-letter agencies. I know you bailed out of spook-central, and you're probably a shade too old to start with the F'bees, although you could pass for someone at least ten years younger."

"Thank you."

Duff paused and made his final assessment. "You showing up today is odd because I don't think you and I crossed paths anytime recently, but I did go somewhere interesting today, and then you showed up. So, I'm going to bet you were part of a team watching Hanley, Dodge & Briscoe for some reason, and you saw my fat ass wandering around in there today. Because of this, I imagine you've taken a job with the IRS because they're the most likely entity investigating an accounting firm. I know you're not carrying a gun at the moment, unless you've got one tucked at the small of your back in a pancake holster, but judging from how you're sitting in that chair, you look a might too comfortable for that. Because of the lack of a firearm, I'm guessing you're not part of any sort of arrest team or someone who gets to mix it up. You're doing analysis or investigatory work, but nothing that might get bloody. How'd I do?"

Mindy's smile went from slightly amused to fully amused. "Correct on all accounts. How do you do it?"

Duff gave her a sheepish half-grin. "Just do. It's like breathing, I guess. If you think about it, you can control it or even stop doing it, but when you're not thinking about it, it's just what happens."

"Still pretty impressive. You would have made a great cop."

"Yes, let's give me a gun and qualified immunity. That will work out well for everyone, I think." Duff turned the focus back to Mindy. "Why the IRS? Get tired of being too loved for being part of the spy brigade?"

Mindy held up her hands like she didn't have a decent answer. "It's a good job. I'm a special investigator now. It's sorta like being a money detective. It's in Chicago. I get to see my brother and his family pretty frequently. It's nice to have family again, as fucked up as that whole situation is."

"You seem happy."

Mindy smiled warmly. "I am, I think. Or, I'm heading toward happy, at least."

"Until my walrus ass waltzed into an operation you were running on an accounting firm, that is."

"You know, I meant to call you guys and let you know how things were going, but I got busy with the new job. I guess maybe seeing you today made me realize I needed to come back here to thank you again before I reamed you a new one for possibly fucking up an on-going investigation."

"Well, I have an ongoing investigation, too. It's not like I would even think to call the IRS about any investigation I was running. Besides, don't you have to be an accountant to be an IRS special investigator?"

"I was a global financial analyst for a couple of years in the spooks. I know my way around money crimes."

"And yet, you're wearing off-the-rack. Shameful. Federal pay scales: that's the true money crime."

Mindy ignored Duff's jab. She knew him well enough to know he wasn't doing it to be mean. He just liked to poke people. "We think someone in Hanley, Dodge, and Briscoe might be running books for Petey Pucillo."

Duff knew the name. "*Il Pulce.*"

The Flea was the translation of Pucillo's nickname on the streets. He was a fourth or fifth-generation member of a second-tier mob family in Chicago's far north side. His father was Enzio Pucillo, called *Ernie* or *Big Ernie* by most people. Enzio was either the man in charge, or he was second to his cousin, Michael, whom people called *Saint Michael* because he was a real Eddie Haskel type—skeezy as hell, but he could turn on the charm and bluff people whenever necessary.

Ernie Pucillo ran a semi-reputable mechanic shop out of the neighborhoods northwest of the city center, with outlets in Montclare, Belmont Cragin, Logan Square, and Dunning. All the Italian families on the northwest corner knew they had to bring their cars to Big Ernie for service, or else they might wake up to find their windshields smashed.

Big Ernie was a good mechanic, though. He hired good men and demanded quality work from them. If you took your car to Big Ernie, he kept the damned thing running, that was for sure, and he didn't screw you on the prices, particularly if you were Italian. Big Ernie was on the verge of actually making his longtime business more successful as a legitimate business than he'd ever been trying to run numbers and sports books. The fact that he was considering expanding from his five existing shops was proof of that.

"The Flea has been slowly taking over his daddy's shops as the old man is galloping toward retirement. The kid was a good mechanic from what I hear, but he appears to be even better with gambling, protection rackets, and loan sharking." Mindy pulled a phone from the interior pocket of her blazer. She showed Duff a picture of Petey Pucillo standing around a table of stereotypical Italian mob types in tracksuits and mechanics coveralls. They seemed to be listening to Petey's rant.

"Pretty standard for the Italian mob, isn't it?" All the different factions of organized crime had their areas of interest and expertise. The Italians kept it pretty low-key and traditional compared to some of the darker stuff the Triads and MS-13 were getting into nowadays. Duff didn't actually mind the Italians. Compared to the other groups, what was left of the Italian mob in Chicago was slowly becoming the racist great-uncle at Thanksgiving. Mostly harmless, and no one paid them much attention; when they did something stupid, everyone just smiled and nodded knowing full well it'd be at least a year before you had to watch them do something stupid again.

"Petey has a group of sycophants behind him, a bunch of boneheaded oregano-eaters who watched *The Godfather* too many times, and they want to bring back the glory days of Capone and the Outfit."

"Hence why the IRS is looking to put him away since he's probably clean as far as the cops can prove."

Mindy touched a finger to the end of her nose. "Petey is dirty; we just need the proof."

"Well, isn't this interesting, then? I might know a little something that could help you out."

"Robert Bloch, right?"

"Abe and I were tailing him, trying to prove infidelity. I saw him get whacked less than twenty-four hours ago."

"I saw the police report. Long gun at range. Clean as crystal."

"Bloch had a Ruger in his trunk. That makes me think he was messed up with something off-center. He also had some weird files on his work computer."

Mindy leaned forward, her eyes were intense. "How weird?"

"Weird enough. I'm gonna have Abe look at them later."

"Can I get a copy?"

"Sure. Why the hell not?" Duff flipped her the thumb drive.

Mindy caught it out of the air, plugged it into her phone, and downloaded the files. Her eyebrows rose as she started to scan them. "I'm going to need a real computer and some time to go over these."

"Call Abe when you find what you're looking for because I'm worthless when it comes to that sort of thing. I know it's probably suspect, but other than that, I don't know exactly what I'm looking at. I don't have the patience to go through a spreadsheet. That's what Abe is for."

"You think Bloch is the guy we're looking for, then?"

Duff couldn't say. It certainly seemed that way, but he had no proof, no hard evidence linking Bloch with the Pucillo family. He threw up his hands in a noncommittal gesture. "Could be. Maybe not. That's why I copied the forms."

"How'd you get in there, anyhow?"

"Just walked in. No one stops you from going anywhere if you're in a custodian's uniform."

"I'll remember that." Mindy stood to leave.

"How'd you spot me? Did you get a warrant to put cameras in the office?"

"We don't have the evidence to get a warrant right now. Turns out, we didn't need a warrant for all the elevators and the hallways outside the office. We just asked the building super if we could tap into the closed-circuit security camera feed. Anything we get won't necessarily hold up in court, but we were watching it in case Petey came in to see someone in the firm. We have a judge who will give us a warrant if we can prove the Flea is working with someone inside. A trip to their floor probably would have done it. This judge is desperate to pull the trigger and shut down the Pucillos, but we just have to find something concrete."

Mindy moved to the door. "Call me if you do find something concrete."

"Will do." Duff tapped two fingers to his forehead in a salute. "Never let it be said I wasn't there when the IRS needed help pinning some fool's nuts to the wall."

"Your government appreciates your service." Mindy opened the door and moved into the hallway. "Thanks again for everything you did last year."

"The best way to thank us is with cash."

"I already paid you fools."

"We also accept gift cards for Culver's."

Mindy closed the door without another word.

Duff sat in the empty office and listened to the rattle of the window AC. What in the hell had he gotten into with this case? There were too many parts to the puzzle, and Duff began to suspect he actually had two puzzles in one box. He didn't like it.

This was where a good detective cat could help put him on the right path.

7

A BE WOKE WHEN the man who lived in the apartment above his decided to practice the electric guitar. The fuzzy crunch of power chords was barely muted through the ceiling because the guy's crusty amp sat directly on the cheap PVL flooring and rattled Abe's ceiling fan. The guy had been teaching himself guitar for more than a year, and he had not improved at all. He was really good at switching between a couple of basic chords, so he just decided to take Harlan Howard's advice and barreled ahead with three chords and the truth. That is, if the incessant repetition of the D4/F4/G4 intro to *Smoke on the Water* was indeed *the truth*.

Abe lay in bed listening to grungy noise while the rotating fan at the foot of his bed blew hot air at him. The fan was better than nothing. He tried to be grateful. As a kid, he suffered for years in an unsavory apartment in a less-than-desirable neighborhood where he and his mother spent many hot summer days without air conditioning. His mother used to fill Ziploc bags with ice cubes and water, and they would hold them to their necks, pressing them on their carotid arteries to lower their body temperature.

It was during the little moments of suffering when Abe missed his mother, a woman who suffered more than most people should. She never got to see her only grandchild. She never got to see Abe become a business owner. He had no pictures of her in the apartment he grew up in because she never owned a camera in the era before everyone walked around with an entire photo studio in their pocket.

There was one good picture of his mother, taken by a stranger on the day Abe graduated from high school. His mother bought one of those disposable cardboard cameras that were all the rage in the early '90s just for the occasion. Abe and his mother were side by side, Abe displaying the most natural smile of his entire life in his black gown and mortarboard with the valedictorian's sash hanging over his shoulders. His mother was positively beaming. She'd splurged and taken the time and money to have her hair done for that special day. She looked beautiful. Happy for once, not exhausted and worried.

Abe took the negative to a drug store and had it blown up to eight-by-ten, and he put the picture in a sterling silver frame. His mother had that picture on her dresser until she died a few years later.

After her passing, Abe kept it. It was one of the few things of his mother's he still possessed. It hung in a place of honor in the old house for years, but after he moved out, Katherine redecorated and put the photo in Matilda's room. As much as Abe would have liked to have that picture in his apartment, it was much more important for it to be in his daughter's room so her grandmother could watch over her.

Abe walked to the window and threw open the curtains. The sun was low in the sky, but it was still bright. The sun didn't fully set until after nine o'clock. It kept the temperatures unbearable. The heat he felt radiating from the glass was akin to a low boil. Abe wiped a gathering of beads of sweat from his forehead with a finger and cast them to the floor with a flick of his wrist. He was shirtless, clad only in his jogging shorts, and it was still too much clothing.

Abe checked his phone. No calls. No messages. He checked the dating app even though he knew what he'd find before he opened it. No messages there, either.

The guitar hero upstairs changed songs. He began ham-handedly butchering his way through the opening lick to Ozzy's *Crazy Train*. Abe began to feel like he was going off the rails a bit, himself.

Fight fire with fire. Abe staggered out of his bedroom and put one of his favorite records on his new turntable. He'd recently picked up the 40th Anniversary remastered vinyl release of Rush's *Signals* album. It was a record about being an outcast, about feeling like you didn't fit in. It was also a record about aging, about fearing you no longer possessed the fire of youth. Abe identified with it strongly.

The sounds of Geddy Lee's voice helped mute the guitar upstairs. It filled the room with pleasant noise that made him think of his time in college, back when he still possessed at least a matchstick's worth of the fire of youth. That inferno never fully kindled for him, but he'd at least been willing to try before he graduated and found out that being a real adult never fully suited him.

A cold shower helped cool Abe down. Then he dressed in shorts and sneakers, a thin, well-worn white T-shirt with WDRV's oval logo on the chest. He'd gotten the shirt for free a few years back. He and Katherine had taken Matilda to some little carnival at one of the nearby parks, and someone had thrust the shirt into his hands. He liked the station, though. They played classic rock, although they tended to go for the more popular stuff like Fleetwood Mac and Journey. They played their forty-song playlist on endless loops while straying away from the harder or less popular classic stuff Abe preferred. Still, it was one of the stations programmed into the six radio presets in *The Bad-Luck Charm.*

Abe left his apartment to get supper. Since moving out of his old house, Abe regretfully followed Duff's bad example of rarely making meals at home. Cooking took a lot of time and effort, and the results were never as good as restaurant food. He tried to balance this sin by skipping breakfast most days or skipping other meals if he failed to skip breakfast. He also tried to spend minimally. No super-sizing. No desserts. Just the basic meal. He used coupons when he could.

Abe walked to DiNonno's, a small sandwich shop a couple of blocks from his place. They were a traditional Italian beef joint. There were dozens of Italian beef joints littered around Chicago. DiNonno's was no better or worse than any of them. They made a good Italian beef, and they had a slew of other sandwiches. Abe liked the Chicago Hammer, a small mountain of various Italian meats on a hard sub roll with mayo, thin tomato slices, and shredded lettuce. He got it slathered with red wine vinegar and oil, as well.

Normally, he brought a book with him so he could sit at one of the little bistro tables outside and read while he ate, however the bistro tables were black metal, and they had been soaking up solar radiation for most of the day, thus turning them from a pleasant place to sit into something that could burn bare flesh. There was a stand-up counter in the shop where people sometimes shoveled down their food, but Abe didn't like eating shoulder-to-shoulder with someone he didn't know. He took his sandwich to go and headed home.

When Abe opened the door to his apartment, Duff was sitting on his couch watching a baseball game on television. Duff didn't have a key to his place, but Duff was a gifted lockpicker, one of many useful little traits he managed to pick up during his time at the boys' home in Canada.

Abe didn't hide the sarcasm in his voice. "Please, enter. Make yourself at home."

Abe shut the door behind him. He should be surprised by Duff's appearance, as this was only the third time his best friend had ever come to Abe's apartment, but Abe had learned never to be surprised by Duff showing up unannounced. The man had his own agenda and his own sense of time and place.

"You need a bigger TV. Maybe an OLED."

"I hardly watch television. It's fine."

"Can we get a bigger TV for the office, then?"

"We don't need a bigger TV for the office."

"Any second thoughts about getting a detective cat?"

"No cats."

Duff nodded toward the package in Abe's hand. "Is that DiNonno's?"

"It is."

"Did you bring me any?"

"I didn't know you were going to be here."

"Can I have half?"

"No."

"Can I have a Diet Coke?"

"They're in the fridge."

Duff held up an open can. "I already got one."

Abe spread his sandwich wrapper on the counter in his kitchenette area. The designers of the bachelor apartment he rented must have anticipated that men would not be using the kitchens much, because they made them functional, but tiny. "Why are you here?"

"I had a visitor about thirty minutes ago. Someone from our past."

That could be any one of hundreds, if not thousands, of people. Abe wasn't in the mood to guess. "Who?"

"Mindy Jefferson."

Abe's eyebrows shot up involuntarily. "Didn't expect to hear from her. How's she doing?"

"She's got a job with the IRS. She's hunting dirty money." Duff held up a flash drive. When he saw Abe tracking it with his eyes, Duff tossed it to his partner. Abe reached out to catch it, but it bounced off his fingers and clattered to the floor.

Abe picked it up. "What's this?"

"I went to Hanley, Dodge, and Briscoe and got on Robert Bloch's computer today. He's got some funky files in there. I made a copy for you to look at, and I gave a copy to Mindy. She reckons that someone at HD-and-B is running numbers for Petey Pucillo, and she thinks little Petey is trying to get his family's fading crime syndicate back up to a level of more influence."

"I thought the Italian mob was more or less done in Chicago. I thought they were content to play in the minors." Abe took a bite of the Chicago Hammer. A blast of oregano filled his sinuses. It was glorious.

"Not anymore, I guess. I mean, I haven't been keeping tabs on them because they've been largely irrelevant for so long."

Abe and Duff had a strong working knowledge of the various factions of organized crime within the city. It was part of the territory, really. There were the Italians, the Mexicans, and the Slavs; they were the heavy operators in Chicago, each with warring subsets and factions. However, almost every racial and cultural designation of humanity was represented in some form. The Irish had a small gang. There was a considerable Jewish mob that tended to operate in the deepest shadows. The Filipinos were active enough to be considered part of the scene. The Chinese Triads were represented, but not as much as on the coasts. The Yakuza had some minor operators in town, as did the Korean Kkangpae. There was a mishmash of Muslim gangs who were beginning to cause a stir, sometimes operating within strict country affiliations, and sometimes operating as more of a melting pot from various countries and regions bound together through common goals and a common religion.

Then there were the smaller, more traditional components of organized crime: the street gangs. The People Nation and the Folk Nation were the most powerful and overriding, each with dozens of sub-gangs controlling various neighborhoods, most of them working two main sources of income: drugs and sex trafficking.

There were the racial power gangs as well, mostly moving meth, cocaine, and fentanyl for income, and then spending that income to upset opposing groups. The whites ran a lot of loosely affiliated outlaw biker gangs, neo-Nazis, and white supremacy groups. The Black Power types styled themselves after the Nation of Islam and their ilk, recognizable by their suits, bow ties, and kufi caps. There were Native American gangs, Arab gangs, and plenty of small-time Asian operators, Vietnamese, Hmong, and Malaysian, and even some Indian and Pakistani gangs running books, guns, and drugs.

Lastly, there were the refugee factions of the recently displaced who were banding together as a source of strength. The Ukrainian gangs, who used to be a subset of the Slavs, were now rising up to be a player in their own right. There were refugee bands from Africa, Afghanistan, and non-Triad Chinese groups.

Abe got a headache when he tried to think about all of them. They were always changing and evolving. Sometimes, one group would suddenly have a power spike, and the CPD or the feds might take them down a peg, and that group would lose considerable ground. A power vacuum would result in several factions competing for territory and money. It was impossible to know who was operating in what capacity at any given time because so much of it happened in the shadows.

There were a lot of people in the Chicago metro who had no clue how much gang activity went down around them every single day, and they preferred it that way. The more the gangs kept to the shadows, the less chance the CPD or the feds would interfere. It kept them at a crispy level of coolness, with none of them wanting to instigate an event that would result in mutually assured destruction from the authorities.

Abe and Duff tried very hard not to have much to do with any of the various mobs if they could help it. They sometimes walked a fine line between being of service to the gangs and being an enemy. It was always best to avoid falling too heavily on either side of that line.

In any city, in any large town even, there is always a world beneath the world everyone else sees. Unless you're part of that world, it was probably best to simply avoid it.

"Ernie Pucillo kept it small-time, didn't he? Preferred his legit business, right?"

"As far as I know," said Duff. "But Ernie is getting up there in years. The old man can't bust knuckles like he used to, and he's got several shops to lord over. I imagine he's making a seven-figure profit from the shops. Why bust knucks if you have a real pipeline the feds won't bitch about?"

"Mindy thinks Petey wants to be a big-time guy. Sounds familiar." Abe and Duff had seen loads of small-timers try to step up a notch over the years. Most of the tall poppies were cut quickly when they stepped on someone else's territory. Petey Pucillo could make a real move to expand his role and take on more ground. Ernie Pucillo seemed content with a couple of neighborhoods of total control and a healthy sphere of influence, but the closer the mob got to the legitimate suburbs like Rosemont and Des Plaines, the looser the control was from the downtown gangs. There was room to expand to the suburbs, where the activity was low and primarily focused on drugs. The only reason they didn't was that there was less demand for goods and services. People in the 'burbs were focused on child-rearing and jobs. They walked a straighter and narrower path. They weren't looking for meth or sex.

Well, most of them weren't. There were always exceptions, of course.

"If Petey makes a big move, it could lead to him pushing out a couple of the other minor Italian families. Might lead to either war or unification," said Duff.

"Petey's moves don't help us solve the Bloch murder."

"True. But it's an intriguing motive, isn't it? Bloch is doing sketchy books. He decides he wants a bigger cut. Petey has him whacked. Makes sense on paper."

Abe knew from the tone in Duff's voice that Duff didn't jibe with that as a solution to the murder. He knew his partner's methods and thought processes better than anyone. "You're not fully behind this theory."

"Are you?"

"I could be. I'd need good evidence, though." Abe retrieved his laptop from where it was charging on the counter. He opened it and plugged the thumb drive into the USB port. The explorer window popped up. Abe used Control-A to select all the files and open them. Dozens of Excel spreadsheets began to populate his screen.

"You would have made a good accountant." Duff turned back to the baseball game. He idly sipped his Diet Coke.

"What makes you say that?"

"Accountants are boring as fuck."

"It's not like you have a vibrant social life, either."

"*Touché.*"

Abe started scanning the documents. Duff walked behind him and pointed out the sketchy files he'd found hidden in the system folders.

"This is going to take me a while," said Abe.

Duff turned up the volume on the game. "That's fine. We're only in the bottom of the second. I got time."

AN HOUR LATER, Abe finally leaned back from the laptop screen and pushed his reading glasses to his forehead. He rubbed at his eyes and yawned. It was the top of the seventh. The Rockies were up 6-2, and it wasn't looking great for the Crew.

Duff muted the TV. "Thoughts, Professor?"

Abe let his eyeglasses fall back to his nose. "He's definitely moving large amounts of cash around for someone, but I have two issues."

"And they are?"

"First, I'm not sure if what he's doing is illegal or just unethical. Second, I'm not one hundred percent certain this is Bloch's handiwork. I mean, I tried to look at the user log data on the files, and it was all scrubbed."

"Say what now?"

"When someone uses an app or a program on a company-wide server like they have at big accounting places, it charts user data. This file has no user data."

"You're telling me that Bloch maybe didn't edit the files, but someone else saved them on his hard drive in his system folder, which isn't accessible by a company-wide network."

"That's a possibility, yes. Bloch might have been the editor and scrubbed his name for plausible deniability or something. He might not. I can't tell."

"That would point us at an IT guy or an exec with considerable privileges, then." Duff's eyes glazed over with the distant, faraway look they got when he had too many inside pieces to the puzzle and not enough edge or corner pieces.

"Or, it's just Bloch covering his tracks."

"Here's another possibility: what if Bloch didn't know about the Ruger in his trunk?"

Abe's eyes narrowed. "Someone else put it there, you think?"

"Maybe Bloch is working for Petey. Maybe Petey has one of his guys hide the gun in Bloch's car just in case. I mean, how often do you check those silly compartments? Maybe if Bloch screws over Petey, Petey makes a call and gets the CPD to stop Bloch on the road, probably for a bullshit violation, and they pick Bloch up on having an unregistered firearm. That's worth a night in jail, at least. Maybe even a couple of nights. Petey knows right where Bloch is then, and it's easy to have the fear of God put into him by some large Italian fella with a broken nose, if you get what I'm saying. Petey has to know people on the inside, even at the local lockups."

"Seems like a lot of work for someone with Petey's connections. Why not just put the fear of God into him with a couple of kneecappers and skip the gun?"

"You're probably right. I was just spinning wild theories."

"That's not like you."

Duff turned his attention back to the screen just in time to watch a player in gray hit a laser beam to the right field gap for a stand-up double and an RBI. Rockies were up 7-2. "I'm just saying, there's a lot of weirdness to this whole thing. Particularly, does the bikini model have anything to do with it? If yes, what? Seems weird that Bloch would go out of his way to hire her once he got that promotion and then be entirely honorable."

"Maybe he tried once, she shut him down, and then she threatened to go to HR."

"Anything's possible, I guess." Duff turned back to the TV in time to watch one of the Rockies swing out of his shoes at a breaking ball.

"How do you want to proceed on this, then? Do we go rattle some cages with the Pucillos, or do we go to the accountants and try them?"

Duff weighed both options in his mind. "I think rattling cages with any mob organization would be bad. We can't really go back to the accountants until Monday, which means we're going to end up spending all day tomorrow with our proverbial thumbs up our proverbial asses, and I hate that. Maybe we should go see Meyer."

Meyer Himmelman was a tiny, wizened little man who owned the building where Abe and Duff ran their operation. He looked like someone built a ventriloquist puppet and patterned it after a 100-year-old Gilbert Gottfried. Looks were deceiving, though. Although Himmelman would never admit it, he was either the highest-ranking member of the Jewish mob in Chicago or one of the top guys. The Jewish mob was good at keeping their organization deep in the shadows, and not even the organized crime guys on the police force knew who did what for them.

Whenever Abe and Duff asked questions about the seedier side of Chicago, Meyer always hemmed and hawed about it, questioning why they would ask him of all people, because he was simply a legitimate businessman and didn't get in with those types. But he always said he would ask some of his friends. Usually, less than twenty-four hours later, an unlisted number would call Abe or Duff on their cell phone with the answers to whatever they needed. It was a weird way to have a man on the inside of organized crime, but it worked. Their landlord had far more knowledge of what was going on in gangland than they did.

"Might be a good idea. Think he'll see us on a Sunday?"

"Do you think he actually takes days off? I've never called him and not had the phone answered by someone. If I needed him, he always got back to me promptly. The man is a devout businessman. He does business. That's all he does." Duff added as an afterthought, "Besides, today is Shabbos. It's not like he has to go to temple tomorrow."

"We could just take tomorrow off like normal people."

"And do what? You spend all your time playing Pink Floyd records and watching reruns of *The Rockford Files* while obsessing over the mistakes and regrets in your life, and I spend all my time watching TV or playing video games. How is doing that all day going to benefit either of us?"

Abe had to concede Duff's point. "We'll go at a respectable hour, though. Maybe noon-ish? I don't want to show up too early."

"Noon-ish is good by me."

Abe's phone began to ring. When he looked at the face, it showed the number from their office telephone. Abe held up his cell phone and showed it to Duff. "Why is my phone getting a call from the office?"

"I usually forward the office telephone to your phone when I go out. I'm surprised you just noticed."

"We don't get a lot of calls to begin with, and even fewer after-hours." Abe hit the button to answer the phone and found himself speaking to Vicky Bloch.

"I'm sorry to call so late, but I just found something sort of weird, and I figured I'd call you guys. Maybe it means something."

Abe summoned Duff with a wave of his hand and put the phone on speaker. "What did you find?"

"Well, my in-laws just left to go to their hotel room, and I decided to go on Robert's laptop here at the house so I could access all the legal stuff I know he had on there. I found out that his old password no longer works. He changed his personal computer password before he died."

Abe and Duff exchanged a knowing glance. "Mrs. Bloch, I'm sure you've had a very long and trying day, but would you mind terribly if Duff and I came over to look at the computer?"

"Not at all. I was hoping you'd say that. If you can't access it, I'm going to have to find someone who can, I guess."

"We'll be there shortly." Abe hit the button to end the call. "You know his new password, don't you? That's how you got the files off his computer."

"I might know his new password. I know the password he used at work. Social engineering tells us people tend to change all their passwords to the same thing because it's easier to function in life that way. However, I cannot guarantee the same password will work on his home computer."

"Better than nothing. Let's go."

Duff checked the score of the Brewers game. They were still down by five at the top of the eighth. He already knew how the game was going to end, barring any late-game heroics. "Might as well, I guess."

8

THE BLOCHS LIVED in an updated but modest two-story row house on one of the nicest streets in the Avondale neighborhood. Their home was only fifteen minutes from the Petersburg building, twenty minutes if traffic was bad. Thirty if it was really bad. The house wouldn't be considered upscale, but it was a little fancier than some of their neighbors. A Realtor might have called it a starter home, but in the current real estate climate, even with Robert's promotion, homes like this were being forced to evolve into forever homes because nothing nicer would be reasonably priced.

The neighborhood was quiet. No kids out playing. No one walking a dog. It was eerily still, but the heat had driven everyone inside. A steady, droning hum could be heard from air conditioning units up and down the street. It was a good day for Netflix, ice cream, and not doing anything to stress the system.

Abe and Duff parked a block away from the house. Street parking was at a premium, so people grabbed spots wherever they could.

Vicky Bloch met them at the door. She looked tired and frazzled. She had aged ten years since that morning. Her hair was frizzy from the humidity. She had given up the linen shirt and Capri pants she wore that morning in favor of a sloppy, threadbare Pixies t-shirt and a pair of black, paint-spattered yoga pants that had seen better days. "Forgive how I look. It's been a long day."

"You look fine," said Abe.

Simultaneously, Duff said, "You look like four miles of bad road."

A man appeared behind Vicky, mid-forties, in shape. He had two days' growth of a blond beard speckling his chin and a blond mop of hair on his head. He was in shorts and a t-shirt. He had a flurry of tattoos down his arms. "I put them in the freezer for you, Vick."

"I appreciate it, Tom." Vicky gestured to the man. "This is Tom O'Brien. He lives next door."

O'Brien nodded a greeting. "Just leaving. Only stopped by to drop off some casseroles."

"The traditional Midwestern meal of mourning," said Duff.

"That was kind of you." Abe stepped to the side so O'Brien could slip past.

"I'm sure Sharon and I will check in on you soon, Vick. Chin up. You'll get through this."

"Thank you, Tom." Vicky gave him a sad half-wave. They exchanged a glance. It was subtle, but Abe noticed it. It lingered for a moment, almost intimate. Was it the odd, uncomfortable situation of the death of a neighbor, or was it something else? Abe chastised himself. *Don't see things that aren't there.*

Vicky stepped back so Abe and Duff could come through the door. "It's kind of funny, I guess. When your husband dies, people come to your house acting like they want to support you, but really, they're looking for their own support. Robert's parents are in their early eighties. This whole thing might just kill both of them. I've never seen two people sadder. His father kept saying he should have gone first. Then, you end up being their shoulder to cry on. It's a lot."

"One of my old professors in college used to say that there are no rules to grief." Abe liked that line. It was true, too. Grief was a long, deep, and wide river, and the currents meandered in strange eddies for everyone.

"I still feel like this is all so surreal. I feel like it shouldn't be happening. Nothing makes sense to me at the moment. I keep wanting to find a reset button so I can go back a day and stop it from happening because it feels like I'm just in the wrong spot in life."

"That's a feeling that may never leave you. It will just get easier to function around it," said Abe. "You're building a new state of being, a new normal."

"I don't know if I can handle a new normal."

"Where's the computer?" Too much talk of feelings made Duff bored and uncomfortable.

Vicky seemed startled by Duff's bluntness. She twitched slightly, blinking as if she were seeing bright lights. She had to make the mental transition from grief to business. She wasn't prepared for it, but she regrouped as best she could. "I'm sorry. It's upstairs in Robert's office."

Vicky led Abe and Duff through her home. Abe was quick to note the plush couch and recliner, a very nice, very expensive OLED widescreen on the wall, and several decorative odds and ends that pointed to the couple having the disposable cash for nice things that a prosperous dual-income, no-kids lifestyle allowed. He also noted photos on a cabinet near the dining room with pictures of Vicky twenty years ago in the old camouflage Army battle dress uniform. There was another photo of her in the standard Class A uniform, smiling with two other girls wearing the same tan skirt and blouse.

The house itself had three bedrooms, a master bedroom with a full bath and steam shower, and two rooms turned into offices. Vicky's was painted a joyous peach with glossy white trim. Robert's office was a sedate, dark gray with matte black trim. It reminded Abe of the corridors on the Death Star.

Duff bulled into the room and sat on the expensive leather chair in front of Robert Bloch's desk. The chair puffed air and groaned in protest when Duff dropped his weight on it. He opened the laptop and was greeted with a generic backdrop of a desert sunset, one of the preset backgrounds included with every Windows laptop.

To Abe and Duff, that said Robert Bloch did not care to personalize his machine. It was a tool. It was not a source of joy. People who spent a lot of time on their computers for fun, be it social media, gaming, or even surfing for porn, tended to personalize a lot of aspects of their machines. People who used them solely for work could rarely be bothered.

Duff cracked his fingers with a flourish and set about entering the password. His fingers moved too quickly for Abe or Vicky to note the new password, but it worked. The laptop's security screen melted away and delivered the desktop screen, the plain blue Windows 11 background. More proof that the machine was a tool, nothing more.

Duff's finger paused over the touchpad. He looked up at Abe. "You want to take over from here, or do you just want me to do what I did earlier?"

"All you." Abe busied himself by walking around the office and looking at all the photographs Bloch had framed and on display. Pictures of Robert and Vicky on a beach somewhere. A picture of Bloch in an ROTC uniform. Pictures of Bloch graduating from Butler University in Indiana. Pictures of him with what looked like nieces and nephews. In all the pictures, he had a big smile, but it was a photographed smile, a *say cheese* smile. The eyes were not engaged with the smile. The eyes were flat and lifeless. It was unsettling to look into the eyes of the now-deceased Robert Bloch.

At the same time, Abe recognized the unhappiness behind those eyes. Why was he unhappy? Was it marital issues? Had they started long before Vicky ever noticed? That was usually the case for long-married couples hitting the rocks. One partner finds out the other has been mentally checking out of the relationship for years by the time things fall apart.

Duff sorted through the file folders with rapid clicks of the touchpad. He went to the systems folder as he'd done when he discovered the files on

Bloch's work computer. No extraneous files were hidden on his home computer. "Strange."

"Maybe he didn't feel a need to hide files here," said Abe. "The only person who could find them would be Vicky, and it's unlikely she'd open his work files for fun or snooping."

Vicky was indignant at the insinuation. "We always respected each other's privacy. I never snooped."

"Never…until you hired us to snoop for you," said Duff.

"I had reasons to believe."

"And you never looked at his phone or computer when you suspected him of having an affair with his secretary?"

Vicky's cheeks flushed red. "Of course I looked. I didn't see anything, so I thought he was just good at covering his tracks. That's why I sought you out. You came highly recommended by one of the HR people at my work."

Duff started going through other files. It was all the typical files people kept on their computers: back taxes, funny pictures, family photos, Word files with resumes and cover letters, one file had the first three chapters of a long-dormant novel Bloch started writing. Duff opened a file titled *Miscellaneous* and found a trove of other files. He opened one and found dozens of nude photos of Vicky Bloch. They were almost twenty years old. She looked fit, happy, and in love.

Vicky saw the thumbnails pop up and shrieked. "Oh, shit! I forgot those existed. Close it, please."

Duff did as he was asked. "For the record, you got nothing to be ashamed of."

Vicky covered her face with her hands. She was flashing a bright crimson from the base of her neck to her hairline. "That was just before we got married."

"Never took more?"

"That's none of your business," she snapped.

"Duff was not asking to see them—" Abe started to say, but Vicky cut him off.

"Yeah, right."

Duff defended himself. "I was just saying, if you never did fun, sexy-time stuff like this after marriage, then maybe that's why he was getting a divorce."

Vicky Bloch flushed bright red, this time with anger, not embarrassment. Tears sprang to the corners of her eyes. She turned on her heel and stormed out of the room.

There was a long silence. Abe leaned down to Duff's ear and murmured, "That was less than tactful."

"Noted." Duff continued to surf through files as though nothing had happened.

A few moments later, he clicked a file and found a half-dozen pictures of Jennifer Rose Carthage staring at him. They were not the glitzy bikini model photos a Google search had rendered. These looked like they were cribbed from her social media. They were simple photos, candids, and she was fully dressed in all of them with minimal makeup. Without the professional lighting and camera work, full glam eyeliner, lipstick, and fake lashes, she looked downright human. Duff was confused by this discovery. "What the hell?"

Abe bent over to look closely at the six photos in the Windows file. "Why does he have her photos?"

"Not just that—why does he have *these* photos? Why doesn't he have all the bikini photos? If I'm a dude with a hot secretary, I'm keeping the sexy bikini photos in a file on my laptop."

Like lightning striking, Abe's mind popped to his own daughter's social media. She didn't have anything sexy or overly suggestive posted, but some of her outfits made Abe uncomfortable as a father—her short Homecoming dress, for example, or the shots of Matilda and her friends when they were all wearing halter tops on a hot day. He tended not to look at those photos.

Abe pointed to one of the social media photos on the screen. "Make that one bigger."

Duff did as he was asked. It was a simple shot, almost a passport photo-style headshot of Jennifer Carthage with a genuine smile. She wore almost no make-up. It was a simple shot, flattering but lovely.

Abe grabbed one of the old photos of Bloch from the nearest shelf. It was a picture of Bloch at a baseball game with a male friend when he was in his early twenties. He wasn't wearing glasses. Even with the Cubs hat shading his face, it was a clear picture of the man. Abe held it up to the monitor. "Do you see what I see?"

Duff looked at the photo. "A rich, northside asshole is a Cubs fan? Hardly groundbreaking detective work, Aberforth."

Abe forgot that Duff didn't see people like he did. Abe had to point out the similarities. He held Bloch's photo closer to the shot of Jennifer Carthage on the monitor. "Look at them together. The chin. The shape of the nose. The brow line. The eyes. She looks like one of those photo filters that gender-swaps someone. She looks like Robert Bloch, but female."

"Are you saying what I think you're saying?"

"I think Bloch might have a daughter."

There was a strangled cry that made Abe jump. Vicky Bloch was in the doorway of the office. She had overheard their exchange. The result was a fresh batch of tears and a tormented wail.

ABE SETTLED VICKY on the sofa in the living room with a cup of tea. Duff sat in the oversized recliner and turned on the TV without asking. He flipped channels until he found the Dodgers playing the Braves in Los Angeles on TNT. He was kind enough to mute the sound, but he was also kind enough to know that comforting a woman in distress was well outside of his wheelhouse. He let Abe handle things like that. Abe was used to female emotions.

Vicky's cheeks were tear-streaked, and she was so upset she trembled. She held a tea towel because facial tissues weren't absorbent enough. She dabbed at her face and fought to hold back sobs. The chance of her husband having a child she never knew about touched a deep nerve. It took her several long minutes to gather herself enough to speak.

"We never had kids. We talked about it. I wanted to, but Robert always said kids were too expensive, and he was too concerned about our incomes. When we first got married, we lived in a shitty apartment near Chinatown for the first six years until we could afford this place."

"What's wrong with Chinatown?" Duff had lived there since he left Canada.

"Nothing. It's fine. It just wasn't a great place to raise a kid."

"Lots of people raise kids there every day."

"It wasn't the type of place where *we* wanted to raise a kid, okay? We wanted the suburbs. We wanted a backyard with a swing set. We wanted a place where our kid could walk to school alone."

"*We* meaning you and Robert, or *we* meaning just you?" asked Abe.

Vicky held the tea towel to her face. More shuddering sobs wracked her body. "Just me, I guess. I had a very clear vision of how I would be a mother. Even after we bought this house, I brought it up a couple of times, but Robert talked about the soaring price of childcare, how expensive a child's education would be, and how we'd lose so much headway on our retirement savings and investments. He wanted to make more money before we thought about kids. And suddenly, we've been married for ten years, and I was in my late thirties and staring down the barrel at forty. I stopped taking my birth control without telling Robert, but I just never got pregnant. When I hit forty-two with no baby, I told myself I probably wasn't able to have kids, and I just gave up thinking about it. Lots of women don't get to have a baby. I was nothing special, right?"

"I imagine the idea that Robert might be a parent is a big shock," said Abe.

"Huge. It explains the distance, though. I think he knew I'd freak out over it."

"Well, let's try not to jump to conclusions without evidence. This woman might not be his child. We know nothing for sure."

There were footsteps on the wooden stairs leading up to the Blochs' front porch. Heavy steps, more than one set. There were muffled voices outside the door.

Vicky Bloch shot out of her seat and tried to put herself back together. "Good lord, who is here?" She rushed to the window and looked out. She let a few good curses hiss through her lips. She turned back to Abe and Duff. "It's my brother and his wife and kids. You have to go. I'm sorry."

"Don't apologize." Abe stood. Duff turned off the TV and pushed himself out of the recliner.

"Don't say anything about this girl just yet, okay? Maybe find out if she's really his kid, first."

"Will do," said Abe. Duff saluted.

Vicky opened the door and was quickly enveloped by a large, stocky man and a plump, middle-aged woman. Three kids tailed after them, ranging in age from early teens to maybe eight or nine years old.

"We came as soon as Mom called." The man's voice was muffled as his face was pressed into Vicky's shoulder.

Vicky tried to return his embrace but was held fast by his arms. "Thank you for coming. It's been a hard day."

Abe and Duff tried to slip out unnoticed, but it was difficult to get around the mass of humanity in the doorway.

Vicky had to make up a story for them. "These are friends of mine. That's Abe, and that's Duff. They were just leaving."

The broad-shouldered man held out a hand to Abe. "Nice to meet you. David Nowak. I'm Vicky's brother. This is my wife Carla, and those are our kids."

Abe shook his hand and forced an awkward smile. "Nice to meet you. We have to be on our way."

"Thanks for stopping by to take care of Vicky. Terrible business this. Very unfortunate." David Nowak held his hand out to Duff, who winced and moved backward a step.

"Ignore him," said Abe. "Most people do."

"Did you find a good place to park? You can use the empty spot in front of our garage in the alley behind the house. Robert's car is still elsewhere. I think the police are holding it for now."

"We got a spot right in front of the house." David jabbed a thumb over his shoulder toward the street.

Abe and Duff squeezed past the kids and stepped out onto the porch. Immediately, there was a twenty-degree difference between the Bloch home and the sweltering night. Duff began to sweat.

They closed the door and heard the muffled voices as everyone spoke at once, everyone trying to mourn and voice their memories and sympathies.

Duff walked down the steps to the sidewalk. His knees were a joke, so he had to robot-leg down the stairs, left foot first, because his right knee had a mind of its own. As he walked, he focused on the big four-door GMC Denali in front of the house. The engine was still ticking as it cooled from the drive. The Denali had Iowa plates. David Nowak and his family had come from somewhere in Cedar County, Iowa. Duff knew this because Iowa put county names on its license plates. Cedar County wasn't very big, but Duff knew Herbert Hoover, the first US President born west of the Mississippi River, grew up in West Branch, Iowa. Estimating the drive time, it was roughly a four-hour haul between Cedar County and the Bloch home, figuring for traffic and restroom breaks. The travel time meant nothing to Duff, however.

The big pickup was an anomaly in the crowded Chicago streets. While big pickups were more common west of the city out in the big, flat nothing of the Illinois prairie, and they were practically mandatory in Iowa farmland, they were not as common as one might think in Chicago's crush of traffic which was dominated by cars, SUVs, and semi-trucks.

Duff could not help but notice David Nowak's pickup had military stickers all over the back. As with so many Marines who like people to know they served in the Corps, an array of yellow-and-red Eagle-Globe-and-Anchor decals were plastered to the back of the pickup window. There was also an NRA sticker and a sticker touting David's belief in the Second Amendment as absolute.

"Hey, Abe—did you know every Marine is a rifleman?"

"No, I didn't."

"General Alfred Gray said that. He was once the Commandant of the Marine Corps. All Marines have to qualify annually on a rifle range."

"How do you know this?"

"I read things. I know stuff." Duff had an encyclopedic knowledge of strange facts and data. Abe never knew how it got into his partner's head, because he never saw Duff do anything but eat burritos and play video games. Abe knew that Duff read constantly as a child and young adult. Any information the fat man gleaned in his youth was subject to instant recall whenever needed. Duff paused and took a picture of the truck's license plate and rear window. "You think a trained Marine could have made that shot to take out Robert Bloch?"

"I don't know how well Marines shoot. Also, why would David drive into Chicago to shoot his brother-in-law?"

"I suppose you're right. It just seems weird that David shows up with this big pro-gun truck, doesn't it?"

"Remember what you always tell me about coincidences, right? Without evidence, they're still just coincidences."

"I know. It's just odd. Hey, tell me something: if you found out you had a kid from before you met Katherine—"

Abe cut him off; Katherine was his first and only so far. No one else had ever been in his orbit, let alone his pants. "I didn't. I am one hundred percent certain of that."

"I know, but humor me. Make it hypothetical. You and some rando hook up in high school, or maybe your freshman year of college. Twenty-some years later, you find out you have a kid. What do you do?"

Abe thought about it. He couldn't imagine the sudden influx of emotions and confusion such a situation would cause. "I suppose I try to see if the kid wants me in their life."

"And then?"

"I guess I'm trying to make up for lost time."

"How?"

Abe thought about it. "I guess I would want to make sure that child was provided for, same as I do for Matilda. I would want them to be happy and healthy, and if I could help them in any way, I would want to do that."

"How?"

Abe could not see where Duff was going with this line of questioning. "What do you mean *how*? I'd want to help them."

"What's the best way to help someone?"

"Money."

Duff touched a finger to the tip of his nose. "Exactly. Would you want to help a child so much that you'd be willing to get into bed with a two-bit wannabe crime lord like Petey Pucillo if it meant a slew of under-the-table cash heading your way?"

Abe considered it. Would he be willing to break laws and risk his job to help Matilda if it meant she could go to Northwestern without incurring student loan debt? Abe hated to admit it to himself, but he just might. He knew far too well how crippling life was when one was being strangled by poverty's grasp. "I guess I would."

Duff said nothing else. He stuck his hands into his pockets and began whistling that same Lovin' Spoonful song that was stuck in his head for the past two days.

9

SUNDAY MORNING ARRIVED too quickly. Abe did not sleep well. With the heat in his apartment becoming nearly unbearable, plus the few uncomfortable hours of sleep he'd had earlier that day, regular sleep had been impossible.

When not thrashing and trying to find a cool spot on the sheets, Abe was plagued by strange, vivid, lucid dreaming. It was like being on Ambien without the sedative hangover. He was exhausted, but not exhausted enough to find that deep, rich, blackness of sleep from whence no dream could escape. Instead, he found himself tormented by all manner of nightmares that felt real because he hovered in that gray area at the edge of sleep where he was cognizant of his dreaming but could do nothing to control it. Worst of all, when he finally woke, sweaty, choking, and panicked, he could remember nothing about any of his dreams other than the fact that they were nightmares, and they were terrifying. It was an amorphous torment from a bleak recess of his mind.

Worse, after being tormented by bad dreams, Abe would often struggle with waking nightmares for the first hour after he got out of bed. While he went through the mundane activities of showering, shaving, and getting together a meager breakfast of an English muffin with peanut butter, he'd be subjected to intrusive thoughts he couldn't control. They usually revolved around Matilda and her health and happiness, or they were about how he'd try and fail to carry on the detective business if something terrible happened to Duff.

Abe was good at the daily tasks necessary to keeping the operation afloat, and he was good at the bookish things like background checks and vetting future CEOs, but the fun stuff like solving the murder cases or finding missing people, the stuff that made being a detective worth all the boredom and monotony—that was Duff's domain. Would Abe even be able to continue the business if Duff suffered a heart attack and died? Or, more likely, what if he lipped off to the wrong guy and got shot in the face?

The worst waking nightmare was when Abe envisioned himself being alone for the rest of his life. He was not a catch, and he knew this. He had a below-average face, a below-average physique, a below-average hairline, and a well-below-average bank account. He was not overly charming. He was not overly romantic. He was not good in bed. He had a hard enough time just dating Katherine in college, and it was crushing when he found out she only dated him because he was non-threatening and kind, and she figured he wouldn't move too quickly to have sex.

She was right about all that, but it still bummed him out that his ex-wife never found him attractive. She loved him, he knew, but it was a different sort of love, more familial than sexual, and that was enough of an ego-crushing disappointment to last a lifetime. You kind of want your spouse to want you.

Abe drove to the office, parking on the street outside their building. The Sunday morning traffic was sparse, and the city was still mostly asleep. Only the early risers headed to the first Mass of the morning were out, dressed in nice clothes as they made their way down the street to St. Peter Canisius Catholic Church.

Cesar Salazar was hanging halfway out the walk-up window of El Muro, the taquería occupying much of the first floor of the building where the offices of Allard and Duffy Investigations were housed. Cesar was a round-faced, good-natured, second-generation Mexican American who was responsible for keeping Duff fed for most of the last twenty years. Whenever food was needed, Abe and Duff never summoned Door Dash because El Muro was down a flight of steps and always ready to help. Abe wasn't certain, but he figured he and Duff had probably given Cesar enough business over the years for him to buy the Cadillac SUV that got him to and from the restaurant every day.

Cesar saw Abe approaching. He waved and barked orders at one of his cooks in the kitchen behind him. He knew their orders by heart. By the time Abe got to the window, Cesar had a small cardboard tub with two foil-wrapped breakfast burritos, two sides of mild salsa, and a couple of squeeze packets of sour cream. He also had a Diet Coke at the ready for Duff and a bottle of water for the more health-conscious Abe.

"*Que pasa*, Stringbean? How's the world treating you?"

Abe slipped a ten and a five across the counter to Cesar. "Another day, another kick in the crotch."

Cesar tilted his head toward *The Bad-Luck Charm*. "Isn't about time you trade in that shitbox on something nice?"

Abe shrugged his shoulders. "It still runs great. It's just not very pretty, sort of like me."

"Van like that scares children, man. It looks like fuckin' Frankenstein over there."

Usually, Duff would engage in some sort of scathing repartee with Cesar where they would fling friendly insults back and forth, typically about having sex with each other's mothers, but Abe didn't have the heart for it this morning. "If you know a guy who can get me a good price on a trade-in, I'm willing to listen."

"I'll give you six bucks and a pack of Tic-Tacs to drive it into Lake Michigan."

Abe smiled good-naturedly and took the food and drinks. "Catch you later, big man."

"Have a good one, Abe. Tell that partner of yours that his mother needs to stop texting me nude photos. It's putting me off my breakfast."

Abe climbed the steps and managed to balance the drinks and burritos while keying the lock to his office through some miracle of coordination.

Duff was at his desk. He was still wearing the same clothes he'd worn the day before. He had assumed his usual position: feet up on the corner of the desk, ankles crossed, fingers interlaced on his chest, eyes cast to the ceiling, his mind a million miles away. He didn't even blink when Abe entered the office. Abe figured he might find Duff dead from a coronary in that position someday, and he probably wouldn't even notice for at least two hours.

Abe stared hard at his friend for a long moment. Duff made no sign of realizing Abe was in the doorway. Abe felt compelled to break the standoff. "Did you even sleep?"

"Sleep?"

"Yeah, sleep: that thing where you close your eyes and your brain plays little movies of things that may or may not have happened to you. I hear it's good to do it on a daily basis."

"I slept a little. Wouldn't recommend it. Had a dream where my mom was my first-grade teacher, and she kept telling the rest of the students I wet my bed frequently."

"I'm sure Freud would have something to say about that." Abe put the burrito and the Diet Coke on Duff's desk.

"Freud had a lot to say about a lot of stuff. That's why he's largely discredited now." Duff picked up the burrito, unwrapped the foil from the top, and applied salsa liberally. "Is it hot out there again?"

"It's Chicago in July." Abe sat at his desk and tucked into his burrito.

"How soon until Mindy Jefferson shows up?"

Abe froze. "She's coming here?"

"She will be."

"She called and said this?"

Duff shook his head. "No, but she's had time to analyze those files I found at Hanley, Dodge, and Briscoe. She'll show up to tell us what she found."

"Why wouldn't she just call?"

"She didn't get to see you yesterday. She'll show up."

"Before or after we go see Meyer Himmelman?"

Duff's turn to freeze. His burrito was centimeters from his mouth. "That's a good question."

"You know, if we're going to go start getting mixed up with organized crime over this, maybe we should buy you a new gun." Abe had been delaying addressing this with Duff. During an investigation a few months back, Duff was shot, but his old Walther PPK had taken the brunt of the bullet, preventing him from meeting an untimely demise. They had yet to replace his gun, partially because guns are expensive and partially because Duff had no desire to do it. Neither Abe nor Duff enjoyed their guns. It was a necessary evil in their line of work, and they strove to do as little with them as possible.

"Here's a better idea—organized crime guys will have way more guns than us, regardless. Maybe we just accept the fact we'll be outgunned by them, and just go in with no gun to show we're unafraid of their guns."

"I am afraid of their guns, though."

"Is your life insurance policy paid up?"

"Of course."

"Is mine?" Duff was only vaguely aware that Abe had put a policy on him just in case. He preferred not to be involved with such matters.

"It is."

"Then we're worth more dead than alive. If they kill us, Matilda goes to Northwestern debt-free. Problem solved."

"I'd like to be around to see her graduate."

Duff inhaled the rest of his burrito. Through a gloppy mouthful, he said, "Me too, but I'd rather have her graduate debt-free."

"How about we look at it this way: we've dealt with these sorts of men before, right? Won't they take it as an insult if we go without guns?"

"They might."

"Then we need to get you a gun."

Duff waved off this suggestion. "Three-day waiting period. It won't help us now."

"We'll go see Jerry Banner. He'll give you the gun and backdate the application."

Jerry Banner ran the gun shop and indoor shooting range not too far from the office. They met Jerry when they bought their first guns more than twenty years ago, when they first hung out their shingle. Jerry taught them to shoot, taught them to care for their weapons, and helped them qualify on the range every year so they could keep their PI licenses current.

Duff knew his argument was defeated. He crumpled the foil of his burrito and chucked it into his overflowing litter basket next to his desk.

"Any new revelations overnight?"

Duff shook his head. "Not yet."

Abe checked his watch, a recent gift from Katherine and Matilda. It was one of those fancy health-tracker deals that connected to his cell phone and counted his steps. He hated it but felt obliged to use it. It was almost 9:00 AM. Jerry Banner's shop opened at ten. Sundays were a big day for the weekend warriors who were compelled to get use out of their home defense weapons.

Abe sighed and picked up one of the many files on his desk awaiting perusal. The jobs that paid the bills for their little shop were all dull, tedious work. They did things for law offices that were too dull to even bother wasting interns on them. It was a lot of Internet searches, phone calls, and emails. The file that Abe opened was a deep background check for a small company about to hire a new CEO. Abe had already completed the search, but he was procrastinating in doing the final write-up because the guy was almost as vanilla as he was. Plain, boring, safe, and professional. That was what they found most of the time.

Duff continued to stare into space with his feet up, nursing his Diet Coke.

There was a knock at the door. For a Sunday morning, this was an extreme rarity. They had no posted business hours, so it wasn't like people could anticipate when they'd be in or out, but a Sunday morning was a strange time for someone to be seeking detective work. Abe and Duff exchanged glances, and then Abe moved to open the door.

Jo Dunbar was on the other side of the steel in civilian clothes: jean shorts, a white tank top with a Chicago Fire FC logo on the front; she had Rayban aviators perched on the top of her head.

"Officer Dunbar, hello." Abe struggled to speak. His throat suddenly felt like it was full of phlegm. He had to clear it with a discreet cough into his fist. "Please come in."

Dunbar smiled politely and stepped past Abe into the confines of the office. Her nose wrinkled. "Jeez, smells like you're baking feet in here."

"That's Duff's fault. And a weak AC unit's fault."

Duff still stared at the ceiling. He had not even glanced at Dunbar. "Don't come here thinking you can steal my recipe for baked feet. I'm taking it to my grave."

"Please, have a seat, Officer." Abe gestured to the chair in front of his desk.

Dunbar slid into the chair and crossed her legs elegantly. They were pale but very toned. "You can call me Jo. I'm not on the clock."

"What brings you by?" Abe took a seat in his chair. "You don't need our help with something, do you?"

Dunbar hesitated as if she were trying to find the right words. "I wanted to ask you about being private investigators. I'm thinking about applying for detective in two or three years, and if I can't be a detective in the CPD, I was wondering if going after it in private life was worth it."

"It's not," said Duff. "Thanks for stopping by."

"Are you always like this?"

"Yes, he is," said Abe.

"I find it keeps people from building emotional attachments to me."

Dunbar was amused. "What if I said I could tell it was a defensive act based on some sort of childhood trauma?"

"You'd be correct," said Abe.

"I am the poster boy for childhood trauma." Duff waggled his fingers at Dunbar and shot her an exaggerated smile. "Thanks, Mom."

"Your mother is Dr. Amity Ableman-Duffy, isn't she?" Dunbar leaned back in her chair and threw her feet up on the corner of Abe's desk to mimic Duff's pose. "I took psychology classes from her at DePaul."

"We're not close." Duff's gaze drifted from the ceiling to the CPD officer in the office. She had his attention.

"She was a battle-axe. One of the toughest professors in the whole school. Nothing was ever good enough for her."

"Sounds familiar."

"Did you know she wrote papers on you?"

"I've read them. They're one-sided and inaccurate; also, they lack many facts and juxtapositions that would paint her in a negative light. However, she had them peer evaluated and published, so what does my point of view matter?"

"Is it true you could have gone to college at twelve?"

"I took the SAT when I was eleven. Got a 1570. My mother wanted me to hold off from matriculating until I got a 1600."

"So what happened?"

"Ask my mother." The tone in Duff's voice told Dunbar she was not going to make headway driving down that road. She changed topics. "Malcolm Betts says you're like Hercule Poirot."

"I'm impressed Betts has read a book. And I bet he didn't just say that. He'd never say something nice. What was his addendum to that statement?"

Dunbar blushed a little. "Truthfully, he said you're like Poirot, but fatter, more annoying, and with less class."

"That's the Betts I know and love."

"How do you do it? How do you see things Betts doesn't?"

Duff shrugged. "I don't know, honestly. It's just one of those things. It's like Michael Jordan trying to teach someone confined to a wheelchair how to dunk a basketball. If you don't have the right development, you're not going to fly."

Dunbar looked to Abe for help. "Can you tell me how he does it?"

"Observation and logical reasoning. It can be taught, but it can never be mastered. You can learn how he does it, but you'll never be able to quite do it yourself to his level."

"Fascinating." Dunbar stood by her chair. She held out her arms and did a slow turn. "What can you tell about me?"

Duff sighed and gave her a long appraisal. "Not much. I mean, other than you work long hours in an outdoor job that requires long pants and a short-sleeved shirt. You like to hang your left arm out the window when you drive. You're right-handed, but you hold pens weirdly. You also don't care for computers; you prefer paper and ink. You had an Egg McMuffin on your way here, with orange juice, not coffee. You're unmarried and uninterested in dating, for the most part. And that tank top was a gift, not a team you like, but you wear it because it's good for hot weather."

Dunbar broke into laughter like a child who had just been shown a magic trick. "That's amazing. Completely correct. Except the tank top wasn't a gift. I won it at a bar raffle. How'd you know?"

"It's too loose. You were very put together at the crime scene, so I assume you are not one for baggy clothing in civilian life, either. I assumed the shirt was from someone who didn't know your size. You'd normally take a medium, maybe even a small. That's a large. So, a bar raffle would be the same idea. I'm sure the guy running the raffle didn't know your size, either."

"And the Egg McMuffin?"

"McDonald's uses muffins with a very fine cornmeal on them. It always falls all over everyone who eats them. If they don't brush themselves off too well, you can see it. You have a couple clinging to the front of your shirt."

Dunbar looked down and brushed the few remaining crumbs of breakfast from herself. "How did you spot that? They're tiny."

"When you are always looking for that thing that stands out, they jump at you. Like the fresh OJ stain in the logo on your tank top."

"And the pen is from the weird callus on my index finger, right? And you know I prefer pen and ink because I have a writer's callus, and nowadays, almost everyone types."

"You're getting it." Duff's eyes drifted back to the ceiling.

"How'd you know I was unmarried and uninterested in dating?"

Duff's gaze left the ceiling and made direct eye contact with Dunbar, a rarity for him. "Because you're here with me and Abe on a Sunday morning. Anyone who was married or dating someone would have had better things to do."

There was a knock at the door. "That'll be Mindy." Duff did not move from his desk.

Sure enough, Special Agent Jefferson was there in a charcoal jacket and black slacks. Her hair was pulled back in a bun at the base of her neck. She cracked a smile when she saw Abe. "How's it going, Slim?"

"I haven't suffocated Duff with a plastic bag yet, so I've got that going for me." Abe ushered Mindy Jefferson into the apartment with a wave of his arm.

"The day is still young. It might still happen." Mindy stopped short when she saw Dunbar. "You have a client?"

Duff made short order of the introductions. "Not a client. Patrol Officer Jo Dunbar, CPD, meet Special Agent Mindy Jefferson, IRS. May you arrest each other in peace."

Dunbar stood to shake Mindy's hand. "I thought special agents were only for the FBI."

"The IRS has them, too. They don't talk about them much because people hate the IRS enough already." Jefferson took a seat in the chair across from Duff.

"What brings the IRS into this office so early on a Sunday?" asked Dunbar.

"Special investigation, actually. That's why the IRS has special agents."

"Well, isn't that special?" Duff dropped his best Church Lady impression. Dana Carvey would not have been impressed.

"Go ahead and tell her, Mindy," said Abe. "Officer Dunbar was on the scene of the shooting last night. She found the sniper's nest."

"Does she know the Kool-Aid Man over there broke into Hanley, Dodge & Briscoe illegally to get knowledge about some sketchy files?"

"I didn't *break into* the place; I slipped in unnoticed like a ninja who simply took advantage of lax security."

"A ninja?" Dunbar's tone questioned the probability of the statement.

"A very fat, but surprisingly agile ninja," said Duff. "Since no one at HD & B has complained yet, technically I have done nothing wrong. What was on the memory stick?"

Mindy sat back in the chair. "Something sketchy as hell. What it is, we can't really say for certain. Our digital forensics guys went over it with all their magic powers, but they struck out. However, the files show someone is tallying large amounts of cash, and it appears they're moving that cash somehow, probably to offshore accounts. That's our estimation, at least. However, since we obtained this file by sketchy means, and since it has no digital fingerprints linking it directly to someone, it's pretty much useless in a court of law. All it does is prove to us everything we already knew is correct, but it doesn't get us any closer to closing the case."

"This is why we need a detective cat," said Duff. "He'd solve the case for us."

"No cats." Abe pulled out his notebook and his favorite Parker Jotter. He clicked the pen to life by thumping the button on his forehead. "I assume you didn't drive all the way to Chinatown to tell us that you don't know anything."

Mindy gave Abe a funny look. "*All the way?* Slim, it's only like twenty minutes back to the office from here. It's not a big deal, especially on a Sunday morning."

"Still. It's a Sunday morning. Doesn't the IRS give you weekends off?"

"Not when we're swinging with a hot investigation, they don't."

"The IRS sounds like a lousy employer," said Duff.

"You both are working, and so is the CPD, it seems."

Dunbar shrugged. "I don't have much of a life."

"I'm pretty sure none of us do; that's why we're all here on a Sunday morning." Duff rose from his chair and walked to the little fridge in the kitchenette where he kept his stash of Diet Coke.

"I'll cut to the chase," said Mindy. "Me and the guys on my team know someone in Hanley, Dodge, and Briscoe is dirty. It might have been Robert Bloch, but it might be someone else who put files on his computer to set him up. We can't audit the firm without some sort of evidence tying them to something dirty. We can't get access to it. So, we at the IRS would like to ask for your cooperation should you come across something that helps us with this case."

"Does your cooperation pay?" Duff's eyebrows waggled.

"There might be a modest consulting fee involved if you provide beneficial information."

"Do we have a choice?" asked Abe.

"Not really. The feds don't play around when it comes to this stuff. If you have evidence and withhold it from us, they'll probably look to put any sort of legal financial squeeze on you as punishment. They're very clever about finding ways to twist your tit."

"Spoken like a true member of the IRS," said Duff.

"I learned the job fast," said Mindy. "Can we expect your cooperation in this matter, then?"

"If we find anything out, we'll let you know." Abe meant every word. The last thing he needed with Matilda on the precipice of college was the Internal Revenue Service running through the last seven years of his financials. He was notoriously anal about his taxes, both personal and professional, and he even did Duff's taxes for him because he knew that his partner could not have cared less about them. Still, he had that pervasive fear of missing a T he should have crossed or double-dotting an I and having the whole weight of the federal taxation system come down on him.

"That's all we ask." Mindy stood up from her chair. "I'll let you get back to your day. I'm going to head back to the office. Did you have any big plans for this miserably hot day? Preferably, any plans that will get you the hell out of this hotbox weather?"

Duff stood as well. "We were gonna go get me a gun, and then we were gonna go ask a mobster about Petey Pucillo."

"Do you guys mind if I tag along?" asked Dunbar.

"I don't," said Abe.

Duff looked at his attire. "Is this a good gun-shopping outfit, or should I wear more American flag?"

BANNER'S GUNS & AMMO was located in a nondescript building a mile north of Abe and Duff's office. It was down an alley off a main thoroughfare, so it wasn't visible from the street. You had to either know it was there or seek it out. It housed a handgun range and a small sales floor. Because it was not in the best of neighborhoods, they used a two-door system where you had to be buzzed into the sales floor at the second door. A security camera watched the foyer at all times. The second door was protected with heavy-duty prison-like bars to discourage people from trying to break the glass to gain entrance. It was an intimidating place, especially since Jerry Banner always wore a sidearm, usually his favorite Colt Python .357 with a six-inch barrel. It was the type of weapon kings carried—both Elvis Presley and King Hassan of Morocco had been fans. It was also the type of weapon that could readily make Swiss cheese of someone's chest cavity, so it demanded respect.

Abe buzzed the doorbell. The first door locked behind them, and they waited for the secondary door to open. A woman's voice crackled over the intercom. "I recognize you and the chubster, but who's the blond?"

Abe knew the voice of Jerry's daughter, Jessica, in an instant. She had been hanging around the shop for more than a decade, starting when she was just a kid. She was in her early twenties now. Abe moved away from Dunbar so Jessica could see her better in the camera. "That's Officer Jo Dunbar, CPD."

"Got a badge?"

Dunbar held up her hands. "Not on me. Not today. I'm not working."

There was a pause. "You guys vouch for her?"

"Sure," said Abe. Duff said nothing. Abe poked him hard in the shoulder.

"Sure." Duff scowled at Abe and rubbed the spot where he'd been hit. "Now I'm crippled. I won't be able to shoot."

The door buzzed loudly. Abe pushed through to the main sales floor. It smelled heavily of leather, gunpowder, and gun oil. Weapons of all types were behind thick glass in locked cases around the edge of the store. Ammo was in the glass cases that also served as sales counters. In the center of the room were shelving units with targets, vests, holsters, t-shirts, and all sorts of other paraphernalia related to guns and shooting things with them. Country music played from a dust-covered boombox on a shelf on the wall behind the cash register.

Jessica Banner was tall, over six feet, with a thin, waifish frame. She had vividly blue eyes and cornsilk blond hair tied back in a single plait. She wore jeans and a black T-shirt with Banner's Guns & Ammo in simple white lettering across the front. Like her old man, she was also wearing a holster on her hip. A sleek Colt 1911 was within easy reach in the black leather pocket, ready to dot someone with .45 rounds if the need arose. She watched the trio walk into the building. "Let me guess: time to re-up your licenses?"

"Surprisingly, no." Abe inclined his head toward Duff. "Duff got shot a few months back—"

Jessica's eyes widened, and her jaw dropped open. "Really?"

"Yep." Duff slapped his left side, under his left arm, where his valiant Walther bore the impact. It gave its life for Duff's. "Right in the PPK."

Abe explained the rest of the story to Jessica and finished with, "So, we need to replace his gun."

"Another James Bond special?" Jessica began to pull a silver-clad PPK from a glass display case behind her.

"Actually, I was thinking more of a modified heavy blaster, preferably a BlasTech DL-44." Duff leaned against the counter and scanned the weapons.

"A DL-44?" Jessica stopped bringing out the PPK. "You want Han Solo's gun from the original trilogy?"

"If possible, yes."

Jessica's eyes narrowed. "Well, Spaceboy, I'm fresh out of weapons from Coruscant. What else can I interest you in?"

"How about a Frontier Model B Liberty Hammer?"

Jessica's eyes rolled. "The gun Malcolm Reynolds carries in Firefly?"

"That'd be the one."

"How about I just shoot you in the thigh before you ask for the Noisy Cricket from Men in Black and save us all a bunch of stupidity? Do you want a PPK or not?"

Duff gave her a syrupy smile. "This is why I like you, Jess. Underneath that crusty exterior beats the heart of a true nerd."

"PPK: yes or no?"

"What do you have in a Beretta 92?"

Jessica's eyebrows went up in surprise. "A Beretta 92? Seriously?"

"What's wrong with a Beretta 92?"

"Nothing. Nothing at all. It's a wise and mature purchase given their popularity and use all over the country by law enforcement and the military. I would have thought you would have tried to get me to find a Webley RIC so you could pretend to be Sherlock Holmes."

"Martin Riggs carried a Beretta 92 in Lethal Weapon." Duff's syrupy smile never left his face.

"Of course he did." Jessica sighed and walked to a different cabinet. She produced a black steel Beretta gleaming with its newness even in the harsh fluorescent lights. She checked to make sure it was empty, cleared the chamber like a responsible gun owner, and handed the gun to Duff handle-first.

Duff took the weapon and turned toward the gun range in the long, empty room beyond the sales floor. He pointed it at a target on the far wall and sighted down the barrel. "It's a lot bigger than the PPK."

"The PPK is for delicate flowers and fictional British spies." Jessica rattled off specifications for the Beretta from memory. "The 92 weighs a little over two pounds fully loaded. Standard nine-millimeter rounds with a fifteen-shot magazine. Effective at fifty meters, maximum around a hundred meters. It's a favored weapon by the military and LEOs the world over. It's a practical, affordable handgun; good for home protection and self-defense."

Duff shrugged. "But does it get chicks?"

"As if you could get chicks with or without a gun," said Abe.

"As if I'd want to get chicks," said Duff. "Are we putting this on the company account?"

Abe dug for his wallet, where he kept the company credit card. "Might as well. I can write it off on the taxes."

Duff handed the gun back to Jessica. "Wrap it up for us, miss. We'd like it to go."

"I know you've got the proper paperwork already on file here, so that's not a problem. A three-day waiting period is standard for new guns. We'll have it for you on Wednesday."

"Could you back-date it for us? We might have to go see some mafia types this afternoon."

"No can do. Both the state and feds look down on that." Jessica's eyes drifted to Jo Dunbar as she spoke.

"I'm not on duty," said Dunbar. "I see nothing. I know nothing."

Jessica kept her eyes on Dunbar, but her shoulders relaxed slightly. "In that case, you guys came in last Thursday, right?"

"I recall we did, yes." Abe slipped the company credit card from its slot in his wallet. He slipped a $50 to Jessica along with it.

Jess pocketed the cash. "Then this little lady will run you about $950 today. I assume you'll need a box or two of ammo as well. The PPK and the Rockford Special Abe carries both shoot .38s."

"Start us with one box. I can't see us using more than one until we have to qualify again."

Jessica dropped the box on the counter and left Duff to fill the magazine manually while she ran the paperwork and charged Abe's card.

Duff finished packing the magazine. He tilted his head toward the range. "Mind if I take her for a spin?"

"Be my guest." Jessica hit a button under the counter to unlock the range door. "Didn't expect anyone to come in until noon, anyhow."

Duff walked to the first booth in the range. A standard pistol target was hanging at seven meters. It was a human shape, black ink on newsprint, with white concentric circles around the heart and forehead area for targets.

Duff donned ear protection and shooting glasses. He rolled his shoulders and stretched his neck from side to side. He held the gun in a triangle stance, arms extended, the left hand supporting his dominant shooting hand. He breathed out slowly and then squeezed three shots. The first shot hit the edge of the paper. The second hit the target at waist level, and the third shot went who-knows-where. The bullet clattered somewhere down at the end of the range, banking off the metal stops and into the stacked bags of sand.

"Nice shootin', Tex." Dunbar was less than impressed.

"Good thing I'm not trying to qualify today." Duff took a breath and squeezed off another round. This one hit the target on the shoulder.

"Mind if I try?"

Duff set the gun down on the booth's ledge and stepped back.

Dunbar stepped into the booth and picked up the Beretta. "Nice gun. I like the balance." She turned partially to the side in a modified Weaver stance. She squeezed off three quick rounds, each one finding center mass. She put the gun on the counter. "It's a good gun."

"It'll do," said Duff. "I'll miss the PPK, but that's only because I always sang the James Bond theme song in my head whenever I shot it." Duff started to hum the James Bond theme aloud and squeezed off three more shots. He frowned. "It's not the same."

"You could sing the theme song to Lethal Weapon."

"It's not as easy to hum." Duff shot once more. He hit the target in the neck. "Ouch. That'll get him one of those electronic voice box things people need when they get laryngeal cancer, the things that make you sound like Twiki from Buck Rogers."

"Who's that?"

"You're too young to know and too pretty to care." Duff shot the rest of the magazine at the target. Most of the rounds hit the paper. At least one went off to its own destination. He popped the magazine from the handle and reloaded it from the ammo box.

While Duff was popping new bullets into the clip, he jutted his chin toward Dunbar. "How about we shoot for real? Me and you. Three rounds, most in the center wins?"

Dunbar laughed. "You sure you want to do that, Big Shooter? Unless you were trying to hustle me, I didn't see much of an aim."

"Scared?"

"Not at all. What are the terms?"

"If you win, you can keep hanging out with us today. Maybe you'll even learn to be a detective."

"And what happens if you win?"

Duff glanced over his shoulder through the window to the sales floor, where Abe was hunched over the paperwork on the counter. "Slim thinks you're cute. Maybe you say yes if he asks you to dinner."

Dunbar suppressed a smile. "Really? That's the bet? If I win, I get to hang out with you some more, and if you win, I have to have dinner with Abe?"

"It'd be nice if you did. That pasty bastard is lonely as hell."

"And you're not?"

"I'm indifferent to loneliness. Yes or no, you want to bet?"

"Fine. It's a bet. If you win, you might go down in history as the best wingman I've ever seen. You shoot first."

Duff squared up to the target and popped three shots. One low, one nicked the ear of the target, and the third hit high and to the left on the white of the paper. Duff grimaced and put the weapon down. "That did not go as well as I hoped."

Dunbar stepped up and squeezed three shots. The first two hit the target where the eyes would have been. The third hit dead-on center mass. "I win."

"I guess you did."

Dunbar turned on a heel and walked back to the main part of the store. She paused at the door. "Abe has to ask me to dinner before I can say yes."

Duff emptied the rest of the clip. He missed more than he hit.

10

MEYER HIMMELMAN KNEW more about the seedier side of Chicago than anyone else in the Windy City, but that fact always had to be a secret. Meyer played his part as a doddering old man, but he somehow always had connections to point Abe and Duff in the right direction when they came to a crossroads involving anything underworld-related.

Meyer knew the various mobs around the city; he knew what they were up to at any given moment, and he knew they knew of him. The depth of the old man's involvement in the various mobs was always up for debate.

The boys knew Himmelman would be at his office because he was there six days a week. Only on Saturdays did he heed the day of rest, and even then, as a more casual practitioner of his faith, he just worked from home.

Himmelman's office was housed in a four-story industrial business building, one of those forgettable, regrettable hulks built in the late '50s, decorated in the early '60s, and hopelessly outdated by 1970. Everything about the place looked anachronistic and shabby. The old man's rationale for not upgrading was the fact that he practically lived there, and if it was good enough for him, it was good enough for everyone else.

Himmelman owned the whole building but rented out most of the offices. He used a large space in the basement level as the headquarters of his empire. There were no windows, just hideous yellow fluorescent bar lights overhead, which buzzed and flickered like something from a 1970s horror movie.

His office looked unworthy of a man of his wealth and stature. It was old, dark, and smelled like dust and tiger balm. The furniture had not been updated since the mid-'80s. The walls had not been painted in more than twenty years. Everything looked a little gray, a little dirty, a little dingy. Himmelman had more than enough money to renovate and update the place, but he was old school. If it ain't broke, don't fix it. He didn't spend money he didn't absolutely have to spend. He once wore a broken pair of eyeglasses for eight months because the tape around the hinges worked well enough, and his vision insurance only paid for one new pair a year.

Judy Breneman was his secretary, but she didn't work weekends. The outer receiving area where Judy worked was dark and quiet. Himmelman's office lay behind a door past Judy's desk. The windows to his alcove were all frosted glass, but there was enough light behind them to show someone was working. A dark silhouette sat at a large desk, dutifully shuffled papers, and paused to type on a computer.

Abe walked to the door and rapped lightly. "Mr. Himmelman, it's Abe Allard and Duff from Allard and Duffy Investigations."

There was a pause. The silhouette froze for a moment. Then, there was a sound of shuffling papers followed by the sound of a drawer closing. An electric lock buzzed when Meyer unlocked the office door from his desk. "Of course, boys. C'mon in."

Abe opened the door and revealed Meyer Himmelman in all his glory at his desk, which now had no papers to be seen.

Himmelman was small and stunted, thin and bony. His skin was pasty and dotted with age spots. He was mostly bald with a few wispy white hairs covering the top of his pate and a thin fringe ringing the sides and back of his head. He wore thick-rimmed glasses with Coke-bottle lenses. When he looked up at Abe and Duff, the lenses magnified his eyes comically, but they were always stuck in a Gilbert Gottfried-esque squint.

"Good day, m'boys! Come in. Sit, sit." Himmelman gestured at the chairs across from his desk.

The old man spied Dunbar trailing them as they entered. He sat up straighter and adjusted his glasses. "What's this? Who is this lovely treasure you've brought to liven up my unworthy office on this sweltering day?"

Abe made the introduction. "Jo Dunbar, Chicago Police. Jo, this is Meyer Himmelman, real estate magnate."

"Come now," Meyer waved away the compliment. "I dabble in the market, yes, but I'm hardly a magnate. I've done well, this is true; I'm comfortable, but I'm hardly a magnate."

Dunbar extended a hand across the desk. "Nice to meet you, sir."

Himmelman grasped her hand lightly with both of his. "Polite and well-mannered, to boot. Abe, this gal is too good for you. Don't spoil her. I hope that you bringing the police here doesn't mean you're thinking of arresting me, does it? I have to admit, I would not object to being placed in handcuffs by such a beautiful and charming young thing like you." He winked at her lasciviously.

Duff remained standing and gave the second chair in the office to Dunbar.

Abe said, "We came because we need some information."

The grand performance they had come to expect from Himmelman began. The old man feigned a shocked look. He clutched invisible pearls at the center of his sunken chest. "Information? Why would you come to me for such information? Who am I but a humble businessman who spends his days in this dark basement, trapped like a mole in a tunnel? What information could I possibly have that you require?"

"Duff saw a guy get popped hitman-style on Friday night, a single bullet to the heart from long range. We're looking into a possible link about the victim being a shady accountant who might have been laundering cash for Petey Pucillo. We don't have proof of such a connection, but the IRS is looking into it as well. There might be something there."

Himmelman sat back in his big chair and laced his fingers together over the tummy paunch so many old men develop, no matter how thin the rest of them were. He squinted hard at Abe and shifted his gaze to Duff. "I believe I might have heard of this Pucillo guy once or twice in my dealings. He's up in the Italian neighborhoods, right?"

"That'd be him. He's the son of Big Ernie Pucillo."

"Big Ernie, he fixes cars. Him, I know."

"You should. He's been one of the top guys in the Italian mob around this city for years," said Dunbar.

Himmelman looked at her with surprise. "Oh, goodness. The mob, you say? I guess the CPD is still keeping tabs on the Italians."

Dunbar held up her hands in a dismissive gesture. "Organized Crime isn't what it used to be, but it's still out there, so we keep an eye on it."

"Good to know my tax dollars are working so well to keep the city safe." Himmelman's tented fingers rose to his chin as he pondered Petey Pucillo. It was all part of his act. Abe wondered what cogwheels were spinning behind the old man's eyes.

Finally, Himmelman spoke again. "You know, I cannot say that I know anything about this young Petey Pucillo fellow, but I do believe I know some people who may be able to shed some light on him."

"We figured you might," said Abe.

"Well, in my business, you know, I meet all sorts. Money is money, after all. Who am I to question how someone else gets theirs?" Meyer Himmelman had perfected the art of deflection. Nothing he did would be construed as being part of a larger, criminally connected organization. His financial books were pristine. He paid his taxes. He never got his hands dirty. From everything anyone with a badge could see on the surface, he was just a little old man who'd gotten lucky with real estate and lived his life as a middling landlord with a small slate of properties.

Abe knew Himmelman was connected. Abe knew the old man called the shots and ran things. He just didn't know *how* the old man did it or to what degree. No doubt, when Abe and Duff left the old man's office, Himmelman would place a call on a burner phone. That call would go to someone a bit more *physical* than himself. The proper gangland information broker's palm would be greased, and within thirty minutes, Himmelman would have his answers.

Organized crime was all about the *organization*, after all. The tit-for-tats amongst the various groups were a prolonged chess match. Pieces had to be moved into position before information could be bartered. A strong position had to be secured before any piece could be moved, and all avenues and outcomes must be considered.

The thing about the world of organized crime most people don't understand is that there are only two things you can be once you decide to mob up: you can be good at it, or you can be bad at it.

If you're bad at it, you're either dead or in prison. If you're good at it, you're out on the streets doing what you're good at. Those who are good at it are always targets. Those who are bad at it don't last long enough to become a target. If you're an old man still in the mix and calling shots, then you're *very* good at it.

"Can I help you boys out with anything else? Is the apartment still in good shape?"

"The AC unit needs to be replaced. Hot as balls in there lately." Duff fanned himself with his hand. Even in the basement of an air-conditioned office building, Himmelman's office was a little warm.

"A new AC unit? I just replaced that one, what, ten years ago?"

"At least," said Abe. "It's done its job, but it can't keep running against this heat."

"I suppose those crazy scientists were right about that global warming stuff, weren't they? I'll see what I can do about your AC." Himmelman opened a drawer to his desk and reached inside it with a pen to scrawl a note. "Anything else?"

Abe shook his head. "No, sir."

Meyer waved them off with a backhanded flick of his wrist. "Don't let me keep you youngsters from enjoying the day, then. Let an old man do his thankless work in peace. You should get out and do something fun. Maybe you could go to the place with all the rides in Gurney Mills. I hear that's fun."

"They don't let fat guys on the roller coasters." Duff's face melted into a pout like a three-year-old. "Abe could go on them, and I could watch and eat funnel cake, though."

"We're not going to Great America," said Abe.

"Aww." Duff kicked at the floor petulantly.

"Yeah, aww." Dunbar mimicked Duff's whine. She got up from her chair. "Funnel cakes, Abe."

"We're not getting funnel cakes, either." Abe opened the door and ushered his companions through it. To Meyer, Abe gave a brief nod of thanks. "We appreciate the help, Mr. Himmelman."

"You're good boys. You always pay your rent, and you don't complain. I'm glad to help where I can."

Abe closed the door behind him. As soon as it latched, Abe heard the sound of a drawer opening and a bunch of papers being brought out and spread around the old man's desk. Abe's natural curiosity was piqued. He wanted to know what was so important that those papers could not even be allowed on the desk while the detectives were there, but at the same time, he knew he'd probably regret it if he ever found out. Some things were better left unknown.

11

DUNBAR PUSHED THROUGH the exit doors of Himmelman's building and into the oppressive midday heat. "What's next then?"

"Next, we wait for some low-ranking crony in the Jewish mob to call us on an unlisted burner phone and drop the knowledge we need." Duff picked up an abandoned copy of a several-month-old *People* magazine from a table in the lobby of the building and began to use it as a fan.

"Is this how they usually do business?"

Abe nodded and shrugged. "More or less. None of the mobs really like us because we're technically on the side of the law, and therefore a threat to their existence, but they put up with us because we're not cops, and we try to stay neutral."

"Neutrality amongst the mobs is critical." Duff was trying to read the magazine cover while he used it to create a breeze. "When it comes to those guys, if you sway too far from being a proverbial Switzerland, some large man in a nice suit might show up unannounced one afternoon and decide to restyle your nose."

"You could probably use it. Yours curves to the left," said Dunbar.

Duff felt his proboscis. It had endured several good beatings over the years. The infirmary staff members at Bensonhurst were good at setting broken noses, but there was only so much they could do. "It's not the best-looking schnoz out there, that's for sure."

Dunbar was taken aback. "Really, I set you up with an obvious dick joke, and you don't take the bait?"

"Mine curves to the right."

Abe checked his cell phone to see the temperature on his weather widget. The little ladybug icon said it was 94. With the ambient humidity,

Abe figured the heat index was at least 101, maybe as high as 109. It was a miserable temperature for any sort of life, but in a megalopolis like Chicago, where people lived in brick buildings that absorbed heat and were surrounded by miles of blacktop too hot for bare feet, temperatures like this would make people get a little crazy.

More shootings happened when it was hot. More fights happened when it was hot. Abe preferred heat to cold because he never walked outside in the heat and thought he might die, unlike heading out on a -30-degree winter morning in Chicago, where the moisture in your eye threatens to frost over. However, a thick, soupy heat like the wave the Windy City was being beaten with was almost as bad as -30 in the winter. Abe wanted to find air conditioning before he melted. "It's too hot to do much outside. We should find a restaurant or coffee shop and have lunch."

Dunbar scanned the street. There were very few people moving on the sidewalks. Those who were outside were moving slowly or hiding in the shade of store awnings or trees. "I know a place. A friend of mine just opened it. It's not far."

Navigating from the back seat of *The Bad-Luck Charm*, Dunbar guided them a few streets over, and Abe and Duff found themselves back in front of a familiar brunch spot.

Abe found an empty spot on the street to park. "Your friend opened this place?"

"Her name is Molly Shipman. She's a redhead, hence the name."

"So's my daughter," said Abe. "She's a waitress here."

Dunbar slipped out of the backseat and into the mire of heat. "Small world, I guess. I didn't see you having a daughter, though."

Duff climbed out of his seat. "Is it because he looks like he's an asexual nematode? That's why I have a problem picturing him having a daughter."

Abe clapped his hand over his partner's mouth. "Please don't listen to him. He's suffered a lot of head trauma."

Dunbar got to the door before Abe or Duff. She held it for them. "You just didn't strike me as the prototypical dad type."

Duff pulled Abe's hand off his mouth. "Are you shitting me? He's got New Balance sneakers in his closet. He thinks khaki slacks are sporty."

Molly Ginger's Morning Spot was becoming popular. Almost every table was taken. Abe asked the teenage girl acting as hostess for a spot in Tilda's section, and the girl obliged by finding them a four-top in the corner by the kitchen.

Duff didn't bother to glance at the menus they were offered. He'd memorized it the day before. Abe and Dunbar perused them, though. Abe didn't bother to use his memory for things like menus.

Duff drummed his fingers on the table impatiently. He spied Tilda carting plates from the kitchen to a table of octogenarians who seemed to enjoy her smile and youthful vigor.

Abe decided to get the spinach-and-feta omelet because it's healthy. Tilda would give him some side-eye, but he would stick to his guns. He indulged the day before; he needed to be good today.

Abe watched Dunbar scan the menu. He couldn't get over how attractive she was. As someone with a psych major as an undergrad, Abe understood how he carried a lot of baggage from his formative years, particularly how girls at his school tended to shun him. He had been awkward, geeky, and white in a majority-Black school. He never cared much about race, but the girls in his school did. So did most of the boys. They picked on him constantly and excluded him at lunch. Somewhere in the back of the lizard-brain portion of his mind, he wished the kids at school could see him having brunch with Jo Dunbar. They would be amazed.

Duff belched. Not a petite burp that could be excused politely. This was a declaration of war. People at several tables near them all turned in disgust and stared. Duff thumped his chest with his fist. "I think I might have just exorcised a demon."

It was a good reminder that Abe was not on a *date* with Jo Dunbar. This was business.

"How long does it take the secret mob info network to grace you with knowledge, on average?" Dunbar didn't take her eyes off the menu. She also said nothing about Duff's belch. She'd been working patrol with a male partner in a heavily male CPD. She was immune to the inherent grossness of the male species.

"Usually an hour or three," said Duff. "Give or take."

"Meyer Himmelman never fails, but he also doesn't work on a timeline. We just have to wait."

At that moment, Tilda swept over to the table, her face lighting up when she spied her dad and uncle by proxy. "Did you guys come back because you missed me, or was the food really that good?"

"Why not both?" Abe smiled at his daughter. He gestured to Dunbar. "Tilda, this is Officer Jo Dunbar of the CPD. Jo, this is my daughter, Matilda."

Tilda shook Dunbar's hand, her smile radiant. "So nice to meet you! You are really pretty."

Dunbar blushed slightly. "Thank you. So are you."

"Why are you hanging out with my dad and this big doofus?" Tilda leaned on Duff as though he were a support column for a building.

"You could take our order, you know. I might starve to death."

"I think that's a physical impossibility at this point. The heat death of the universe will occur before you can die of starvation." Tilda silenced him with a wave of her hand. "Now, hush. We're making conversation."

Dunbar continued unfazed, "I'm thinking of becoming a detective someday, either for the force or as a private business. Some people told me these guys were the best detectives in Chicago."

"They are, but they will never admit it." Tilda readied an order pad and pulled a pen out of her apron pocket. Like her dad, she thumped the button off her forehead to pop the nib from the barrel. "What can I get you to drink?"

They all placed drink orders. Tilda fetched the three Diet Cokes in seconds since they were next to the fountain where the wait staff filled cups. Then, they placed food orders. Abe and Dunbar chose healthy omelets. Duff ordered an abomination called *The Afternoon Nap*, a concoction of beef, rice, gravy, and eggs. It was served with biscuits and extra butter.

Duff's phone rang. The programmed jingle was the Quizno's Subs song popular on TV a few years back. That was a classic rock hit to Duff. He pulled it from his pocket and showed the screen to Abe and Dunbar. Unlisted number. It was Himmelman's guy. Duff answered without speaking.

A man's low growl came out of the speaker. "This that fat detective?"

"I don't know about fat. How about pleasingly plump?"

"Pucillo might not be the guy you're looking for. Word is, the accountant was working for Pucillo, but someone else might have popped him."

"Who?"

The phone was already dead. Himmelman's guys never hung on the line. They dropped the necessary info, and that was that. They were done with the call. No goodbyes, no pleasantries. Efficient.

Duff knew from experience that the thumb-breaker Himmelman had make the call had already snapped the burner phone in two and chucked it into the Chicago River. Good luck tracking him. He was a ghost. This is why Meyer Himmelman was in his declining years and still at the top of the pyramid.

Duff relayed the call to Abe and Dunbar, and then he thumbed a text to Mindy Jefferson about what they had learned. "We're gonna have to talk to Petey Pucillo. We need to figure out who might have wanted his accountant dead."

"That's how you get new leads?" asked Dunbar.

"Sometimes. Sometimes, we have to work for it by doing actual detective work. Sometimes Duff can just figure it out based on the evidence in front of him," said Abe.

"This is why we need a detective cat. We could just follow the detective cat's lead, and he would figure out everything for us."

"What is it with you and a detective cat?" Dunbar was squinting at Duff. This was not an uncommon reaction.

"It worked for Jim Qwilleran, Charlie Harris, and Kathleen Paulson."

"Who the hell are they?" Dunbar looked even more confused.

"They're characters in books Duff has been reading. My daughter got him into reading cozy mysteries where the sleuth has detective cats, and he decided we need one."

"That would be kind of cool. Maybe you could rebrand your agency as Allard, Duffy, and Mittens."

Duff snapped his fingers. "That's god-damned genius. Abe, write that down."

"No detective cat."

Matilda wheeled over carrying plates of food. "What's this about a cat? I thought you were allergic, Dad."

"I am. No cats."

"Your dad is a killjoy, Matilda. He does not love animals. That's the hallmark of a psychopath."

Matilda put Duff's food in front of him. "Says the guy who would rather play video game baseball than sleep."

"I'm accomplishing the Lord's work by taking the Milwaukee Brewers to the World Series since the club will never be able to afford to buy a Series win in real life." Duff grabbed the salt and pepper shakers from the little basket in the center of the table and used both liberally.

Matilda set the other two plates in front of Abe and Dunbar.

"This looks wonderful." Dunbar picked up a knife and fork.

"It is." Matilda gave Dunbar a pleasant smile before she skittered off to another table.

Abe suddenly became very self-conscious. He didn't usually dine with women, not since Katherine, really. He had, in the past, of course, but it was always informal—food from wax paper wrappers or aluminum foil while they were working on a case, or a business lunch with several people from a law firm. This felt more intimate, despite the presence of the three-hundred-and-fifty-pound cockblock next to him. Abe had a habit of accidentally dropping food on his chest. Most of his shirts had a small, faintly visible stain on them in the exact same spot, right where spaghetti sauce or a hollandaise would drip when he least expected it. He did not want to embarrass himself in front of Jo Dunbar. He knew the chances of him ever having a real dinner with her without Duff anchoring a third seat were nonexistent, but he still carried that deeply ingrained middle school fear of having a woman laugh at him. He managed to ditch some of his childhood baggage over the years, but that particular angst was going with him to the grave.

Neither Abe nor Duff could be considered loquacious, nor were they particularly good at conversation. Too many years together in a small office had basically ended any need to verbally communicate. They had worked out a system of nonverbal communication for the little stuff. Now, their conversations usually consisted of Duff complaining about something or someone on TV he didn't like and Abe trying to understand why Duff felt the need to watch that thing or person instead of changing the channel.

Abe felt the pressure to say something. It was awkward. They didn't know Dunbar well, and yet there she was. And the worst part was that she was so attractive. She was still vibrant and full of life. Abe and Duff had the life squeezed out of them over the years like a tube of Crest in a laundry wringer.

It didn't help Abe's case that Duff was eating next to him. Duff's inhalation of food was a sight to behold, but it wasn't for the weak of heart. Duff did not enjoy food, despite what someone might think about a man his size. Duff ate like he was angry at the meal, like it had wronged him in some way.

Abe swallowed a bite of his omelet and wiped his mouth with his paper napkin. He tried to summon some sort of conversation starter. Nothing intelligent came to him. This is why he shouldn't date, he'd told Matilda. She kept insisting he try. No part of this was natural for him.

Dunbar must have sensed his unease because she swooped in and rescued him. "In my research about you two, I saw you have multiple degrees, Abe. How'd you end up in the PI game?"

Bless her.

Abe jabbed a thumb at Duff. "I was not cut out for the courtroom, and this guy rescued me on my first and only case as a trial lawyer. Afterward, he said he was starting a PI firm and needed help. The rest is history."

Dunbar eyed Duff with a raised eyebrow and a hint of fear on her face. "Does he always eat like that?" *The Afternoon Nap* was almost completely gone from Duff's plate.

Abe could only nod. "Sadly, yes."

"Reminds me of my brothers." Dunbar had to shake her head to get the image of Duff's feeding out of her mind. "You were never interested in being a detective before meeting Duff?"

"Unless you call watching Humphrey Bogart movies as being interested, no. I was determined to be a lawyer ever since I was a kid, and I learned that a lot of lawyers were rich."

"Going after the big attorney money, eh?"

"Until I learned I had crippling stage fright, yes."

"Ouch. You and he—you just started solving crimes, then?"

"We had to be licensed first. Luckily, Duff had worked for a guy for a little while and learned the ropes, and he knew some people who signed some papers. We didn't solve crimes right away. We had to build up a client base with a lot of boring work at first. Duff hounded the CPD whenever there was a case he felt he could solve, and eventually they started contacting us when they were stuck."

Dunbar leaned forward and planted her chin on her fist. "That's really fascinating. They just started believing you were worth a consulting fee, then?"

"It took a few years, but they came around."

Dunbar switched her gaze from Abe to Duff, who had finished his plate of food and was folding his napkin into an origami Yoda. "What about this case? What's your thought process on it?"

Duff did not respond. He finished his little art project, erected a soggy, stained Jedi master, and set it next to his plate. Only then did he bother to speak. "I'm not sure why a hitman would take out a valuable asset like an accountant. If he were moving money for the mob, you'd think he'd be more valuable alive than dead, especially if he knew where the money was hidden. I'm also wondering why Bloch had the gun in his truck, what the redheaded model with the perky cans has to do with anything, and why that guy across the restaurant from us is cheating on his wife."

Dunbar frowned and looked over her shoulder until she located the broad-shouldered Italian-looking fellow having dinner with a petite woman of Chinese descent. "They both have rings. They look like they know each other. How's he cheating?"

"Keep watching." Duff sat back in his chair and laced his fingers over his belly. In a few moments, when the woman was distracted by her food, the man casually leaned back and checked his phone, which was hidden in his lap. He smiled and started responding with a single-thumb typing method while making half-hearted eye contact with the woman across from him.

When the gal got busy dipping her Spam musubi into an intriguing orange sauce, the guy double-checked his message and hit send. Then, he tucked his phone back into the lower part of his shirt and turned his full attention to his wife, all smiles and bright eyes, with her none the wiser.

"I'll be damned." Dunbar sat back in her chair and marveled at Duff for a moment. You just picked that up out of all the actions in this very hustling and bustling crowd and pinned him for cheating without so much as breaking a sweat."

"He wasn't hiding it too well." If Duff processed the appreciation in Dunbar's voice, he didn't show it.

"How do you know he's not texting a buddy?"

"He wouldn't hide that. The phone would be on the table, or he'd be more obvious about it. He doesn't want her to know who he's texting. He doesn't want her asking questions. Besides, I caught sight of something on the screen when he looked at his phone earlier. Unless his buddy has massive jugs he's exceptionally proud of, some other woman was texting him dirty pictures."

"That's impressive." Dunbar turned to Abe. "Is he like this all the time?"

Abe held up a hand and tilted it back and forth. "He does weird things a lot, but this is the only one we have been able to monetize."

"You say weird things, I say I'm just a bold thinker."

Dunbar forked more of her omelet. "He had a good idea with the detective cat."

"You should have been around the week he decided I needed to grow a huge mustache because of Kenneth Branagh's Hercule Poirot movie."

Duff stiffened. He stood. His whole demeanor changed. His voice was low, almost a whisper. "Stay here. Don't look up. Don't follow me."

Abe froze. "What's going on?"

"A large gentleman in a nice suit just walked in, looked around, and walked out after he spotted us."

"Would this gentleman be dark-haired and olive-skinned?" asked Abe.

"I believe he's eaten more than his fair share of Nonna's red sauce, if that's what you're asking."

Dunbar leaned across the table toward Duff. "Are you telling me one of Petey Pucillo's guys is here and looking for you already?"

Duff touched the end of his nose. "They probably heard Himmelman was looking into them this morning. The information brokers in this town have no loyalties. They trade to the highest buyer."

Dunbar reached for her phone. "I could text some guys I know are working in this neighborhood today."

Duff shook his head, a slight, almost imperceptible movement. "Don't do anything. Sit. Talk. Stay here. They're going to put me in a car, take me somewhere, and make me tell them what I know. Then, they'll let me go."

"I'll go with you." Abe started to rise, but Duff put a heavy hand on his shoulder and forced him back down. Duff had surprising strength for a guy who only did curls with cans of diet cola.

"I've got this. Worst that happens is they punch me a few times." Duff pulled a pair of twenties from his pocket and threw them on the table. "For the kid."

OUTSIDE MOLLY GINGER'S Morning Spot, Duff took a half-dozen steps before the rear door of a Lincoln Navigator idling at the curb swung open. An Italian guy in a red Adidas tracksuit emerged. Mid-twenties, rail-thin, with a face like a map of Palermo. "You're the fat detective, ain't ya?"

Duff's hands went protectively to his generous belly. "Why does everyone start descriptions of me with fat? Why don't they say handsome or intelligent or witty?"

"Because you ain't none of those." Tracksuit gestured to the rear door of the SUV. "Get in."

"You know, it's such a nice day, I figured I'd go for a stroll. I could use the exercise; apparently, people think I'm gaining weight."

A hand landed on Duff's right shoulder from behind. Thick, meaty, and smelling like Jean Paul Gaultier cologne—the cheap, knock-off brand, not the real stuff—the hand clenched on Duff's deltoid just hard enough to prevent him from running off, but not hard enough to hurt.

"Since you seem to be insistent on taking me somewhere, I'll just have you know that I don't put out on the first date, even if you buy me lobster."

"Goddamn, man. No one likes your mouth, you know. Just get in the fuckin' truck."

"Do the thing where you show me your gun first. Isn't that how you properly intimidate someone?"

Tracksuit sighed. He glanced around, saw no police, and lifted the front of his tracksuit top. The handle of a small handgun was jutting out of his waistband. Like any two-bit hood, he was dumb enough to have the barrel pointing almost directly at his penis.

"If that thing goes off, you're going to be the new countertenor at Haymarket."

"Yeah, yeah. I've heard it before. The safety is on, dipshit."

"Or so you'd better hope." Duff walked to the car and climbed into the back seat. There was another guy in a tracksuit at the wheel, this one dark blue. The air conditioning was on full blast, and there was a thirty-degree difference in temperature between the exterior and interior of the car. Duff sat in the backseat and looked around the cab. "This is the worst Uber I've ever been in."

The big thug in the nice suit sat next to Duff. Between his broad shoulders and Duff's girth, the pair of them filled the space. The two tracksuits sat in the front. The driver stomped on the gas pedal. The Lincoln's big V-8 roared, and the Navigator shot down the road.

The driver turned on the radio. Some horrible nu-metal band started blaring from the speakers, power-grunting and chord-crunching their way through some song about love and loss.

Duff was not a fan of music in general. Music annoyed him, particularly when it had lyrics. Even with some long-haired dude screaming a song at him from the sound system of the Navigator, John Sebastian was still dominating Duff's thoughts. *Hot town, summer in the city...*

"I never would have guessed you guys were into Nickelback."

None of the dime-store hoods reacted.

"Or is this one of those bands that sounds like Nickelback, but has even less talent?"

Still no reaction. They stared straight ahead. The guy in the nice suit was bobbing his head to the kick drum.

"Listen, are you really going to drag me all the way to the northwest side? That's like thirty or forty minutes from here. How about you just do your silly mob guy speech here and save all of us a lot of time? Or, better yet, call Petey and tell him we can meet halfway at this great Italian restaurant I know. You guys ever heard of Olive Garden?"

The thick thug's hand shot out with such speed that Duff only had time to turn his head a fraction. The man connected with Duff's cheek hard enough to rattle Duff's teeth. If he hadn't turned his head a little, the impact would have driven his lips into his teeth and cut them. This was something he'd learned as a kid at Bensonhurst over the course of many, many beatings from teenage boys with rage issues. Better to take it on the cheek. More padding. Less chance of your teeth piercing your lips.

Duff winced and shook off the pain. If Bensonhurst taught him anything, it was the ability to take a punch. He had to learn it the hard way, but he knew he could handle a lot of damage. He wasn't a fan of pain, but spending the entirety of his teenage years in a sketchy boys' home in Canada taught him that crying or acting hurt only resulted in more beatings. He learned not to react when he got hit. The bullies wanted the reaction. It was a drug to them. They loved to see the pain, the frustration. Duff learned to put his brain somewhere else and let his face go dead. No reaction meant the bully got frustrated. Best-case scenario, the bully would go find a smaller kid who would howl more. Worst case, the frustration turned into blind rage, and Duff would be beaten nearly unconscious before the orderlies could intervene.

Duff rubbed at his cheek. "Okay, no never-ending pasta bowl for this greasy bitch, I guess. Too bad for you, really. I bet it's tons better than your grandma's recipe anyhow."

Another punch.

Duff was better prepared for this one. It hit him fully in the part of his cheek capable of absorbing the most impact. It still hurt, but it was more manageable, dissipated the pain faster.

"No Italian, then. How about gyros? I mean, let's face it, Greeks are basically a better, more intelligent, and cleaner version of Italians, anyhow."

The next punch rocked Duff hard enough that he saw stars. He had to blink away the pain and shake his head to clear the cobwebs.

The thug in the seat next to him never even looked at him. He kept his gaze straight ahead. He showed no outward signs of emotion. He kept bobbing his head to the drumbeat.

Duff settled back in his seat. "Fine. I'll go to the suburbs. Seems like a waste of time. I'm ninety-nine percent certain Petey could have handled whatever he wanted to tell me with a fifteen-second phone call. Instead, he sends you three Rhodes Scholars almost to Chinatown to drag me to strip mall central, and for what? Just so he can play mob boss?"

No reaction from Moe, Larry, or Curly. Duff let the nu-metal wash over him for a minute or two.

"Any of you guys John Sebastian fans?"

There was no reaction from the trio.

"How about cats? You guys like cats?"

ABE WATCHED DUFF leave Molly Ginger's. He watched his partner get into the SUV. He watched the SUV disappear down the road.

"They're not going to hurt him." It was a statement more for his own reassurance than Jo Dunbar's. Duff had tangled with small-time crime lords in the past, he reminded himself.

"He just threw himself at a lion for us." Dunbar refused to let Abe pay for her meal. She was signing the credit card receipt that Tilda had brought her.

"He has a way of doing that. I'm not sure if it's some sort of deep-seated sense of nobility that makes him do that, or if it's just so he can lord something over me in the winter when he doesn't feel like leaving the apartment to buy more Diet Coke for the apartment."

"Still, he willingly got into a gangster's car. He's tougher than he looks."

"Or dumber. One of the two." Abe shucked some cash onto the table to cover his bill and a tip for Tilda.

Matilda saw them leaving and swept over to the table. "You haven't finished your omelets. Were they not good?"

"They were great. Something came up, though." Abe kissed the top of his daughter's head. "Duff was kidnapped by a couple of goons from the Italian mob."

"Again? What did he do this time? Did he tell someone their ravioli couldn't compete with Chef Boyardee?"

"Something like that, I'm sure."

Dunbar was confused. "You're not panicking? I'm panicking."

Matilda shrugged. "Duff's like that. You just need to know him, I guess." Matilda gathered up the plates from the table, but she paused after a moment. "It's like, when I was a kid, I used to get scared that something bad would happen to my dad because of his job, and he tried explaining to me that they rarely got into trouble like that. It didn't help. I was still scared until Duff took me aside and told me that if there was ever serious trouble, he'd make sure my dad never got hurt. He pinky-promised, so I never worried about my dad after that. I do worry about Duff, though."

"We all worry about Duff," said Abe.

To Matilda, Dunbar said, "It was nice meeting you, at least. Good luck on the job." Dunbar got to her feet. To Abe, she said, "What do we do?"

"We go back to the office, call Mindy Jefferson and let her know what's happening, and then I guess we wait. Not much else to do." Abe hated feeling useless. He hated being in limbo. There were so many moving pieces to this murder, and none of them made any sense.

The Bad-Luck Charm started right up, but the interior had become dreadfully hot from being out in the sun. The rickety AC unit tried to push cold air, but there was only so much it could do.

Dunbar grabbed the hem of her tank top and fanned it out, flapping it against her body to generate a breeze. Abe caught sight of a flat stomach, toned and smooth. He tried not to think lascivious thoughts.

"Is this typical?"

Abe was thinking of her stomach. "No. No, it isn't."

"You don't tangle with mob bosses a lot, then?"

"Mob bosses? Oh, no...almost never." Abe felt himself blushing. "We've actually been hired by them on occasion."

"You've worked for the mob?"

"A couple of times. We take jobs as we can. Sometimes, someone connected with a group rolls in and asks us to find something that went missing or find out what happened to one of their guys. As long as it's not criminal for us to do it, we've taken those cases. Money is money, after all. Crime boss money is just as good as anyone else's money. Plus, it kind of helps us walk that line between crime and justice. We're not out to stop the mob. That's not our role in this world. We're just keeping ourselves afloat."

"Doesn't working for a crime organization conflict with your work for the CPD?"

"Probably. But money is money. If the CPD wants to pay us more and more often, we could start turning down the crime lords." That was the phrase Abe and Duff always repeated in such circumstances. Green spends equally everywhere. It made Abe a little squirrelly thinking about where the large stacks of cash given to him by crime outfits came from, or how they acquired them, but the CPD were no angels, either. They might have badges and claim to uphold the law, but there were just as many rule-breakers and criminals in the CPD as in any crime outfit. They were just harder to prosecute.

That was the saddest and most depressing fact Abe learned about the world: no matter where you go, laws were pretty arbitrary for a lot of people. Especially the closer you got to the top. It was something touched upon briefly during his law school days, but Abe had been mixed in with the justice machine long enough to know it was true. Laws were there to keep the majority of people in line, but there were always those who got to be outside of them on both sides of the thin blue line. He didn't mention it to Dunbar. No cop likes to have that sort of thing pointed out to them; good cops were already all too aware of it.

"Duff told us Pucillo probably didn't have Bloch killed, so why does Pucillo still need to talk to him?"

"That's just how these guys operate. They catch wind of someone looking into their business, and they need to know why. They need to know if they should dig in and put up the shields, or if they're in the clear."

"You seem so calm about this. How can you be so calm?"

"Duff can handle himself."

"What about you?"

"What about me?"

Dunbar adjusted the vents of the AC, which were just beginning to trickle cool air. "Can you handle yourself?"

"Not really, no. Duff had to grow up fighting. I was goony, awkward, and painfully shy, so most kids left me alone."

"Goony and awkward guys don't get to get married and have beautiful kids."

"They do when they marry a closeted lesbian."

They lapsed into awkward silence. Dunbar looked out the window at the long mash of buildings and cars. Abe stared at the road. He wanted to say something else, something that didn't sound so negative and off-putting, but he came up dry. Talking to Katherine had always been easy. They had college in common. And then they got married and had married things to talk about, like home repair, bills, and jobs. When Matilda was born, every conversation they'd had for sixteen years centered solely on the baby or what they should have for dinner. Abe didn't know how to talk to women anymore.

Abe thought really hard but couldn't find a single topic to breach with her. "I guess I could take you home."

"Trying to get rid of me already?"

"Well, there's not much to do until Duff calls and tells me where he is so I can go get him. He might just take a cab or a bus home, too. I don't know."

"He's an odd duck, isn't he?"

"He had a tough life. It ruined him. All things considered, he's actually doing amazingly well for someone who went through what he went through."

"I've heard about his origin story. Is it true?"

"Every word," said Abe.

Dunbar shook her head. "I couldn't imagine it. And he really does what he does because of that little girl he liked?"

"Loved. He loved her. He won't say he did, but he loved her because she was the only kid in his school who was nice to him, who played with him, who stuck up for him. Losing her meant losing the one thing he enjoyed in life."

"And he never moved past it?"

"He never wanted to move past it. Big distinction."

"Sad. It's like a melodramatic Mills and Boon novel."

Abe never thought of Duff like that. He was more of a Shakespearean tragedy. "He gets by."

"What happens if he solves her murder? Like, what happens if something comes into the cold case department, breaks open the case, and finally gives her family justice? What then?"

"Honestly?"

Dunbar nodded. "Honestly."

Abe took his eyes off the road long enough to meet Dunbar's gaze. "I think Duff probably kills himself the day the guilty verdict is read. He doesn't like being here. He only exists because her death is a fire that keeps him going."

There was a long silence after that. Abe felt bad for revealing the truth of Duff's situation to Dunbar, and she felt bad for asking. What else was there to say?

Dunbar moved to a new topic. "Are you going to do some work today?"

"Probably not." Abe would be too preoccupied with thoughts of Duff's safety and well-being to worry about vetting some dull future CEO who would make more in the next year than Abe would in the next twenty.

Dunbar's gaze didn't leave the window. "I guess you can take me home, then. Maybe I'll get some work done."

Abe did as she asked. Dunbar gave him directions to get her back to her apartment building, a modest three-flat in an improving neighborhood. "All the benefits of gentrification without the rent increase," she said.

Abe parked the van, fully intending to walk her to the door, but it was the middle of the day, and she was a Chicago cop. It seemed like a pointless gesture. He would remain in the van and watch until she got inside, though. That was just good manners.

"Thanks for letting me tag along today." Dunbar unbuckled her seatbelt and popped the door. "Text me when you get Duff back."

"I don't have your number," said Abe.

Dunbar reached over and grabbed Abe's phone from the little cubby in the van's console where he stored it while he drove. She swiped a finger across the screen and shook her head with an admonishing click of her tongue. "You should have a lock screen on this thing in case you lose it."

"Sometimes I do if I know I'm not going to need it for a while."

Dunbar keyed something into the phone. A second later, there was a beep from her pocket. "Now you've got my number."

Abe caught the phone when Dunbar tossed it back to him. She gave him a quick smile and shut the car door. Abe watched her walk back to the lobby door of her building. When she got to the glass, she looked back and gave him a wave. Abe waved back.

Psychology classes told him a look back was a common display of interest. If a woman looked back once more before disappearing from view, if she made a second effort, it was her showing intent, or at the very least, it was friendly, a way of extending a moment between two people for a few extra seconds. It was meant to give the person watching a gesture that would instill a final memory. The textbooks were very clear about look-backs and waves. Abe had read those texts in college and knew the meanings. He was also very good at shrugging off things that were not meant to be romantic. Dunbar was, after all, far too young for him.

Abe shifted into drive and headed back to the office. He did the only thing he could think to do to be of service, and that was researching the crap out of Hanley, Dodge, and Briscoe. The whole time he compiled data, he worried about Duff while he sipped a Diet Coke and wished he were a drinker because a little booze might have calmed his nerves.

Even with the research and the constant worry, he couldn't get the image of a sunlight halo on Jo Dunbar's hair out of his mind.

12

THE THUG IN the suit only punched Duff in the face twice more before they got to Big Ernie's shop in northwest Chicago. As far as wannabe mafiosos went, they were pretty tolerant of Duff's prattle. He'd dealt with far less lenient guys in the past.

Big Ernie's was closed, being a Sunday, but there were always cars stacked around the place waiting for service. A couple of guys were picking up overtime by working on Sunday afternoon. The Bears don't play in July, so there wasn't much reason for some of those guys to stay home. The shop had tunes, pals, and cold beer. The Cubs game was on the radio. Getting paid time and a half to fix a suspension was a good deal, despite the relentless heat. A pair of five-foot-tall hurricane fans kept air moving around the shop to help cool it down.

Blue Tracksuit drove the Lincoln to the rear of the shop and parked next to a couple of nicer cars, a refurbished early '80s Cadillac, a Corvette Stingray, and a few memorable pieces of Detroit's finest from the '70s.

Blue Tracksuit killed the engine and looked over his shoulder at Duff. "Get out."

Duff did as requested. He started mapping details. This was an involuntary action for him. He scanned and memorized license plates. He matched the plates to the cars by make and model. He scanned the faces he saw, noted visible tattoos, and cataloged the scene in his head down to the number of cigarette butts littering the ground near the shop's rear door.

Thirteen: ten Marlboro Reds, two Kool menthols, one Parliament Light.

In the few seconds it took Duff to walk from the Lincoln to the shop, he had a perfect picture of the entire scene in his head. That picture would remain in his memory forever. He would be able to access it at will and glean information from it, should it ever be necessary. This was how Duff processed the world: in perfect snapshots in his memory, each capable of being scanned and accessed at his leisure.

Red Tracksuit opened the rear door of the shop and ushered Duff inside. There was a large break room for the shop's mechanics. Two long tables sat in the middle, ten brown metal folding chairs occupying slots along the length. A couch sat in one corner. A large TV was mounted on the wall. Fox News was on, but the sound was muted. A pretty blonde was reading headlines. The scrolling ticker on the bottom of the screen spewed information about the heatwave in the Midwest.

"Have a seat." Red Tracksuit pulled one of the folding chairs from the table.

Duff sat. In the three steps from the door to the chair, he mentally mapped the room.

The big thug in the suit sat on the couch in the corner. Duff caught sight of a gun in a shoulder holster under his left arm as the guy sat. It was a big gun, a hand cannon. It was the sort of gun that ended arguments just by being drawn. As Duff's mentor, retired Waukesha County Sheriff Buddy Olson, liked to say: *No one mouths off to a .44 Magnum.*

Blue Tracksuit disappeared into the shop. Beyond the break room, Duff heard the sound of power tools and chatter, a mix of English spoken in Chicago and Mexican accents.

Duff sat back and tried to enjoy the moment. At least he wasn't bored. He jutted his chin toward the TV. "Any chance we can kill Rupert Murdoch's propaganda machine and find some sort of baseball game to watch instead?"

The big thug glanced at the TV, shrugged, and got up to find the remote. A few seconds later, he found a game on one of the channels, the Nats and the Pirates in the final game of their current series at PNC Park. Duff always liked that stadium. If he was more of an adventuring sort, he could see traveling around the country to catch games at a couple of the more famous parks like Fenway and Yankee Stadium. But staying home and seeing those stadiums on his PlayStation was almost as good as being there, he reasoned. It cost less, and he didn't have to deal with the crush of people at the park, $20 beers, and urinal troughs.

Red Tracksuit returned a few minutes later with a guy in a blue mechanic's jumpsuit behind him. Duff had only seen pictures of Petey Pucillo before, but this was him. Rail-thin, with a big Italian beak made to look all the bigger because he was so thin. He had a mop of jet-black hair, but it was starting to thin and recede, so he styled it forward in a vain attempt to disguise the loss.

Duff fought that battle a decade ago, losing most of his hair in his mid-thirties. At a certain point, he had a monk's tonsure with a little tuft hair at the front of his head like Charlie Brown. He gave up the fight and shaved his head after that. Sometimes, you just have to admit defeat. Genetics always wins.

Pucillo pulled out a chair and sat across from Duff. "So, you're the dick. I've been meaning to meet you for a few years. I heard good things."

Red Tracksuit brought out two cans of cold beer from a fridge in the corner, Silver Bullets. Not Duff's favorite domestic, but a free beer was a free beer. Duff popped the tab when Red Tracksuit set one in front of him.

"I haven't heard all that much about you, strangely." Duff took a pull from the Coors Light. Given the heat of the day, it tasted good, light and icy cold.

Pucillo drank from his own Coors. "I heard you got a mouth. I hope Dante didn't have to get too rough with you."

"If Dante is the gorilla on the couch, then no, not too rough. Truth be told, I've been punched by better and stronger guys. He did all right, though." Duff's hand massaged his cheek. He could feel a bruise starting to swell.

"I also heard you asked the old Jew to look into me today."

"Word travels pretty fast, doesn't it? That's the Internet age for you, I guess."

"Why are you prying into my business?"

Duff shrugged and took another sip. "I dunno. Seemed like a good way to pass the time. Wikipedia can only tell me so much."

"I hear you're investigating the hit on the accountant."

"Was it a hit?" Duff raised an eyebrow. "All I know for sure is he was shot."

Pucillo laughed, a wheezy, hiccuping sound. "C'mon, man. Dude took one to the chest from a sniper, is what I heard. That's a hit. You know it, and I know it."

"I heard the accountant was on your payroll."

It was Pucillo's turn to raise an eyebrow. "Who told you that?"

"I have sources, same as you."

The big guy on the couch started to rise, presumably to smack Duff in the mouth again, but Pucillo stopped him with a gesture. "S'alright, Dante." Pucillo adjusted himself in his chair. "I already know who you're talking to. It's that Black chick from the IRS, right? Whatever her name is. Minnie-verva or something."

"Minerva," Duff corrected. "You can call her Ms. Jefferson, though."

"Do me a favor and tell the IRS chick she's barking up the wrong goddamn tree."

"Bloch wasn't on your payroll, then?"

Pucillo finished his Coors and crushed the can in his fist. He flung it to the far corner where a fifty-five-gallon trash can was almost full of crushed cans. Red Tracksuit had a new beer in front of Petey in seconds.

"I know the IRS lady thinks I'm dirty, but she got it wrong."

"The IRS isn't well-known for mistakes."

"In this case, she is."

Duff's curiosity was piqued. "How so?"

"Bloch was on my payroll, but not how you think."

"Now I'm intrigued." Duff took another sip of his beer. He was not a drinker by nature. He only ever drank beer, and when he did, he nursed them. He'd been drunk twice in his life, both in the same week he left Bensonhurst. He decided it wasn't for him and took care to avoid doing it again. He was not an accomplished drinker like Pucillo.

"Someone is making major moves, lots of cash." Petey cracked the pop-top on his second can. He immediately took another healthy swig.

"That's what I heard. The IRS is under the impression it was you."

"Any moves I'm making are defensive, not offensive. We believe someone is building up their stores of guns and ammo, as well as bringing in some more illegals from their home country. You know what that means, right?"

"Territory war?"

"At the very least. Someone is making a play to expand business, and someone at that accounting firm was laundering money for them."

This all gelled with what Himmelman's guy told Duff on the phone. Bloch was on Pucillo's payroll, but not how Duff thought he was. "Not Robert Bloch, then?"

"Me and Rob knew each other from way back; we had friends in common. I learned who was moving money, and since I knew Rob, I called him up and asked him if he wanted to make some fast cash. I told him if he could find out who was moving money in his firm, and who was paying to get that money moved, I could make it worth his while." Pucillo paused to drink again. "He turned me down at first. He's a pretty straight arrow."

"But he did agree?"

"Said he needed money."

"How long ago was this?"

"A year or so, I guess. It's been slow going. He was working on it, but he couldn't make real progress until he got that promotion a few months ago."

"What did he find?"

"Not much. Enough to let me know I was right, and he had a good idea of who was probably doing it, but that's about it. Nothing concrete."

"The IRS tells me you guys are the ones making a play for territory.

They say you're moving money. How can I be sure that you didn't have Bloch killed because he found out about your activities? Seems to me that's a more plausible scenario than what you're selling."

"The cops search his car at the hotel?"

"They did."

"They find the Ruger in the trunk?"

Duff had enough professionalism not to show surprise on his face, but Petey had just surprised him.

"That Ruger—it got no numbers on it; it's a ghost gun. I gave it to him because he started feeling like someone at the office was onto him. He was carrying it in his briefcase during the day, but storing it in the trunk of his car at night so his wife wouldn't find it. I told him it was probably paranoia, but he was sure someone was watching him. Said someone was putting shit on his computer at work. The gun made him feel a little better."

In his head, Duff scrawled a line through Petey Pucillo's name on his suspect list. It was highly unlikely that someone would arm someone they planned to kill. It also lent Petey some credibility because he knew things even the cops didn't know.

"No one in your organization took the shot at Bloch, then?"

Pucillo took another long draw on his Coors Light. "Hell, no. Look, I know my role in this world. We ain't the Outfit no more. Would I like a little more power and respect? Absolutely. But my old man, he built something special with these repair shops. We don't need to break thumbs like in the old days. This ain't the '70s no more. We're not trying to run this town. I know my place. My loyalty is to my family first, always."

"That's not what I heard. People are saying you're trying to bring back the glory days."

Petey shrugged. "People are wrong a lot."

"So why look into the money, then? It wasn't going to change your business practices."

Petey shook his head. He leaned toward Duff. "You don't get it, do you?"

"Explain it to me."

"All these fuckwits with pistols in their pockets in this town think they're players. They're not. The real players don't need guns to prove they're players. However, that don't mean the fuckwits can't do some damage. Bullets are bullets, after all. I'm trying to limit that damage."

"You're telling me you're trying to prevent a territory war."

"I'm trying to help people keep the balance."

"You sound like a saint." Duff's tone was wry and sarcastic.

"I'm no saint, but I'm also no devil. You know what happens if one of those groups makes a big push?"

"People die."

"For starters. Then, neighborhoods will shift. New bosses will move in and start pushing product. Starts with a little weed, maybe a little coke, then before you know it, it's meth and fentanyl. Suddenly, teenagers are hooked on drugs, and that's when the sex trafficking explodes. Neighborhood prices start dropping, there will be white flight, and shit gets really bad for those who can't afford to run. It ain't good, man. Cities are all about balance. There will always be drugs and prostitution, but we need to keep that shit in check so it doesn't get out of control. That's the first thing my old man taught me about running neighborhoods: balance is key. If all your customers bail out, you don't got a business anymore."

Duff hated to admit it, but he was starting to like Petey Pucillo. He wasn't the two-bit crime lord Mindy Jefferson pegged him to be. Pucillo seemed to see the bigger picture, to understand the delicate web of how the underworld moved beneath the safe, surface world. "So, who do you think is moving money for this hypothetical territory war?"

"It's either the Koreans, the Venezuelans, or the Chinese. Most of them fuckers ain't from here. They don't give two shits if Chicago burns. Me—my family's been here since before Capone. This is home. I'm more Chicago than I am Italian. My loyalty will always be to my family first, but the city second."

"And you think someone at Hanley, Dodge, and Briscoe is moving money for one of those groups?"

"I know someone is. I just don't know who. Rob never gave me that info. Said he was close, though."

"Why bring me here to tell me this?"

Pucillo finished his second beer, the crushed empty flung to the garbage can in the corner. "Because I heard good things about you. I heard you get shit done. I know you probably wouldn't consent to coming into my organization 'cause you're all noble and shit, but I'm hoping you'll figure it out and tell me who is moving cash and who they're moving it for so I might be able to arrange a meeting to *redirect* their efforts."

Duff understood the emphasis on the word. It was a subtle way of saying Petey would have him killed if he didn't go with the flow. Whoever was moving money would disappear one day. It was the best way to take care of such a thing in the mobs. The Italians were good like that; nothing flashy, just a subtle message to the other crime syndicates that they could still flex muscle when necessary. Lake Michigan was long and deep, and a few yards of heavy metal chain attached to a cinder block was a cheap cost of doing business.

Duff took a pull from his can. "Why not let the cops handle it?"

"Because they're the fuckin' cops. They're not well known for their efficiency and competence."

"Do you know why Bloch needed money?"

"He never said, and I didn't ask."

"Did you know he was heading toward a divorce?"

"We didn't exchange a lot of pleasantries about our personal lives. It was all business."

Duff knew he had a thousand reasons not to trust Petey Pucillo, but he also knew that Petey seemed logical and reasonable, as far as mob guys could be reasonable and logical. "A hit like this—long distance—it's not really how organized crime works."

"I know."

"You know what it says to me?"

"What's that?"

Duff finished his can of beer. He crushed it in his hand and threw it to the corner like Petey had. Of course, Duff, being painfully nonathletic, missed wide right, and the can clattered off the wall to the concrete floor, making a racket as it did. Red Tracksuit rolled his eyes and picked up the can. He did not get Duff a second beer as he had for Petey.

"This was either hired, or it was done by someone who knew him and owned a long gun. Either way, it was personal. It wasn't related to people in your line of work, if you catch me."

Pucillo cracked a smile. "That's exactly what I told Dante. I heard Bloch was killed, and I says to Dante that it wasn't one of us who did it. It was personal."

On the couch, Dante nodded to confirm Pucillo's story.

"Do we have a deal, Mr. Detective?"

Duff shrugged. "I'll let you know what I find out. Best I can do."

"That's all I ask."

"How will I contact you?"

"Dante will give you his number before he and Leo drop you off."

Red Tracksuit, whose name was apparently Leo, hopped to his feet from the stool along the wall where he was perched. Dante stood as well. Duff took that as his cue to stand, too.

Petey got up from his chair. "If you need any work done on that shitbox your partner drives, swing by. I can't help the body on that thing, though."

"I'll keep it in mind. It's a little out of our way to get to the northside for auto repair."

"For now. Things keep going in my favor, maybe one day you'll have a Pucillo's shop down near you."

Pucillo did not say goodbye. He did not extend a hand for Duff to shake, not that Duff would have taken it. He just turned on his heel and went back to the shop. A few seconds later, Blue Tracksuit reappeared.

"Let's go," said Leo.

They walked back to the Lincoln. Duff got in on the rear passenger side. "Where are we going now?"

"Oh, we got a special place for you," said Leo. "You're gonna love it."

ABE FOUND DUFF at the Olive Garden in Forest Park. Duff was at the bar with a Diet Coke and a never-ending bowl of fettuccine Alfredo.

"They were pretty nice guys. They knew what I liked."

Abe sat at the bar next to his partner, refusing a drink and a menu. He didn't want to stay long enough to eat anything; he was still full from brunch. He noted the darkening bruise on Duff's cheek but said nothing.

Duff informed him of the conversation between himself and Pucillo. "This goes back to what I said about it being personal. This doesn't feel mob-related."

"But it is mob-related. Someone is moving money for some mob, and some mob is looking to expand territory by force. It has to be mob-related."

Duff waved off Abe's concern. "Doesn't mean Bloch's death was mob-related."

"Do you have evidence of it being otherwise? Because the mob connection seems to be the strongest evidence we have going at the moment."

"True. Maybe pursuing the mob angle will provide something that will get us closer to the real killer."

"If you needed to kill an accountant, getting a professional to do it is efficient, even if you're in a crime outfit."

Duff had to concede that point, as well. "It just doesn't feel very mobby, if you ask me."

"What would feel mobby?"

"I dunno." Duff slurped down another twirled forkful of noodles and sauce. "I think tying someone to an old mattress frame and hooking his nuts up to a car battery feels mobby. At least Richard Kuklinski would approve."

Abe didn't want to think about it. "Who do we know in the Asian syndicates?"

"Archie Vang. That's where I'd start." Duff finished his fettuccine and threw a few crumpled bills to the bar to cover the check.

Vang was a longtime source for Abe and Duff. He was their age and vacillated between the various Asian syndicate gangs when they needed extra muscle. Arch was Hmong, a group that had their own organized mob but never really rose to the same level of power as the Japanese, Chinese, and Koreans.

Vang had gotten into bodybuilding as a teen. While he never amassed the physique that would have put him into competitions, he was still a brick shithouse of a human with a neck as thick as Duff's thigh. He was also a Northwestern grad, like Abe. He never really sought a proper job after earning his bachelor's in Economics, preferring instead to help out in his mother's little grocery store during the mornings. This left his afternoons open so he could spend several hours at the gym each day, and it kept his evenings free so he could work piecemeal for whichever crime boss needed someone to loom intimidatingly in the back of a room to scare potential rivals. He wasn't wealthy, but he wasn't broke, either. Syndicates paid well enough. Arch probably banked more than he would have in a standard nine-to-five, but didn't get the perks or a retirement plan.

"I don't think the head of a syndicate is just going to talk to us, even with Archie vouching for us."

"I figured as much." Duff did not seem concerned about it. "We have cards to play, though."

"What if that doesn't work?"

"Then I'll probably do something stupid and get hurt."

The boys walked to their van, which baked in the afternoon sun. The asphalt sent as much heat back at them as the sun sent down. It was like a river of sticky, hot dampness no matter where they went.

While they walked, Abe told Duff what he'd learned about Michael Hanley and Arlo Dodge.

"They met in the Army when they joined at the very end of the Vietnam era, but neither got sent overseas. They finished their stint, used their GI Bills to get accounting degrees, and joined a practice started by another ex-Army guy, Walter Briscoe. Briscoe was a few years older, did two tours in 'Nam as a staff sergeant in the Quartermaster Department, and went into accounting when he got his degree after getting out of the service. Together, the three built a hugely successful firm thanks to being quick to adopt computers and marketing their efficiency toward the bigger corporations in Chicago."

"They rich?"

"Obscenely." Abe started *The Bad-Luck Charm*. The AC blew hot air at first. It cooled to merely warm air once Abe began driving, but it was better than nothing.

Abe guided the van out of the parking lot and pointed it south. "From what I could gather from the Internet, their net worth was somewhere around five million apiece, probably more."

"I guarantee they have more. Creative accounting hides a lot of cash, I'm sure. I'm certain they've both got overseas accounts. Must be nice."

Duff rolled the passenger window down to get some air flowing to cool the van, but it only succeeded in equalizing the heat. "There are a lot of Army people around this case, isn't there?"

"Could be a coincidence."

"True." Duff pulled his phone out of his pocket and called Vicky Bloch. She answered on the first ring. Duff didn't do pleasantries; he went straight to the question. "Was Robert in the Army, too?"

Vicky was taken aback momentarily, but she came through with an answer. "He was, briefly. He was in ROTC in college, of course. Got a commission after he graduated for a few months, but he got in a car accident just before he was about to be shipped to Iraq. Wrecked his knee. They gave him a medical discharge, so he never really saw action."

"Interesting." Duff hung up on her without saying goodbye. "Very interesting."

"What does it mean?"

Duff was staring at his phone. "Might be nothing. Might be everything. We're missing something somewhere." Duff's gaze drifted from his phone to the window. He watched buildings passing by with a vacant stare.

Abe knew Duff was no longer present. He was scanning through his memory banks, trying to find some clue he had missed. Abe knew better than to interrupt him. It wouldn't matter if he spoke, anyhow. Duff would never hear him.

13

A RCHIE VANG WAITED for Abe and Duff at the gate of a dilapidated warehouse near the Chicago River, just south of Chinatown. Most of the Asian gangs worked out of Chinatown or the surrounding neighborhoods in some capacity, except for a few minor groups who worked more exclusively out of the northside 'burbs and the southern Wisconsin city of Racine.

The Koreans owned the warehouse. It was a garment mill for several decades before World War II, but had fallen into disrepair and disuse. Now, it was mostly empty. Last Abe heard about the place, the building had been up for condemnation, but no one had shown up with a wrecking ball.

Archie gave them a lackadaisical salute as they parked. He wore a light gray suit with a white tank top beneath the jacket. His chest was broad, shoulders large and rounded even beneath the padding of the coat. His hair was thinning on top from a combination of the questionable hormonal *enhancements* weightlifters sometimes used and the natural progression of time and age. Archie slicked back what he still had up top with some hair oil, but it left an expansive forehead as evidence of rampant recession.

"You guys sure you want a tilly with these boys? They aren't exactly happy-go-lucky fellas."

"The case has led us here." Duff climbed out of *The Bad-Luck Charm.* The haze of a streetlight illuminated the area. The sun was low in the western sky, but it was nearly dark. The heat of the day relented slightly, but the air was still thick and soupy with humidity.

"Leave your guns in the van. If they find them, they'll take them, and you won't get them back." Archie started heading toward the darkened warehouse.

"See! I told you I didn't need a gun." Duff had to remove his shirt to remove the shoulder holster with his new Beretta.

Abe ditched his Jim Rockford special under the front seat and climbed out of the van. He wondered why he always had to meet gangsters in odd locations late at night. Did gangsters have something against brunch? Or perhaps a nice early afternoon iced latte at a fair-trade coffee shop? As a middle-aged man staring down the barrel of fifty, Abe liked an early bedtime. He was no longer built to be doing shady investigations after 10:00 PM.

Archie directed them to a graffiti-covered door at the base of the warehouse. A dozen cars were parked at the building. There was no cheap steel in the lineup. All of them were expensive, most with custom additions like fins or wraps, and the majority were smaller, high-powered imports with five-speed manuals. They were cars driven by men who were serious about speed, typical of the Asian syndicates.

American gangs, both Black and white, preferred muscle like Hellcats, Mustangs, or Chargers, but the triads and the Korean gangs liked their compact Mazdas, Nissans, and Hondas. Either that or they went with the Lincoln Navigators because there was no middle ground; it was either low and fast or the biggest damn thing on the road.

Archie opened the door and ushered the boys inside. They were greeted by an immediate thumping they hadn't heard outside the warehouse, a tight, fast, rhythmic beat of heavy drums.

A large man was on a stool just inside the door. Actually, *large* would only begin to describe him. He was Samoan, with a big, wild mane of black hair standing off his scalp in every direction. He had neck tattoos. He was easily four bills and change, but it wasn't all fat. There was a scary amount of muscle in the man's build. He stood when the door opened and saw two middle-aged white guys, but relaxed when Archie appeared and gave him a signal. He patted Abe and Duff down roughly before he gave them the go-ahead.

Beyond the door was a long, dark tunnel lit with tiny blue LED lights every ten feet. It gave the hall a strange, icy look.

"I thought this was just a distribution center." Abe tried not to show fear, but this was a little disturbing to him. Why was there a massive bouncer at the door?

Archie strode past Abe, wide shoulders filling the narrow tunnel. "Distribution isn't as profitable as you'd think, so they pivoted into something more profitable after hours."

Archie opened the door at the far end of the tunnel. Immediately, the throb of the electronic dance music became unbearable. A strobe of green and blue laser lights illuminated a nightclub-like space that once was a warehouse. A long runway stage was in the center of a large, open floor, and three topless Asian women, all thin and toned, were gyrating against tall metal poles mounted to the floor of the stage. It was hot and damp in the warehouse. The women were slick with sweat, but the haze of cigarette smoke and flashing LED lights only made them look sexier and more athletic.

A few dozen men waving cash crowded the stage, most of them Asian as well, but a few whites, Blacks, and Latinos were represented in the mix. A full bar along the far wall was tended by several large men, all built like Archie Vang. A small casino was on the far end of the warehouse with multiple tables running various games, everything from roulette to baccarat, but the poker tables were getting the most action.

A DJ in an astronaut helmet was stationed at the far end of the stage behind several monitors and two laptop computers. He was thrusting and dancing to the music, waving his arms and trying to hype the crowd even though no one was looking at him. There were boobs to be seen. No red-blooded man in the place would dare cast a glance at Commander Space Cadet and his turntables of doom when there were jiggling, surgically enhanced C-cups to stare at instead.

Duff shook his head with mild disgust. "I remember when being in music meant you had to have talent. Now these assholes push buttons on a MacBook and think they're Quincy Jones."

Archie Vang shrugged as though apologizing. "People used to want to be in a band. Now they want to be TikTok famous. We have failed as a society."

"How do the police allow this place to run?" Abe was genuinely curious. Normally, any illegal gambling and liquor operation gets slammed to the turf within a day or two by the feds. They hated it when the mobs tried to cut them out of the license fees and taxes those establishments generated.

"Same way as always: Han Sang-Wook has the right people in his pocket."

Archie led them past all the vice activity on the main floor and up a set of steel stairs guarded by a heavily muscled Korean man in a black suit. When he turned sideways to let them pass, Abe caught a glimpse of a mini Uzi in a shoulder holster under the man's left arm.

Abe couldn't help but remember the rate of fire on that thing: 950 rounds a minute. A standard clip only held twenty rounds. An extended clip could hold thirty. Either way, the entire clip could be emptied in less than two seconds. That was a lot of hot death spat downrange at a moment's notice. It reminded Abe of how much he didn't like guns. It was sad that humanity had so many ways to destroy each other and so few ways to save each other.

The second story of the warehouse held the operation's offices. Abe noticed that all the windows leading to the outside world were blacked out to keep the lights and noise from leaking to the public. This wasn't a resort. It was a place to which you had to be invited. It was a place that did business with a select clientele.

Archie Vang walked them to the corner farthest from the DJ's speakers. It was quieter, but not by much. He opened a door leading to a large office along the north side of the building. The office was lined with soundproof battens to minimize the sound. It was still audible, but more of a dull, muffled static in the background.

The room was mostly dark, lit only by neon beer signs on the north wall and an 80-inch flat screen playing highlights from that day's Cubs game. A half-dozen men stood along the walls of the room. Each looked Korean, all of them wearing either a business suit or a tracksuit not dissimilar from the ones the Italian knuckleheads sported. The business suit guys were packing handguns in shoulder holsters. They did nothing to hide them. One guy sat on a large couch in the center of the office in a black-and-gold tracksuit and sneakers that cost more than Abe and Duff's entire operation would make in two months.

Han Sang-wook was wearing sunglasses as if he needed to protect his eyes from the bright glow of the massive TV. He disguised his fifty-plus years with a smart, modern haircut, longer on top and faded on the sides. He was probably using Just For Men to hide the gray at his temples. He looked like he was in tremendous shape for a man his age. He wasn't a muscled meathead like his bouncers, but even under the loose-fitting clothes, Abe could see sinewy, taut muscle. Han had the reputation of being a fighter, and a good one. Abe heard the man had studied several forms of martial arts throughout his life, favoring Chinese Wing Chun and Indonesian Pencak Silat. Still, he had no qualms with switching to a barbaric, formless, brutal ground-and-pound when necessary.

Archie motioned for Abe and Duff to be silent and took two steps forward, waiting for the leader of the Korean syndicate to address him first. It was like dealing with royalty, especially for a hired goon like Archie. He knew his place, knew how to play the game.

Han never looked away from the TV. He took his sweet time. He admired his fingernails for a second, pushed back a cuticle, switched channels to see some highlights from a women's soccer match, and then switched back to baseball. He picked up a can of beer from the coffee table and took a drink. Finally, after he felt Archie had waited long enough, Han deigned to address him.

Han spoke without looking away from the TV. "Archie Vang, my man with the plan. What brings you by tonight?"

"I brought Abe Allard and Duff to meet you. They're detectives. They got questions about some accountant who got merked on Friday night. They heard you were the man with all the answers."

Han removed his aviators and tossed them onto the coffee table next to the can of beer. He rose to his feet. He was trying to appear intimidating, but he was at least two inches shorter than Duff. His posture and stance were exaggerated to make him seem larger and tougher.

"So, you are the detectives I keep hearing about, the ones who got the office in the old Jew's building in Chinatown."

"And you're the..." Duff trailed off, searching for the right word. "Low-level mob boss wannabe who can't bring the Korean mob to the same level as the Yakuza or the Triads."

Before Abe could warn his partner, one of the suited thugs moved on Duff like a striking viper. He was fast and silent. In a single, concerted motion, the thug swept a leg at Duff's ankles and used an arm to sweep the fat man's upper body in the opposite direction. It was an elegant maneuver with no wasted motion or strength.

Duff, caught completely unaware, was knocked horizontally in midair and slammed unceremoniously to the concrete. His body slapped the floor with the same sound a dropped spiral ham makes when it hits pavement. The thug finished the move by grabbing Duff's right arm, twisting it into a joint lock, and kneeling on the side of his neck. Despite the size difference between the two men, Duff was completely incapacitated. His face was pressed into the concrete.

"Da toof hurds, dozen it?" Duff's mouth couldn't form the words correctly because it was pinned against the floor.

Another guard took a step toward Abe, in case Abe tried something to help his friend.

Abe held up his hands to indicate he had no plans to do anything even approaching heroic. Instead, he said, "I'd like to apologize for Duff." Abe was used to apologizing for Duff.

Han walked over and squatted in front of Duff, craning his neck so his face could approximate the same angle as Duff's face. "You're the guy who went crazy, right? Got stowed away up north with a bunch of other crazy fucks, right?"

Duff said something, but it came out as a garbled mess. Han made a gesture, and the hired thug took his knee off Duff's neck but maintained the joint lock on his arm.

Duff licked his lips and tried again. "They weren't so much crazy as they were psychopaths incapable of empathy or human decency."

"Is there a difference?"

139

"There is if you're locked in an asylum with them."

"I suppose you think you're some sort of tough guy, then?" Han reached down and flicked Duff's nose hard with his middle finger.

"He doesn't," said Abe.

"I really don't." Duff tried to point at the thug holding him with his fingers, which were contorted at an odd angle due to the wrist-lock being applied. "In fact, I'm so much the opposite of a tough guy that if this guy lets me go, I'll probably just continue to lie here for a while. Might even cry a little. I'm not sure. It's been a long day."

Han gave a small gesture with his fingers, and the thug dropped Duff's arm. True to his word, Duff made no effort to pick himself up from the floor. He remained in repose and took in the details of the room from his vantage point.

Han Sang-wook was amused. He sat on the floor before Duff, crossing his legs in a yoga pose. Abe was impressed by the man's flexibility. He was maybe five or ten years older than Abe and Duff, but he was in far better shape. Abe once read that you could measure a man's health by his flexibility. Abe was as flexible as dry spaghetti, and Duff was even worse. Abe once saw Duff drop a five-dollar bill on the ground, shrug sadly, and watch as the wind blew it down the street.

Han leaned toward Duff. "I hear you had a little girlfriend who died. People say it made you lose your mind."

"*Lose* is a relative term."

Abe felt a strange, fraternal need to defend his partner. "It honed his mind, sharpened it."

"I didn't ask for help from the peanut gallery." Han held a finger to his lips and gave Abe a lethal stare. Abe continued to hold up his hands in a state of compliance and surrender.

Han adjusted his position so he was lying on the floor like Duff. "They call you Fat Sherlock on the streets, you know."

"I've heard better nicknames. My friends call me Thor."

"No, we don't," said Abe.

"They used to call me Viper."

"Never did that, either," said Abe.

Han propped his head up on his hand. "You know what they call me?"

"Is it Zeppo? I feel like it's Zeppo."

Han Sang-wook inhaled through his nose, flaring his nostrils for emphasis. His voice was low, it rumbled in his throat. "They call me *jug-eum*. Death."

"People on the street call you *jug-eum*? Like, random people do that? Even if they don't know you? Because I'm betting almost no one in greater

Chicago speaks Korean, so for them to wander around calling you some Korean word is really weird. I'm betting they call you Zeppo, and you just haven't heard it."

Han lashed out with a kick that moved faster than Duff could react.

It caught Duff square in the nethers and forced him to groan and curl into a ball, clutching his crotch. "Well, there goes my dreams of being a father, but you just did wonders for my dreams of being a castrato soprano."

"You have a mouth on you. It's a disrespectful mouth. I wonder if you might need it shut permanently."

"That'd make it hard to eat Swiss Cake Rolls. I imagine I could still blend them in a Vitamix and use a nasogastric tube to take them in, but that kind of kills the fun of eating them, am I right?"

Rather than getting angry, Han seemed amused. "You don't much care about dying, do you?"

Duff shrugged. "I mean, it's not on my list of things to do today, but I don't fear it."

Han stood and extended his hand. "Get up."

"Are you sure? I mean, if you want to monologue with some shitty villain clichés some more, I'd be willing to play the straight man in this act."

Han laughed. Gone was any trace of his heavy Korean accent and anime villain voice. He was no longer Han Sang-wook, the notorious Korean mobster; instead, he was magically turned into Sammy Han, who graduated from Teddy Roosevelt High in the '80s. He had a Chicago accent and a bit of a nasal twang to his voice. "I heard you fuckers were crazy. I guess it wasn't a lie."

Duff let Han help him to his feet. He rubbed his shoulder where it had slammed into the floor. "I heard you were crazy, too."

"Crazy's a relative term. Given what I do for a living, sometimes crazy is preferable to sane." Han snapped his fingers, and one of the tracksuited guys started pouring drinks. "You guys want something?"

Archie stepped in. "Abe doesn't drink, and Duff only drinks unpretentious beer."

"Teetotaler?"

"Never liked the taste," said Abe.

The tracksuited guy magicked a bottle of water out of a fridge disguised as a cabinet, along with a bottle of Miller High Life. He handed the water to Abe and the beer to Duff.

"Not my usual brand, but it's hard to turn down the champagne of beers." Duff twisted the cap and took a sip. "Of course, it's only the Champagne of Beers when it's from the Champagne region of Wisconsin; otherwise it's just sparkling piss water."

Han collapsed on the couch again, his attention on the TV. "Why did you have Archie bring you here?"

Duff took another slug of beer. "Robert Bloch got shot and killed on Friday night. It's looking like it might have been a hired hit. We hear you might know something about it."

"Robert Bloch. Doesn't ring a bell." Han Sang-wook took a drink of a brown liquid in a Glencairn glass. He sat back on the couch and rested the glass on his belly.

"Accountant. Worked for Hanley, Dodge, and Briscoe."

Han shrugged his shoulders. "Sounds like white guys."

"The whitest," said Duff.

"Never heard of 'em."

Abe was watching Han's face and features. Abe's background in psychology gave him an edge when it came to reading people. If he studied features closely enough, he could usually detect a lie or at least an attempt to deceive. Things like that wouldn't hold up in a court of law, but they could help an investigation. It wasn't an easy thing to do, especially against characters like Han Sang-wook. They were practiced liars, but there was a difference between lying and deception. Lying was easy. Deception was harder to do. Little clues always emerge when one is trying to deceive.

Han wasn't making eye contact with Duff. He kept his gaze on the sports highlights on the TV. That could be a power-play move, but it could also be an attempt to prevent someone from seeing his eyes. Eyes gave away the most when trying to deceive. A slight flare of the pupils when a subject hears a word that means something to them, for instance, is involuntary.

Duff switched to a new topic. "The Italians say you might be stockpiling guns."

Han wasn't fazed. "I say the Italians might be the ones who are stockpiling guns. See how that works? Anyone can say anything about anyone. Doesn't make it true. Have you not been watching politics for the last fifty years?"

"I didn't figure you'd tell me if you were, but I figured you'd flat deny it if you weren't. You kind of pussyfooted around the topic a little. That might lead me to believe you are lying about it."

"Believe whatever you feel like believing if it makes you feel better."

"I think the Italians had some solid info. Said it might have been you or the Venezuelans."

Han waved this off with a flippant attitude. "You know how them Chicago-born Guidos are. Anyone who ain't alabaster and blue-eyed all look alike to them."

Duff flicked a glance toward Abe.

Abe knew what that look meant. After all their years together, this was part of their unspoken language. Duff knew Han would never give him a straight answer. The man was the head of a syndicate. He was anti-authority. He had nothing to gain from answering a detective's questions. Duff needed to escalate things. The glance told Abe that Duff was about to do something incredibly stupid.

Without being asked, Duff moved to sit on the couch next to Han. The same thug as before came off his spot on the wall and hit Duff like a whirlwind, sweeping his feet out from under him again and slamming him to the floor face-first. Duff's bottle of Miller flew out of his hand and shattered against the cinder block wall. The Champagne of Beers ran down the wall and pooled on the floor.

Han took another sip of his liquor as if a man being beaten in front of him was a common occurrence. "You'll have to forgive Mr. Pak, Fat Sherlock. He takes his bodyguard duties very seriously."

Duff blew out a hard breath through his nose. He painted the floor with a fine spray of blood. "I'm going to feel that in the morning."

Han waved Mr. Pak back to his place against the wall. The bodyguard moved like a jungle cat. His suit hid his muscles, but Abe could see the man was an extraordinary athlete. There was a strange, unnatural grace about his movements. He probably never tripped over uneven sidewalks or missed a step when descending a staircase. Meanwhile, Abe had done both of those things in the last two days.

Duff sat up and swiped his wrist beneath his nose. His hand was stained with blood. "I've had my nose broken by better men, but never with as much flair."

Han made another gesture. The guy who made the drinks tossed Duff a roll of paper towels.

Duff caught them in the air. "I hope they're two-ply." He tore one strip in half, rolled the two strips into little wound bandages, and stuffed them into his snout.

"Another beer?" asked Han.

"Sure, why not?" Still sitting on the floor, Duff accepted another Miller High Life from the tracksuited guy. He held the bottle out toward Han. "To blood-flooded sinus cavities."

"I'll drink to that." Han leaned forward and tapped his Glencarin against Duff's bottle.

Abe glanced at all the men in the room. All were indifferent toward the attack on Duff. They were used to such things. Abe noticed one of them adjusted his stance, though. The rest were leaning against the walls, even the extremely swift Mr. Pak. They looked like they were relaxed. Alert, but relaxed. One of them, the one nearest the door on the far side of the office, was no longer leaning against the wall. He was standing upright, feet close together. He was watching Duff, not Han. That meant something. It showed concern. Why was he concerned about Duff?

The thug's eyes flicked from Duff to Abe. Abe was caught staring. He did not look away. He locked eyes with the young man and noticed the kid did not look away, either. It was not a challenge like locking eyes sometimes became. The young man saw Abe looking at him, moved his eyes, tilted his head slightly toward the door next to him, and then returned his gaze to Duff. The young man knew something. He wanted to talk.

Abe couldn't communicate anything to him. He looked to his left and tried to get Archie's attention without anyone else noticing, but it was too much of a risk. Abe could not chance it.

"I guess we've been misinformed, then." Abe locked his eyes on Mr. Pak and held up a hand. "Don't slam me to the floor, please. I'm just going to help Duff."

Abe pulled his partner to his feet. "We should probably get out of your hair."

Duff adjusted the bridge of his nose with his fingers. There was a stomach-churning sound of something clicking into place. "Yeah, I suppose we should go. Clearly, you know nothing. Nothing about guns, nothing about the accountant, and definitely nothing about which of the six men in this room is ripping you off under your nose. Thanks for your time."

The last comment landed. Hard.

All the men in Han's group were suddenly at attention. No one was leaning against the wall anymore. Several reached inside their jackets to grab handguns.

Han Sang-wook barked a command in Korean, and the men moved to parade rest, but all of them were shooting daggers at Duff. Except the kid next to the door, Abe noted. The kid was different. Why?

Duff moved toward the door, but Han held up a hand. Mr. Pak positioned himself between Duff and the exit. A slim pistol appeared in his hand.

Han gave Duff a long, hard stare. "What do you mean, Fat Sherlock?"

"I didn't mince words. You're oblivious. We're going to find someone who might know something that will help us because you're too dense to see what's going on in front of your face. That's how investigating crime works."

Han stood and put his liquor on the coffee table. "Tell me what you know."

Duff shook his head. "Nah, I'm not calling out one of your guys in front of you. They know who they are, and they know what you'll do. It's better for everyone that you stay oblivious."

Han was on Duff like gochugaru on kimchi. He grabbed him by the front of his t-shirt. "You will tell me what you know."

"Get rid of your guys, first. Clear the room, and I'll let you know."

"Why should I have them leave? You think you can kill me without my bodyguards?"

"God, no. I don't have that kind of fight in me."

Han eyed Duff suspiciously. He gave another order in Korean. The guards protested, replying in Korean. Han's anime villain voice returned. He said something Abe didn't understand, but the tone was more than enough to convey his meaning.

The guards walked to the exits, all of them angry. They filtered out one by one, save for Mr. Pak, who maintained a sentry position at the door.

"There. They're gone. I assume Mr. Pak was not the man who was stealing from me. I know Mr. Pak very well, and I pay handsomely for his loyalty."

"No, it wasn't Mr. Pak." Duff limped to the windows overlooking the rest of the warehouse. He stood at Han's side. One of the guards in a tracksuit was hustling toward an exit, but he was trying to look casual while doing it. Duff pointed him out. "There's your thief."

Han murmured something in Korean to Pak. The bodyguard nodded and slipped out of the office with a panther's grace.

Duff pinched the bridge of his nose again. "Figured he needed a running start. It's only fair."

"How did you know?" The cartoon villain's voice was gone again. The Chicago accent was back.

Duff tapped his wrist. "The idiot was wearing a Rolex. None of your other guys was wearing a Rolex. They had some nice pieces, but all of them were under a thousand dollars. They were not Rolex Sky-Dweller nice. That's a forty-thousand-dollar watch. If all of them were rolling that large, I'd just think you were paying your men well. I asked you to clear the room because I wasn't positive. I knew if he ran, then I was right. The fact that he was comfortable wearing it around you tells me he liked flaunting it in front of you. He either thought you were a dim bulb, or he thought you were so full of yourself that you wouldn't deign to look at the wrists of your men."

"He was right. I will note their watches from now on."

"Shoes, too. Expensive shoes are a dead giveaway about how much someone is making," said Duff.

Han crossed his arms in front of his chest. He stared out the window at his club. "You have properly humbled me. I guess I owe you something now."

"You're the mob boss, not me. I don't know how your world works." Duff popped the two makeshift nose plugs from his nostrils. They were coated with deep, almost black blood.

"Sorry about your face."

"I've had worse."

"You guys are basically the Diet Pepsi of cops, you know."

Abe tried to deflect that thinking. "We're private eyes. Our mission is to our clients, whoever they are, not to the police. Not to justice, either."

"One calorie cops," Han said.

"Look, Sang-wook—can I call you Sammy?" Duff said.

"No."

"How about *My Little Dumpling*?"

"That's racist."

"I'll let you call me your favorite honky."

"You're not, though."

Duff smiled sweetly. "But I could be."

"Make your point, Mr. Duffy."

"Just Duff is fine. And my point is this: we're not cops. We get that society has a lot of layers, and sometimes, people in your position have to make some decisions that those in higher legal standing might find distasteful. But those decisions still need to get made, right?"

"I fail to see the point you're trying to make," said Han.

Duff crossed his arms in front of his chest and stared out at the floor of the warehouse, mimicking Han's stance. "I remember when Lee Yu-Jun was the leader of your group."

"Do you?"

"It's a shame he disappeared like he did."

Han took in a sharp breath of air. "Yes, it is a shame. He is missed."

"The OCD asked us to look into it when he disappeared." Duff knew referencing the Organized Crime Division of the Chicago Police Department would get Han's attention.

The gangster's eyebrows raised involuntarily. "Did they?"

"They did." Duff waited for a moment, a dramatic pause. "*Pyohyo.*"

That was the Korean word for *drifting*. It was also the name of the modest yacht Han Sang-wook kept at Burnham Harbor. Duff pulled an ace out of his sleeve. He and Abe had briefly investigated the Lee disappearance as a favor to Malcolm Betts. They learned a few things.

They knew the elderly Lee Yu-Jun, former head of the Korean Syndicate, had most likely been unceremoniously executed, hauled out to some deep trench on Lake Michigan, and dumped overboard with a couple of old car tire rims chained around his body to keep it from popping to the surface for at least a few years.

The problem was that they never found hard evidence for the killing, so any information was only conjecture and not useful for a conviction. They weren't positive Lee Yu-Jun was in the lake, nor were they positive Han Sang-wook either killed the old man or had him killed. They could only speculate.

"I could have told the police that a homeless man near the Shedd Aquarium was watching the water just before dawn four years ago, and he witnessed your boat hauling ass out of the harbor, but I figured that was information they didn't need to know because there's a balance to be maintained in the city. No hard evidence would have meant they were just going to bother you, and cops sniffing around too much is bad for commerce. Business is business, right?"

Han knew what Duff was saying. "Business is indeed business."

"And some business is not any business of the CPD, am I right?"

"You are correct, Mr. Duffy."

"Just Duff is fine. So, here's the deal: we don't give two shits about the guns you're probably stockpiling. That's not our case at the moment. We just want to know about the accountant."

Han Sang-wook turned to Archie. "Mr. Vang, would you be so kind as to escort your friends out of the club? Take them to the north door."

"Yes, sir." Archie opened the door closest to them. "This way, guys."

"Mr. Vang will see you out." Han walked back to the couch and returned to his SportsCenter clips. "I trust you will find something to your liking outside."

THE NORTH DOOR exited the building on the side of the warehouse closest to the river. An expansive rail yard stretched between the building and the water, where decommissioned cargo train boxes sat rusting in silence. The place was walled off with ample *No Trespassing* signs tacked at 12-foot intervals to the chain-link fencing.

A dozen lights illuminated the rail yard, but there were no other lights on the north side of the building. From the outside, the throb of the music could no longer be heard. Coverings over the windows blocked the laser light show from being seen by unknowing passersby.

Abe scanned the rail yard. "Was this what Han wanted us to see?"

Archie Vang gave the view a hard scan before shrugging. "Han can be a little inscrutable at times."

Duff was still holding the bottle of Miller High Life. "He said we would find something to our liking out here. He wouldn't have said it if he didn't want us to see something."

The big man slowly surveyed the entire scene, slugging back another sip of beer while he did. "The rail yard is too obvious, too big. He knows I see things; this is a test. He wanted me to see what he was talking about without being obvious. It needs to be something related to the case. He knows something important. If he doesn't know exactly who did it, he was telling us something that'll lead to the next step."

The door behind them opened. The kid in the tracksuit who locked eyes with Abe exited. He was thin, almost scrawny. He had a mop of black hair that looked as fluffy as the feathers on a baby chicken. "You guys are the Chinatown detectives, right?"

"We are," said Abe.

"I'm Ha-joon. People call me Harry."

"I'm Abe. That's Duff. And you already probably know Archie Vang."

"You guys helped my great-aunt last year."

"We did?" Abe exchanged a glance with Duff.

"Her name is Rose. She runs the little Asian grocery store down the street from El Muro. She got robbed last year, and Duff figured out who did it and got all her money back. You guys refused to take any money from her."

Duff had been able to pin the theft on one of the burgeoning juvenile delinquents the woman's grandson hung out with. Got the kid to admit to it and give back the money when Duff pointed out the cameras on the streetlights across the street from the grocery store. Give the money back or go to jail. Easy choice.

"She made us like a metric ton of homemade pork mandu. That was better than money," said Duff. He and Abe had lived off those dumplings for weeks.

"Anyhow, I want to pay back that favor. I don't know who pulled the trigger on your guy, but a dude came to us about a week ago and asked for help on a problem. He didn't want to cough up the money Han wanted, but he did give Han something. It was done behind closed doors. Only Han and Pak know what he got."

"You saw the guy?" Duff's interest was piqued. "Older? Younger?"

"Middle-aged, I think. Leaning toward older. Fifties, maybe? I don't know. Blond. Scruffy. Tats."

There was only one guy on their radar fitting that description so far. Abe's nose wrinkled in thought. He scratched at his bald head. "Tom O'Brien? Vicky Bloch's neighbor?"

Duff blinked twice. "Maybe. Was he even on the list of suspects?"

"He wasn't in my book. We just passed him at her house that one time. We had no rational reason to suspect him."

"I told you this felt personal from the beginning."

"What's the motive, then?"

"An affair." Duff's answer was blunt. "She was projecting. She was the one cheating on Robert. I'm betting Robert found out, confronted her, and she wanted to believe he was cheating on her because they were both unhappy in the marriage."

"Do you have evidence?"

"Hell, no. This is a brand-new schism in this already screwed-up mess. I'm boldly guessing based on common reasons married people murder each other."

Abe had difficulty wrapping his mind around this new flux in the investigation. "All the evidence gathered so far points to something corporate: the money being moved, the handgun, the potential mob involvement. Corporate makes more sense, doesn't it?"

"It does, but I feel like we're missing something." Duff thought for a moment. "Aberforth, when you researched Hanley, Dodge, and Briscoe earlier, did you see what they looked like?"

Abe hadn't. There was no need to look at pictures of them. What people looked like rarely figured into whether or not they would commit murder.

Duff pulled out his phone and searched for Michael Hanley and Arlo Dodge. Michael Hanley was the first image to pop up on his screen. Hanley was in his late sixties but could have passed for someone in his late forties. Money could buy youth. He was handsome with a square jaw and piercing eyes. He seemed to favor a beard trimmed very close to the skin. He also kept his hair slicked back with a sheen of gel-based product in all his professional photos. If he had not used hair gel, it might be scruffy in its natural state.

Duff showed the picture to Abe and Archie. "This could be our guy, too."

Abe had to squint at the image on the phone screen. "Tattoos?"

None of the pictures of Hanley showed his bare arms. Duff considered this for a moment. "He was in the Army. He could have tattoos."

"What about Arlo Dodge?"

Duff scrolled further and found pictures of Harrison Arlo Dodge, addressed on the company website and in all business press releases as H. Arlo Dodge or simply Arlo Dodge.

Duff almost choked when he saw the man. Dodge had a recognizable oval head devoid of hair, a sad-looking, slack visage with a painfully familiar resting bitch face. It was like looking at a slightly older version of Abe.

"Abe, how much do you know about your father?"

"I've told you this before."

"I know. I'm saying this for Archie's sake. Tell him."

"Almost nothing. My mother only said she met him during her freshman year of college. She never told me anything beyond that."

Duff held out the phone again.

Abe froze. For a moment, he felt like he was falling, his legs became jelly. The world spun. A piece of his brain broke off from reality and spiraled into the ether. He could not, for all his education, experience, and logic, fathom what he was seeing. It was like looking into a mirror.

When he could speak, he could only stammer. It was hard to get through the sentence. "What are the odds that he is my father, though?"

For all his mental strengths, questionable or not, Duff wasn't a mathematical genius, but he was good at estimating odds. "Slim. But what are the odds that Jennifer Carthage is Robert Bloch's daughter?"

Abe took the phone and stared at the picture. The age of the man was right. His mother would have been sixty-five if she had not lost her battle with cancer. She was nineteen when she gave birth to Abe. This man looked like he was in his mid-to-late sixties. The timing was right. What if his mother had a fling with a young man who had joined the Army at the tail end of Vietnam? What if that young man had left to serve overseas, and his mother had not found out she was pregnant until after he had gone? It was the mid-1970s when she got pregnant. Contacting people then was not as easy as it is now. Abe always knew his mother had decided to go through with motherhood alone after discovering she was pregnant. She never mentioned trying to find his father. She deflected any questions Abe asked about his father, telling him to concentrate on his studies instead. *What's done is done, Abe. Wishing for change won't change anything.*

Abe realized Duff and Archie were watching him. They were waiting for him to dictate the next steps. Abe wanted to find Arlo Dodge and ask him if they might be related. That wouldn't help anything at the moment.

It might not help anything in the future, either. He knew what the responsible play was. "I guess this is a twist unrelated to the case, so it's unimportant."

Abe tried to sound brave, but in reality, he was spiraling. Could this man be his father? The odds suggested he wasn't. Abe leaned into the odds. Stay the logical course. Abe had a common head shape and a familiar face. It was one of the gifts of possessing such obvious Midwestern features. He was easily forgettable because there were a thousand guys who looked like him in every city in America. And even if Arlo Dodge was his father, so what? He was old now. It wasn't like they were going to go out and chuck a football around the yard or talk about the facts of life. The man had missed every point in his life when Abe really needed a father. It made no sense to play forgive and forget now.

Duff turned to the cityscape splayed out before them again. He sought what Han Sang-wook wanted him to see. His eyes processed the visible buildings in the distance. After several seconds of silence, he raised a hand. "There."

Duff pointed at a darkened lot in the distance. A slew of white trucks and white vans were lined up around a small building. "That looks like a rental place if I've ever seen one."

"The white van in the parking ramp," said Abe. "The shooter's van."

"Han Sang-wook might not have sent a hitter or pulled the trigger, but he might have taken cash for something the police would never be able to charge him with, like renting a vehicle for a crime."

"Plausible deniability," said Archie.

"We need evidence. Han directed us to that rental place. I'm betting we find something to move this case along inside." Duff finished the last of his Miller High Life and tossed the empty over his shoulder. The bottle shattered against the ground behind them, more broken glass for the already littered asphalt. "Let's go rent a car."

Abe checked his phone. It was past ten on a Sunday night. "They're closed."

Duff slipped a hand into the back left pocket of his jeans. He pulled out his trusty lock-picking kit. "That's never stopped me before."

"If you guys are going to be breaking and entering, I think I'm going to bounce. I don't need to deal with the CPD tonight." Archie jabbed a thumb over his shoulder. "There are titties in the building, and I think I'm going to take Ha-Joon inside, and we're going to go watch them."

"I don't blame you." Abe patted Archie on the shoulder. "If I was intelligent, I'd go with you."

Archie slung his arm over Ha-joon's shoulders, and they walked into the club.

Abe and Duff started the long walk to the rental place in silence. Duff was trying to piece together the parts of the investigation in his brain. Abe was trying to wrap his head around possibly having a father after all these years.

Neither one of them felt like talking.

14

E ZEE TRUCK & VAN Rental was half of a legitimate front for one of the Korean mob's biggest businesses. Yes, they rented vehicles like vans and box trucks. Yes, they made legit deliveries all over the metro area and even out into the other major cities in Illinois, Indiana, and Wisconsin. Yes, those parts of their business were legal, above-board, taxed, licensed, and kept uncooked books capable of passing any inspection the IRS could throw at them on both a state and federal level.

It was also how the Koreans controlled a lot of the drug trade around the city. It is easy to move products when you already have a legitimate shipping business, and there are plenty of ways to keep the product moving without the boys in blue catching wind or getting too interested. Buying cops was one way. Buying local aldermen and city councilmen was another. When all else failed, it was simple business to have some of your boys hit a nearby convenience store with a grab-and-go stickup, make it look messy, and then, while the police were distracted with that site, you simply drove your drug-loaded trucks past them, and waved as you did it.

Guns were just as easy as drugs to transport around town when the opportunity presented itself. There might be truth to what Petey Pucillo said about the Korean mob. They certainly had the warehouse, the vehicles, and the necessary cops and politicians purchased. They could move any amount of anything around the city without causing so much as a ripple on the surface of the collective society, be it meth, ghost guns, or even people.

Abe didn't like to think about the last one. Human trafficking was a problem the world over, and Chicago, with all its Midwestern charm, was not absolved from the issue.

EZEE was walled off from the world by high, wrought-iron fencing, complete with sharp, waggly spikes reminiscent of medieval torture devices on the top of the fence. Blocking the road access for the lot was a heavy sliding gate locked with a thick chain and a Masterlock the size of a man's fist.

The rental office was safely ensconced behind the fencing. A pair of cameras watched the lot with all the vehicles, and a single camera watched the main gate. Duff's sharp eyes took in the surroundings, even at a distance, and quickly realized the rear of the office was not on camera, nor was the right side of the gated area. All they had to do was get over the fence without getting torn open by the spikes on top, pick the lock at the back of the building, and they'd be inside where they could rummage through files for what they needed.

Getting over the fence was the challenge, though. It was ten feet tall. Even with Abe standing on Duff's shoulders, it would still be a challenge for him to get himself over the fence. And then, even if he made it without being impaled on the spikes, how would Duff follow? Abe could not pick locks like Duff. That was a skill the big man learned in the darkest pits of Bensonhurst from juvenile career criminals.

"How do we get in there?" Abe started scanning the area around them. Garbage. Scrap wood in a small drainage ditch. A Chick-fil-A bag. Nothing that would get them over the fence with any ease.

"I don't suppose you've learned the art of levitation and not told me, have you?"

"It was on my to-do list. Haven't gotten to it, yet."

Duff grabbed the bars of the wrought-iron fence and shook them. They were sturdy and did not even rattle. The gaps between the bars were small. "We could lose a lot of weight in the next ten minutes."

"Short of a miracle, I don't foresee that happening."

There was a crackle of noise, a hiss of static. Abe and Duff froze, both ducking low. Duff's knees cracked like a shotgun blast.

Han Sang-wook's voice came over a speaker mounted on the exterior of the rental office near the door. "Hey, dumbasses—the cameras don't actually work. Just do what you gotta do."

Duff stood up again. His knees cracked a second time. He spoke to the air. If Sammy Han could see them, then Duff figured they were on mic somewhere, too. "If they don't work, how are you seeing what we're doing?"

"Different cameras, ones you can't see. Don't worry about it. No one will get the footage."

"Trusting gangsters isn't really in my nature, but I think you and I were having a real *Christmas on Walton Mountain* moment together when you had your hired thug break my nose, so I'll trust you."

The static hiss from the speakers clicked and cut short. Han was no longer listening, but Duff said it anyway. "Good night, John-boy."

With assurance from the gangster, Duff made short work of the Masterlock on the gate with his lock picks and swept the old, well-worn lock on the door of the rental agency in seconds. The older the lock, the easier the tumblers and pins gave up their secrets.

The rental office had a dense, thick smell, a mixture of cigarettes, stale beer, oil, and gas. The walls were dingy from time and exhaust. The floors were filthy with dark paths showing the most-used routes through the building. The front of the building was a service counter, with the rear of the building being an office, a bathroom, and a storage room for basic repair supplies like new oil filters, cases of motor oil, and gallons of windshield wiper fluid. It lacked a full mechanic's bay, but a large metal door at the rear of the building could be opened to allow part of a vehicle to pull halfway into the space for more comfortable repairs during storms or the coldest parts of winter.

Abe used the light on his phone as a flashlight. In the old days, they always carried pocket flashlights. Times change. Methods change. Abe missed the pocket flashlights, though. You felt more like a detective while dagger-gripping a five-inch Maglite. Waving around a Pixel 7 in an Otterbox case was not quite the same level of cool.

Duff wasted no time. He headed straight for the file cabinets along the wall behind the service counter and pawed through the folders.

Abe went to the opposite end of the line of file cabinets. If either Michael Hanley or Tom O'Brien rented a truck or van through EZEE, there would have to be some sort of paperwork. Even if Han Sang-wook did it as a favor to the guy, EZEE was a legitimate business. They wouldn't let someone borrow a truck for a few hours without some sort of paperwork. There would have to be a rental agreement, a signature, a credit card receipt —something would have to exist to explain the absence of the truck on Friday night, or it would have been pointless for Han to send them there.

Duff moved to the next drawer in the file cabinet after coming up snake-eyes on the first. His voice was low, just in case there were microphones in the office. "You realize, of course, Han sending us here basically means that Petey Pucillo was right about Hanley, Dodge, and Briscoe moving money for the Koreans, right?"

"I assumed as much."

"You think Han Sang-wook is going to start a gang war?"

Abe didn't know and couldn't answer that. The days of the mob going to the mattresses against each other were long gone because they had become far more strategic about their attacks, but in the current culture, with hostilities being ramped up over any perceived slights, anything was possible.

Even if it was true, what could they do about it? Who were they? Powerless PIs with bad joints and worse aim. The police and the FBI had jobs for a reason. "That's not the case we are being paid to solve."

Duff pulled a file folder from the cabinet and handed it to Abe. "Check this one out. This looks right."

Abe took the file and found a rental contract for the same type of white van they saw on the security cameras after the shooting. The time of rental and return were recorded on the sheet: out at 4:45 PM on Friday and back at 7:00 AM when EZEE opened on Saturday morning. The rental fee was paid in cash, but a credit card was used as a holder. The receipt for the credit card was stapled to the corner of the rental agreement. The agreement had been signed with an illegible scrawl. It wasn't even a name. The card receipt was unsigned, but the last four digits of the card were printed on the receipt. It would be simple work to get a court order to find the rest of the number and match it to either Hanley's or O'Brien's card. For all the shooter's planning, leaving a credit card receipt, even an unsigned receipt, was a silly mistake. Abe had to believe the shooter thought no one would use the card or print anything connecting the card to the van.

Duff squinted at the scrawl on the rental agreement. "I don't see an O or a B or any sort of apostrophe. The letters are all jags, no curves. I'm betting this is Michael Hanley's scrawl, even if he tried to fake his signature."

"What's the next step?"

"We take that with us, number one." Duff used his phone to take a photo of the document and zoomed in on the receipt for a second photo. "That'll give Betts enough to at least question Hanley about the shooting."

"Still looking for a definite motive, though. We need proof of the money. We need proof he was up to something shady. The little hidden file with no markings won't prove anything to anyone."

Duff walked to the small waiting area where an old wing chair sat in front of a newspaper-covered coffee table, its stubby arms worn to shredded nothing from years of use. Duff tossed the manila file folder onto the coffee table, flopped into the chair, and leaned back into the broken springs and dilapidated padding.

Abe was simultaneously impressed and disturbed by Duff's ability to not care about germs, dirt, or how many backsides of questionable cleanliness and greasy heads had been in that seat over the years. Abe was not obsessive when it came to cleanliness, but he also didn't want to sit in a waiting room chair that looked like it had been used daily since Carter was President.

Duff put his fingers on his chin and looked to the ceiling, piecing together the details of the case. "Robert Bloch was in a state of paranoia and worry. He was stretched between his career and the money he was taking from Petey

Pucillo to investigate his employers. He was also dealing with a marriage that was slowly dissolving, and may have been dealing with finding out he was a father and never knew about it. He found evidence of his employer doing something shady. He had no evidence in his car, in his briefcase, or at his house that we could find."

"Which means if there is evidence, it's somewhere else."

"But where, is the question." After a moment of silence, Duff looked at Abe. "If you have evidence that proved your employer was taking mob money, would you give it to Tilda?"

"Never. That would put her in danger."

"What if no one knew Tilda was your daughter?"

"I still wouldn't do it, because I wouldn't want to put her in danger."

"So, you'd send it to Katherine?"

"No, I'd send evidence to you. You're my business partner. That would be our business."

"I'm asking if you think Bloch would have sent the evidence to Vicky Bloch."

"No, because he couldn't trust her. Their marriage was falling apart."

"Was it, or was that just Vicky's interpretation of it?" Duff stood up from the chair. "Is Vicky hiding something from us? If you're Robert Bloch, you have exactly no one in the world to trust at this moment. You would send your evidence to someone you trusted: your secretary, who might also be your daughter."

"You really think so?"

"I do. It only makes sense, right? She is all he had, even if she doesn't know it. Besides, she's in the company. She would know whom to turn in if she found the evidence. If he sent it to someone other than Vicki or Jennifer, would they even know what it was?"

Duff bent to grab the folder from the coffee table, and there was a gunshot from outside. The floor-to-ceiling glass window at the front of the store shattered into a cascade of shards and crashed across the filthy tile floor.

Abe dropped behind the counter. Duff, in a surprisingly athletic move for the big man, threw himself backward, over the counter, and crashed to the floor. A split-second later, another shot rang out, and the bullet sank into the wall just above the counter over Duff's head.

Abe was pressed to the floor like a snake.

Duff ducked as another gunshot rang out. "Is this the part where we do something awesome and heroic, or is this the part where we pee ourselves? Because I'm leaning toward the latter."

ABE USED HIS phone to text Archie Vang, the only person in his contacts list near enough to offer any aid. *Being shot at. Help!*

Another gunshot rang out, but Abe didn't see where the bullet went. Abe and Duff were not shot at often, but when they were, Abe's first thought was always a terrible one: did he text Katherine and Matilda to tell them goodbye, or did he refrain from it, knowing there was a chance he might survive and would not want to worry them?

Duff scrambled on his hands and knees down the hall toward the maintenance bay. Due to Archie Vang's suggestion that they leave their guns in *The Bad-Luck Charm*, they were weaponless. "There has to be something we can use in the garage. A big wrench or a long-handled ratchet or something."

Another shot hit the wall above the counter over Abe's head. A scattering of drywall and dust fell on him.

From the darkness outside the rental agency, a voice taunted them. "You sons of bitches could have kept your mouths shut." Fluid English with the barest touch of an accent. The speaker wasn't a native speaker but had been in the country long enough to pass for American.

From the garage bay, Duff called out, "It's your fault for flaunting the watch, man. Han would have seen it eventually."

The Korean man in the tracksuit emerged from the darkness. He stepped through the shattered window and stared down the hallway of the rental shop. He held a black handgun in front of him. "You are an idiot."

"Not the first time I've been called that."

Abe wished he had a gun on him. He wasn't a crack shot by any metric, but the man was only ten feet from him. He could land a couple of shots at that distance if he dumped all six rounds.

The shooter moved forward, sighting down the barrel of his weapon. "I didn't steal from Han Sang-wook."

"You got lucky with Bitcoin?" Duff's voice rang out in the maintenance bay. The echo made him sound tinny. He was rummaging through boxes.

"Where my money comes from is no concern of yours."

"You're working for a rival syndicate, then. You're a mole." Duff darted past the open door of the hallway from one side of the bay to the other. The shooter took a single shot. He missed Duff, but the bullet hit the rolling metal door and made a cartoonish noise when it ricocheted.

"What I do is none of your business." Another step forward.

He was dangerously close to passing the counter and seeing Abe cowering on the floor. Abe was desperate for a weapon.

Something flew out of the maintenance bay. A can of something. It blitzed out of the darkness, but it was not a challenge for the gunman to dodge. The can rattled to the floor behind him.

The thug paused. "You don't have a gun, do you?"

"What makes you say that?" Duff threw something else. A wrench. It came at the gunman with more speed, but he sidestepped it.

"If you had, you would have shot by now."

"You've never seen me shoot. I could miss at point-blank range."

The gunman was getting bolder, encouraged by this new information. "What kind of shitty detectives don't carry guns?"

The only thing behind the counter Abe could find was a can of Lysol. If he had a lighter, he could have made a makeshift blowtorch. However, Abe didn't smoke. He had an emergency kit in the car with a magnesium block and a flint striker in case he needed to start a fire in the woods—really handy for downtown Chicago—but that was it. If nothing else, he might be able to blind the shooter with the cleaner. Abe readied the Lysol like a can of mace.

"What kind of shitty henchmen wears an expensive watch around the boss they claim to not be stealing from?" Duff hucked another can out of the darkness.

The shooter slapped it away and raised his gun. "Come out now, and I'll make it quick and painless."

"Nice dialogue. What DC comic book did you get it from? I'm more of a Marvel guy, myself."

"You're brave. I'll give you that."

Duff winged a tool down the hallway. His aim was off, and the tool hit the hallway wall and fell to the floor with a heavy clunk. "Funny thing about bravery—it's often indistinguishable from stupidity."

"I'll agree with that." The shooter ducked behind the counter and prepped for his shot using the counter to steady his aim.

The muzzle of the handgun was just above Abe's head. He could see it poking out, glossy black in the shadows. Abe's stomach tightened. He felt that familiar full-body twitch that preceded a fear-induced adrenaline rush. It was now or never.

Something in the back bay crashed on the concrete floor: a toolbox, a crate of old metal parts. It was the hellacious sound of something making a massive mess.

Duff's voice called out from the darkness in his best Steve Urkel. "Did I do that?"

"Come out and take your bullet like a man." The tracksuited thug sighted down the barrel of his gun.

"You can't come back here because you don't know what I've got planned for you. I'm not coming out there because you'll Swiss cheese my chest cavity. We are at an impasse," said Duff.

"I don't have time to play this game all night."

"I do."

Abe knew if Tracksuit walked around the counter, he'd be a sitting duck. He moved as silently as he could, getting a foot under him, and then he launched straight up as fast as he could. He grabbed the barrel of the gun with his left hand, making sure to slide it as close to the trigger as possible. He sprayed the Lysol with his right hand, pressing the trigger for all he was worth and aiming directly in the thug's eyes. He kept pressing, even when the man in the tracksuit discharged a bullet. The powder burned the palm of Abe's hand, but the panicked rush of adrenaline kept him from feeling it.

Like a wounded buffalo, Duff charged out of the darkness of the back bay with a foot-long ratchet handle in his hand. He smashed it down on the thug's forearm as hard as he could. The man screamed and thrashed, blinded by Lysol.

Since he knew where Abe was without needing to see, the man spun in a tight circle, putting Abe on his back, and he executed a textbook hip-toss, sending Abe flying.

Abe landed flat on his back on the dirty floor with force. It hurt. Abe also lost his grip on the gun and the can of Lysol as he was flipped. He was nothing but a target. Abe knew the man would shoot straight down, so he rolled at the far wall as fast as possible. The first bullet missed him by centimeters.

Duff was about to swing the ratchet again when a shadow darted into the room, leaping through the space where the window used to be with the speed and precision of an arrow. The shadow slammed into the tracksuit thug, sweeping the man's legs from beneath him and driving him hard to the floor in a move Duff recognized all too well.

With a surgeon's touch, Mr. Pak grabbed the man's gun, bent it out of his hand, breaking the man's trigger finger as he did, and quickly ejected the clip and cleared the receiver. The weapon then broke into two pieces in the bodyguard's grasp. They clattered harmlessly to the floor.

The tracksuit man started to move, but Pak twisted the man's arm in a circle and applied pressure to the man's wrist in such a way that the man began to emit ear-piercing wails reminiscent of a cat in heat yowling for attention.

Archie Vang appeared in the broken window a moment later. He was breathing heavily. Weightlifters tended to shy away from cardio due to the hit they'd take on gains. "You guys all right?"

Abe lay on his side. He was miraculously free of bullet holes and only had a smarting powder burn on his left hand. It was barely noticeable at that moment, but Abe knew it would get nasty later on. "I'm fine."

Duff dropped the ratchet handle and disappeared into the back of the shop. A moment later, he returned with a small bag of Cheetos, the kind parents pack in their kids' lunches. "I'm good now."

"You found snacks?"

"They have a whole box of them back there. Can't blame 'em. They're tasty and give you orange fingers, which is always fun."

Archie Vang squinted at Duff. "You almost died, and your first thought was to eat something?"

Duff patted Archie on the shoulder, leaving faint orange dust stains. "*Good food is a celebration of life.* Anna Thomas said that."

"She said it in a vegetarian cookbook as a reason for why she didn't eat meat." Abe rolled to his feet.

"And Cheetos aren't meat, so I doubt she'd have an issue with me eating them now. It's a salty orange celebration of life."

Archie squatted by the tracksuit man's head. "Aw, Larry. Why'd you do it?"

Larry didn't dignify Archie's question with an answer.

"Ol' Larry there is a mole." Duff crunched heavily on a thick Cheeto. "He's reporting to someone else. That's where his money was coming from, I bet. That's why he has the nice watch. Double-agents in gangland don't tend to last too long."

Mr. Pak mumbled something to Archie in a language neither Abe nor Duff could understand.

Archie stood and brushed the dirt from his hands. "You guys get what you needed?"

"I think so," said Duff.

Archie jabbed a thumb over his shoulder at the night beyond the parking lot. "Well, then you might want to get gone."

"Whatever you do, please don't kill him." Abe felt a weird need to step in and help the man, although he couldn't understand why. The guy tried to kill Duff, and certainly would have killed him, too.

"That's not up to me." Archie inclined his head toward Mr. Pak. "It's up to the big man."

Abe hated knowing that the thug's life was worth less than a plugged nickel at that moment. That was the dark side of the underworld. They had their own code, their own rules, and nothing Abe said or did would change anything. It had been that way since the industry of violence called the Cosa Nostra rose out of back alleys in late-1800s Sicily, and no doubt that same code had existed in the eons before that.

If prostitution was the world's oldest profession, then organized crime was probably the second-oldest. Wherever there was money to be made by preying upon society, some version of the mob would be there. Abe didn't want to think about Han Sang-wook's yacht making another early morning fishing run to some point in Lake Michigan where no one could see them dump a chain-wrapped, body-shaped form into the deep water.

Duff put a Cheetos-dusted hand on Abe's shoulder and directed him through the broken glass window of the shop. "Forget it, Abe. It's Chinatown."

Even quoting one of Abe's favorite movies didn't make him feel better. "We really should do something. They might kill him."

Duff continued to walk Abe away from the scene. "They probably will. Let the mobsters do mobster stuff. That ain't our world. The less we see, the better."

Abe conceded. He knew Duff was right, no matter how much it bothered him. Bad people do bad people things. That's the way of the world. "I hate this planet sometimes."

"I hate this planet all the time, but we don't have time to worry about that guy now. We focus on the job. It's all we can do. We're not gonna run in, guns blazing, and save some two-bit hoodlum. We need to go see Jennifer Carthage."

"Now?" Abe glanced at his phone. It was almost midnight.

"She's young. I bet she'll be up. Those kids today, always with the screens and the YouTube and the influencing."

They trekked back to *The Bad-Luck Charm*. Abe unlocked the van with the key fob. "No twenty-something woman is going to open the door to two creepy middle-aged guys in the middle of the night, no matter what badge we wave at her."

Duff already had that covered. "It's not going to be two creepy middle-aged guys."

15

JO DUNBAR KNOCKED on Jennifer Carthage's door. She wore her full uniform, the bright silver shield of the CPD blazoned high on her flak jacket just below the mic of her radio. Abe and Duff stood behind her. Abe was sweaty and dirty from rolling on the floor of the rental place. Duff's face looked like an MMA fighter's mug post-match. The clock inched past midnight.

Dunbar straightened her vest and tried to look professional. "This couldn't wait until a decent hour in the morning?"

"By morning, everyone at Hanley, Dodge, and Briscoe will know of Robert Bloch's death if they don't already. We need to find the evidence we're missing, something that ties everything together, and I am willing to bet money that Bloch gave it to this gal." Duff looked haggard. He had been running on zero sleep since the shooting, and the effects were showing on his face, mingling with the swelling and bruising.

Abe straightened his polo shirt, for all the good it would do him. His left hand was burning like crazy, and he wanted to hold a bag of something frozen for a while.

Dunbar knocked again. "Jennifer Carthage? This is Officer Jo Dunbar of the Chicago Police. Could I ask you a couple of questions, please?"

There were footsteps in the apartment. The light behind the peephole in the door flickered away for a moment. Jennifer's voice was muffled through the door. "If you're really CPD, why are there two men with you?"

Abe held out his Illinois PI license. "I'm Abe Allard. That's Duff. We're private investigators. We're here about Robert Bloch."

There was a long pause. "What about Mr. Bloch?"

Duff nudged Abe with his elbow. Abe stepped closer to the door. "If you haven't heard, Mr. Bloch was shot and killed Friday night. We've been looking into his murder. We're sorry for being the bearers of bad news, but we think you might have a missing piece of this investigation, and we'd sure like a chance to talk to you before you go to work tomorrow morning."

There was a pause. Then the rattle and clack of someone undoing the safety chain was heard through the door. A moment later, a rumpled Jennifer Rose Carthage stood before them, eyes wide. "Someone killed Mr. Bloch?"

"Can we come in and talk?" Jo Dunbar gestured past Jennifer with her chin.

Jennifer opened the door and let them step inside.

FOR A FORMER bikini model famous enough to have dozens of glossy glamor photos splashed across the Internet, Jennifer Carthage's apartment was surprisingly sedate and spartan. It was a single bedroom with a kitchenette and a tiny living room in a decidedly unglamorous part of the city, not far from the Petersburg Building, but far enough to make her commute a hassle.

The apartment was decorated with a nice couch, a modest flat-screen TV, and a cheap laptop computer on a small folding table next to the sofa. She had no art, no bookshelves, no hobby materials. The kitchenette had a bistro table with two mismatched chairs. Abe couldn't be positive, but he believed they were bought from a thrift store or salvaged from the garbage.

Jennifer closed the door after Duff entered the apartment and gestured for them to sit on the couch. She brought out one of the chairs from the kitchenette and set it in the middle of the living room for herself. "I'm sorry, I don't have more chairs."

She wore a knee-length nightshirt made of soft fabric and decorated with palm trees. She adjusted the nightshirt to cover her bare knees.

"Your apartment is a little empty. I thought modeling would have paid better," said Duff.

Duff squeezed himself onto the small couch next to Abe, pushing Abe tighter against Jo Dunbar.

Abe felt himself blushing because of this. He tried to play it off by pretending to ignore it completely.

"Modeling doesn't pay what you think it does, sadly. Especially the small-time stuff I did." Jennifer shrugged and looked around her apartment. "There are a million pretty girls and only so much money to go around. If you're lucky, you get a few pictorial spreads in some magazines, and then you have two choices: get famous from those few spreads, which happens to very few girls, or start doing nude stuff, which many do. I didn't feel like doing nude stuff. Bikinis were bad enough. How'd you know I was a model, anyhow?"

In her middle-of-the-night-just-rousted-out-of-bed state, Jennifer looked like an exhausted, slightly raggedy young woman, and nothing like a model. In all fairness, everyone looks exhausted and ragged when woken by strangers in the middle of the night.

"We're detectives. We do our homework," said Abe.

"We checked out your background because Robert Bloch's wife thought you were shtupping him." Duff didn't break out Yiddish too often, but his mother was an Ashkenazi Jew, so many choice words and phrases were in his back pocket.

"Shtupping? She thought I was sleeping with him?"

"Amongst other things. We know you weren't."

"Not in the least."

"Why not?" asked Dunbar. "Seems like he was a decent-looking guy. He was a little older, sure—but he had money. Guys like that hire girls like you with the hopes that something will happen between them."

"How did you get the job with Hanley, Dodge, and Briscoe?" asked Duff. "Nothing in your background says you're an accomplished executive assistant. You bypassed a lot of more qualified people for that role. How'd you get it?"

Jennifer blushed and smoothed her hair with her fingers. Nervous habit. Her mouth pursed for a second, as if she was thinking about whether or not she should tell the truth. Then, she relaxed. She looked down at her feet. "I'm not qualified. Not in the least. I mean, I wasn't qualified. I only got this job because Mr. Bloch took pity on me."

"Why would he do that?" asked Abe.

"I have no idea." Jennifer fidgeted in her chair. She looked uncomfortable, embarrassed. "About eight months ago, I was depressed. Like, I wasn't getting offers for modeling anymore because I'd been in the industry for eight years and only had things like tool calendars and swimsuit calendars on my resume. I still had a day job working at Hooters and hated it. My modeling career was heading for stripping or porn, and I didn't want to do either of those things. I can't dance at all. The window I had to be successful in modeling was shrinking, and since I barely graduated from high school, I didn't have another plan."

Jennifer looked at Abe, Duff, and Dunbar on the couch. "I got on Instagram live one night, depressed and crying, and I poured out my heart to a dozen people who happened to be on at three in the morning. One of them was Mr. Bloch. He got into my DMs and sent me a message that said he would give me a regular job if I wanted to start over.

"I thought he was nuts, to be honest. Who would want me? I barely graduated from high school. But he offered again the next day, and I guess I decided something was better than nothing. I moved to Chicago, and he gave me the job. I was making more money working for him than I ever did before. He taught me what I needed to know and signed me up for online classes so I could learn more. He was so kind."

"And he expected nothing from you? No sex? No implications?" asked Dunbar.

"Nothing."

"No flirting? No errant touches?"

"Nothing, honestly. In fact, when I first started working there, my wardrobe was a little too California for the office, and some of the other girls were talking, I guess. Mr. Bloch called me in, explained proper business dress, and gave me five hundred bucks to buy more appropriate business clothes."

"Just gave it to you?" said Dunbar.

"Yes. He called it a *Welcome to Chicago* gift."

Abe needed to breach the possibility of Bloch being her father. "Would you say he took on a paternal role toward you?"

"What does that mean?"

"Fatherly."

Jennifer sat up a little straighter in her chair. "Yes, exactly. He was fatherly. He wanted me to succeed and do well. He was kind and supportive."

"Why? Do you think the other men in that office treat their receptionists that well?"

Jennifer considered this for a moment. "I guess you're going to tell me they don't."

"It's not typical, no. He was going above and beyond for you." Abe moved forward on the couch, putting his elbows on his knees and adopting one of the caring and concerned postures they had taught him during his undergrad degree program in psychology. It was a posture meant to make the person you're addressing feel at ease, to show you are supporting them by leaning in and giving them your focus. "Jennifer, what do you know about your father?"

"Not much, I guess. My mom was a single mother. She said she got knocked up in college at the very end of her sophomore year by some senior who went off to the Army after he graduated, and she didn't know she was pregnant until about three months later. She said it was just a fun little fling, nothing serious. She never bothered to tell him because she lost contact with him when he graduated. She said he was a nice guy, though. She liked him a lot."

"She never told you his name?"

"No. She said it wasn't important."

"But didn't you want to know?"

"I guess I did. I mean, I submitted a cheek swab to one of those DNA data banks a couple of years ago, but I never heard anything back."

"Could we talk to your mom?" asked Duff.

"She died about a year ago. Breast cancer."

"I'm sorry," said Abe.

Jennifer tensed and stiffened. "Why are you asking about my mom and dad? This is weird."

Duff pulled out his phone and found the picture that made them think she might be Robert Bloch's progeny in the first place. "This picture of you —you look very much like Robert Bloch. Same eyes. Same nose. Same chin. We thought you might be his daughter."

Jennifer slumped back in her chair as if she had just been punched.

Duff slipped the phone back in his pocket. "Your mom, she went to Butler University, didn't she? So did Robert Bloch. He graduated from Butler about twenty-seven years ago and then did a short stint in the Army. That would line up with your unplanned entrance into this world, wouldn't it?"

Jennifer was shocked. Her eyes were round, her mouth slack.

"It makes sense, doesn't it?" said Abe. "This guy comes out of nowhere and gives you a job offer, he gives you money for clothes. He teaches you what you need to know to survive. To me, it sounds like he was making up for the years he wasn't there. I'm sure it was a shock for him to learn he had a daughter."

"But how did he find out?"

"Well, only one person in the world knew who your father was, and she's been deceased for about how long Robert Bloch started acting weird toward his wife," said Duff. "I don't think it takes much brain power to think your mom reached out to Robert before she died and told him."

"I would want a clean conscience if I knew my time was short," said Dunbar.

This revelation stunned Jennifer into silence. She could only stare at the floor, fully bewildered in the moment.

Abe saw cracks forming in the young woman's facade, little twitches at the corner of her mouth and eyes, a tremble in her fingers, a curving of the shoulders. She was seconds from letting all her emotions go. It was a lot to accept. Your boss being dead was bad enough, but to suddenly learn the man who might have been your father is now dead—well, that's just too much for any one person to handle.

"I don't—why are you here? Why are you telling me this?" Two big, fat tears freed themselves from Jennifer's eyes and rolled to the corners of her nose. She wiped them away with the tips of her fingers. "What's wrong with you?"

"We're not doing this to be cruel." Abe felt a fatherly urge to hug the young woman. It probably had something to do with her red hair. It reminded him of Tilda. "Someone killed Robert Bloch on Friday night, and we think he might have given you something that has evidence on it that might prove who the killer was."

"He didn't give me anything like that." Jennifer fought to regain her composure. Dunbar went to the kitchen and retrieved a small box of tissues from the counter. Jennifer took them and dabbed at her eyes.

"Something tells me he did, even if you didn't know it." Duff stood and looked around the cramped apartment. "He didn't have anything of value in his desk, his car, or on his person when he was killed. That means he had to put that evidence somewhere else. It was evidence detrimental to someone at Hanley, Dodge, and Briscoe, so he probably didn't hide it at work. He needed it somewhere he could access later, or somewhere you could access it without the office knowing."

Duff walked to a small door near the apartment entry. "I take it this is a closet?"

Jennifer nodded. "For what it's worth. Hardly enough room to hang a coat in there."

Duff opened the door and peered inside. After a moment, he pulled out a large, leather tote bag. It was a sedate shade of beige with looping handles and a flat bottom spreading to voluminous sides. Expensive, but not overly so. It was a better bag than someone paying rent for a tiny apartment could afford. Duff held it up. "Tory Burch. What's the retail on this? Four hundred? Five?"

Dunbar squinted at Duff. "How does someone who dresses like you know a Tory Burch bag?"

Duff pinched a small metal bar on a leather tag hanging from the corner of the bag. "It says Tory Burch on this thing."

"But how do you know who Tory Burch is?"

"I'm not completely ignorant of mid-priced couture." Duff held the bag out to Jennifer again. "How much?"

The secretary shrugged again. "I have no idea. I didn't buy it."

Duff twirled it slowly. "It was a gift from Robert Bloch, wasn't it?"

"He said it made me look more professional."

"He gave it to you, what? Two weeks ago?"

"Yes. How'd you know?" Jennifer asked.

Duff turned the bag upside down and dumped the contents in a cascade of papers, pens, and all the other odds and ends that end up in a purse a woman carries daily. It was a mess of crumpled tissues and old granola bar wrappers mixed in with the paperwork Jennifer needed for the office.

"What are you doing?" Jennifer slid out of her chair and to her knees, trying to gather up the mess. She was embarrassed by having so much clutter in such a nice bag. "There's nothing in this bag, I'm telling you."

"Nothing you know about, at least. Think about it, though: your boss gets some information that is highly detrimental to a colleague. He needs to get you the information as an emergency measure. The easiest way is to give it to you in something elegant, something you will use daily. That way, if he needs to get it back from you, he knows where it is every single day."

Duff thrust his hand into the bag and felt around the bottom of it. In one corner, barely noticeable, he found a gap in the seams of the fabric sealing the flat plastic piece that made the bag's bottom stay wide. A moment later, he pulled out a small, slim silver flash drive. It was barely big enough to fit into a USB port. It must have been the smallest flash drive Robert Bloch could find.

Duff held his prize aloft between two fingers. "The missing piece."

Dunbar gave Duff a golf clap. "Impressive."

"Not so impressive," said Duff. "A detective cat would have found it faster."

"No cats," said Abe.

"What about cats?" Jennifer was confused again.

"Never mind." Abe tilted his head toward Jennifer's laptop. "Can we please borrow your computer?"

Jennifer, still in a daze, gestured vaguely toward the machine. Abe took that as a go-ahead.

Abe pulled the laptop onto his lap. It was a cheap HP model. Good enough for basic Office applications and web-surfing, but it won't run heavy-duty programs. It was the sort of computer you got because computers were necessary for daily existence in the modern world, not because you liked them or were good with them. He loaded the flash drive into the USB port on the side and waited for the machine to find it.

Jennifer moved to sit on the couch and watched as Abe worked. "I don't get why Mr. Bloch would give me a flash drive. I never would have thought to look for it in a bag like that."

Duff had already considered this. "Robert Bloch had recently seen a lawyer to draw up divorce papers. It would not be much to leave a letter with the lawyer to be mailed in the event something happened to him. He was already paranoid about seeking evidence of something illegal at his office, and he was dealing with some heavy-duty crime lords. It's what I would do if I needed someone to learn some information after my passing."

Abe turned toward Duff. "What information are you hiding that you'd need a lawyer to pass it on?"

"Not a damn thing. If I did, I'd get a lawyer to send you a letter after I shuffled the mortal coil, though." To Jennifer, Duff said, "You'll get a letter in the mail by Wednesday or Thursday. The letter will tell you about the flash drive and what to do next. Mark my words."

Abe opened the file explorer on Jennifer's computer and found the flash drive's location. He clicked into it and found a dozen files, including .pdfs, Excel spreadsheets, and two Word files.

"What are you looking for?" asked Jennifer.

"Whatever Robert Bloch was hiding on that drive," said Abe.

Duff expanded on Abe's answer. "We think Michael Hanley was moving money for the Korean mob. Bloch found out about it, and Hanley learned Bloch knew. That made Bloch expendable."

Jennifer's mouth twitched, and Abe saw it. It was a tell. A twitch like that, a quick pout, was often a sign that someone was going to say something but reconsidered it before they could verbalize their thought.

"Go ahead," said Abe. "Say it."

Jennifer's mouth wrinkled at the corner. She crossed her arms, a defensive gesture. She was building a wall. "I liked Mr. Hanley. He seemed really nice. He invited me to see his place in Wisconsin sometime."

"Invited you? Sounds like he was coming on to you," said Dunbar.

"He has three daughters, all of whom are older than I am."

"Yes, because no old dude would ever want to bang someone forty years younger than himself if he has daughters. Especially not old rich dudes," said Duff.

"Mr. Hanley is really nice. He was the one who told me to get Mr. Bloch a hotel room on Friday morning."

Abe, Duff, and Dunbar all froze, ears perking at the mention of a hotel room.

"Did you get the room at the Hotel Afton?" said Dunbar.

"Mr. Hanley insisted. He said Robert was working too hard and going through some things at home. Said he needed a night away from the world. He told me to get him a high floor facing the street because the views were impressive."

Abe and Duff exchanged a glance.

"Yes. He told me to tell Bloch that it was a thank-you gift from the company, if he asked. Because the executive board knew he was going through a difficult time in his marriage."

"Would you testify to that in court?" asked Dunbar.

"If I had to. Why?"

"It looks like Michael Hanley killed Robert Bloch." Abe turned his attention back to the laptop.

Opening one of the .pdfs, Abe found dozens of pages in the file filled with receipts, money transfers, and other incriminating evidence gained at great personal risk. The spreadsheets showed large quantities of money being moved.

The first Word file was a letter to Jennifer Carthage explaining the phone call Bloch received from her mother shortly before her untimely passing and the resulting fallout. He apologized for not telling her, but given the mess surrounding him, he hoped she would understand. He said he was doing it for her, to get her money to help her chase her dreams.

The second Word file was a three-page explanation of everything Robert Bloch had learned over the last year about the nefarious activities within his accounting firm. He pointed a finger at Michael Hanley for being the mastermind, and the .pdfs would prove it. Hundreds of thousands of dollars were being laundered and funneled to offshore accounts to benefit various mobs in the city, all while lining Hanley's pockets.

Bloch claimed Hanley was washing cash for criminal organizations for years. When Petey Pucillo hired Bloch to look into it, Bloch found the depth and breadth of the money. It was big. National news big.

Abe's stomach tightened the way it did when he knew he was looking at something well out of his depth. This was a big deal. This was one of those major white-collar crimes that facilitated so many other blue-collar crimes. Without the money being moved to the pockets of the biggest players, the drugs, guns, loans, gambling, racketeering, extortion, and prostitution would decrease exponentially.

Abe closed the files, closed the laptop, and immediately used the USB dongle he carried with him to plug the flash drive into his phone and clone it. He uploaded the files to his personal cloud drive and sent a link to Duff.

Duff watched Abe with interest, an uncharacteristic grim look on his face. "Is it that bad?"

Abe could barely bring himself to nod. "This is a file worth killing over. Call Betts. Call Gates. Call Mindy. We have a lot to do before Hanley, Dodge, and Briscoe opens."

16

IN THE HUSTLE and bustle of the Monday morning commuter traffic, a series of four black SUVs, three with federal plates, one with state plates, pulled in front of the Petersburg building at exactly 9:00 AM. As if someone had choreographed it, all the SUVs stopped, doors opened, and men and women poured out of each vehicle. The men and women in the vehicles with the federal plates wore sedate gray or black coats and ties. Malcolm Betts was behind the wheel of the state ride. Diana Gates rode in the passenger seat. In the backseat, Abe and Duff bookended Jennifer Carthage.

A Ford Explorer with CPD badging and a light blue stripe down the side pulled up behind Betts's unmarked car. Jo Dunbar and Keith Schrader got out, both in full, finest kit, and followed the detectives into the building.

Four more CPD units pulled into place in the line, lights flashing. Eight more cops rolled out, following the group into the building. This was not a casual proceeding. This was as official as it gets.

The lobby of the Petersburg building ground to a halt as the federal tax troopers stormed the lobby. Warrants were produced, and security was forced to wave them through.

The first group piled into the first available elevator and rode up, followed shortly by the second group. Twelve IRS special agents, Minerva Jefferson in the lead, swept down the hallway from the main elevators to the offices of Hanley, Dodge, and Briscoe. They walked quickly with no wasted movements.

There was something uniquely terrifying about a cadre of forensic accountants. The IRS did not mobilize a spreadsheet squad like this unless they intended to do some heavy damage. Just hearing the synchronized clicking of heels on the ceramic tile floors put the fear of god into Abe's angst-ridden soul.

Abe and Duff brought up the rear. Abe's heart was in his throat. He was about to witness something that would be front-page news tomorrow. It would be the lead story on the local newscast that night, and it might even get a nod on the national news.

Not to mention, he was about to enter the same office where a man who might be his father would be.

Abe used to daydream about who his father might be. A jet pilot or a Vietnam War hero was his most frequent daydream. Occasionally, he pictured his father as an itinerant drifter, *a la* Bill Bixby's take on Dr. Bruce Banner—just a guy roaming the country putting wrongs to right with a forlorn piano medley playing as he hitchhiked to the adventure.

He never once pictured his father as a millionaire accountant.

The cadre paused a dozen steps from the entry to Hanley, Dodge, and Briscoe. Mindy Jefferson was running the take-down operation. She summoned Betts and Gates to her side. "I'm going to announce the shutdown of operations. As soon as I do, I'm going to tell Mr. Dodge that we'd like to question him back at the office. You can sweep in and place Mr. Hanley under arrest after that. Questions?"

"I imagine he's going to lawyer hard." Betts pulled his service weapon, double-checked it, and slipped it back into the holster under his left arm.

"I wouldn't doubt it."

Gates also checked her service weapon. They weren't likely to need the guns, but it was procedure to make sure they were ready, just in case. "We're going to let Dunbar and Schrader put the bracelets on him. They earned that."

"Do whatever you've got to do. We're going to hit this hard and fast. If anyone runs, take them down." Mindy glanced at Abe and Duff. "Slim, Biggie—just stay out of the way."

Duff flashed the okay sign with his fingers. "That's what I do the best."

Abe wasn't about to do anything stupid where the IRS was concerned. They scared him as much as the mob did.

"Everyone ready?" Mindy looked from face to face with all the members of her team. There were nods all around. Everyone was armed, but this was not a storm-in-with-guns-blazing sort of takedown. It was orderly. It was efficient. It wasn't about intimidation or threat. Just business. Mindy flung open the door and stormed the lobby.

Everything after that moment was a blur of people, noise, and confusion.

THE WOMAN AT the receptionist's desk tried to stop the storm but was quickly waylaid by the warrant Mindy shook at her. Like hawks diving on mice, the other IRS special agents began sweeping up laptop computers, bagging them before anyone could delete evidence. They moved with speed and efficiency. They had done this many times before.

They moved into the bullpen area and found the entire staff gathered for a meeting. Michael Hanley, dressed in his best black suit, was giving the staff the notice of Robert Bloch's untimely demise. His white-blond hair was smoothed, gelled, and combed back. He had four days' growth on his chin and jowls. He looked tired.

Next to Hanley, Arlo Dodge loomed like a wraith, arms crossed in front of him and head down, projecting the proper somber bearing befitting the moment and wearing a black suit with a dull gold tie.

When Abe saw the man, it put a chill through his body. It was like looking at an older version of himself. Same posture, same bearing, same face. Abe felt a hand on his lower back. He looked over his shoulder and saw Jo Dunbar standing at his side.

She flashed him a small, reassuring smile. "Steady there."

Abe nodded a thanks. He saw the handcuffs in Dunbar's hand, ready for her moment.

Mindy roared into action. Her voice boomed through the room, all business. "Everyone, if I can please have your cooperation. I am Special Agent Jefferson with the IRS. We have a warrant. All computers in this facility are going to be appropriated and held as evidence in an ongoing investigation. We ask for your complete cooperation in this matter."

Hanley and Dodge looked stunned, then outraged. Staffers looked around confused, some scared, as the IRS agents began bagging laptops. Another man in a dark suit stepped out of the line of executives. He produced a wallet and flashed an ID at Mindy. "I'm Don Fitzgerald, the firm's legal counsel. What is the meaning of this?"

Mindy simply handed him the warrant and pushed past him, moving toward the executive offices with another agent. "We're going to need these doors opened immediately."

"Hold on!" Hanley rushed to position himself between Mindy's accounting squad and the executive hallways. "I will not have you rushing through my office."

Mindy stopped short. "That's too bad. I just handed your legal eagle a sheet of paper, and it says that on this day, I can do whatever the hell I feel like doing in your offices. Now step aside."

"On whose authority?"

"Uncle Sam. Now move."

Hanley started to protest, but Arlo Dodge laid a large hand on the man's shoulder. "Mike, relax."

Dodge's voice had a low, dull quality with a slight nasal tone. Abe hated the sound of his voice, but his voice didn't sound too different from Dodge's. When Matilda took videos of him, he'd hear his voice in the playback. It was almost identical to Arlo Dodge's.

Hanley let himself be pulled aside by Dodge. He was about to say something else, but Betts swooped in with Dunbar and Schrader behind him.

"Michael Hanley, we are placing you under arrest for suspicion of murder."

There was a collective gasp from the gathered staff, and more voices rose in hissing confusion. The IRS agents continued to bag computers. Police swarmed the cubicles to assist. It was chaos, all noise and motion.

Dunbar swiftly gathered one of Hanley's wrists with a cuff before he knew what was happening. When she went for the other, Hanley yanked his right arm from her grasp.

"Wait just a minute—"

"Mr. Hanley, please don't resist. Come quietly, and we'll deal with this at the station." Dunbar reached for his other wrist again, but Hanley moved.

At this point, Keith Schrader stepped in and grabbed Hanley's right arm. Hanley tried to fight, but Schrader and Dunbar simply lifted the man off his feet, spun him, and dropped him on the floor. It was a hard drop, but not a slam. The impact took the fight right out of him. The two officers locked up his wrists before he could gather a second wind.

"This is ridiculous." Hanley wanted to protest, but it was difficult to do anything more than complain when two Chicago police officers were kneeling on his arms and pinning him in place.

Fitzgerald stepped up to Betts, but quickly backed down when he read the warrant. "Go with them, Mike. This is serious."

"This is seriously stupid." Hanley allowed Dunbar and Schrader to lift him to his feet. "I've done nothing. This is a farce."

Betts snapped his fingers at Duff. "Tell the man what you got."

Duff tilted his head at Abe. "Let this guy do it."

"I don't give a shit who does it. Someone say something."

Abe stepped forward and began listing the points of evidence on his fingers. "We got a receipt that says you rented a cargo van like the one the killer drove on Friday night. We have a secretary who says you told her which hotel to rent a room for the victim. We have a history of being good with long rifles. We have police at your farm in Genoa City, Wisconsin, currently searching your private shooting range for bullets whose ballistics will match the bullet that killed Robert Bloch. Two hundred acres is a lot of land, but it's not big enough to hide the sound of rifle fire from your neighbors. They say they can hear you shooting almost every weekend. Almost like you're staying in practice for something."

Hanley's eyes were crackling with fire. His lips twitched in an angry sneer. "I was at my place in Wisconsin all weekend. I never left it. This is ludicrous."

"Do you have anyone who can vouch for you?" asked Diana Gates.

"My daughter, Christina, was there."

"Well, I guess we'll have to talk to Christina and hope her story matches up with yours because right now, we have motive, we have opportunity, and we have proof of this company doing some money moving for some questionable members of our fine city."

"Mike?" Arlo Dodge's face was slack. His shoulders were slumped. It was the look of a defeated, betrayed man, and Abe knew that because it was exactly what he saw in the mirror every morning.

"This is insanity, Arlo. You know me. I'm straight as an arrow."

Dunbar and Schrader started walking Michael Hanley toward the doors. Hanley began to struggle, still not willing to accept the situation.

"This is ludicrous. Don, get me out of this. This is insanity."

Dunbar and Schrader looped their arms through Hanley's and forced him to move faster.

Fitzgerald looked flustered. This was not his area of expertise. "Mike, plead the Fifth. Say nothing—not a single word! I'll be there as soon as I can."

Arlo Dodge sat in the nearest chair, deflated and beaten.

"I still need someone to open the executive offices." Mindy Jefferson's team was still bagging laptops.

Dodge reached into his pocket and pulled out a small electronic key fob. He tossed it to Jefferson without a word.

Jefferson caught the key, and her team progressed down the halls, a member swooping in to gather up computers and files as they saw fit. It would be a long day, and an even longer week, as the IRS, the CPD, and any other state or federal agency that wanted to pile on would be employing the best cyber squads around the clock to scour every last piece of incriminating evidence from those machines along with the company's central servers.

Diana Gates handed Dodge one of her business cards. "We'll need to speak to you, as well, Mr. Dodge. You can come to the station at your leisure this afternoon."

Dodge nodded glumly. He was as stunned as everyone else.

Abe watched as Arlo Dodge sat in a chair and looked at his feet. Abe noticed the man wore cowboy boots, black and polished. They looked expensive. Ariat. Maybe Rujo. Possibly alligator-skin.

Abe wanted to go up to the man and ask him questions, but this was neither the time nor the place. Abe backed into a corner where he was firmly out of the way, and watched as the offices of Hanley, Dodge, and Briscoe were stripped of anything that might contain information by a swarm of IRS locusts.

17

MICHAEL HANLEY WAS delivered to the nearest station. Dunbar and Schrader turned him over to lock-up. He was booked, photographed, fingerprinted, and held in a cell until he could be arraigned the following day.

A murder-one charge would be proffered before the judge. If accepted, it would mean an instant trip to Cook County Jail to await trial.

Normally.

Wealth had its privileges, though.

If the judge was feeling magnanimous, and depending on how slick Hanley's lawyer was, anything was possible. That wasn't part of the investigation, though. Abe and Duff had no control over anything once the CPD stepped in to take the reins. Their part in the proceedings was over unless they were called to testify during the trial.

Abe and Duff went to the station to give official reports and deliver the collected evidence. Nothing with the CPD moved quickly when compiling cases, so it took the rest of the afternoon. They gave their statements in separate rooms, Abe speaking to Malcolm Betts, and Duff speaking to Diana Gates.

For the sake of efficiency, Duff kept his non sequiturs and sarcasm to an absolute minimum. Gates only had to threaten to shoot him twice. Duff considered it a new high-water mark in their relationship.

After his deposition with Malcolm Betts, Abe excused himself to call Vicky Bloch and tell her the news of Hanley's arrest. She was both relieved and confused, unable to fathom why Hanley had to kill her husband.

Abe also revealed that Vicky had a stepdaughter, telling her about Robert's communication with Jennifer Carthage's mother before her death.

The news brought about a fresh round of tears. Abe hated hearing her cry. The problem-solver in him wanted to be the shoulder to cry on, to be the guy who fixed the issue and got everyone back on a steady course, but there are some problems larger than anything he could do to help, and this was one of them.

Sometimes, you have to know when to shut up and let someone cry.

When Vicky Bloch gathered herself, she asked Abe for a favor: "I'd like to meet her."

"I'll see what I can do," said Abe.

"If we had known earlier, she would have been in my life. I would like her to know she has a family if she wants one."

JENNIFER CARTHAGE SAT in a chair in the station lobby. She was peeling the label off a bottle of a coffee drink she'd bought from a vending machine. Her left leg bounced in quick, jerky movements. Anxiety. Nervousness. Exhaustion. She had not slept since being woken after midnight. Her hair was a wild tangle of red held back by a rubber band.

Abe finished his phone call with Vicky Bloch. He saw the young woman looking wan and nervous. Something parental within him needed to check on her. He and Duff blew up her world in the middle of the night, and that was unfair. The world was unfair. It would forever be unfair, and that would never change. It was something he hated to tell his own daughter. Something deep within every father is a desire to make the invisible karmic scales of the world balance in favor of their child, and there is always a hollow and painful frustration when you know you can never shift those scales. They have their own will and bend how they please.

Abe crossed the busy lobby and sat next to Jennifer in the cheap, barely padded waiting room chairs. He resisted the urge to reach out and pat her leg like he would have if she had been Matilda. They sat in silence for several minutes. Jennifer finished peeling the label and stuffed it into the empty bottle. She capped it and set it on the ground at her feet.

Abe could not stand the silence any longer. "You going to be all right?"

Jennifer said nothing for a time. She looked over her shoulder at one of the windows and watched the activity in the parking lot. Then she shook her head. "Probably not. I don't know what to think right now. Yesterday, I didn't have a dad. And then I find out I have been working with my dad for six months, and now he's dead."

"It's a lot. I understand."

"Do you? Is your dad dead?"

"I don't know."

Jennifer pulled back a bit. "I'm sorry. I didn't—"

"It's fine. Don't worry about it."

"I just…" She clenched her fists. "I don't have a job anymore. The firm is going to be shuttered during the investigation. They've already let the interns go. One of the older women told me to polish my resume and start looking elsewhere. My resume is crap. I don't have any real experience, and a semester of junior college with a 2.2 GPA isn't going to impress anyone."

Abe knew the IRS was not going to leave the firm unscathed once they found all the evidence of moving money for the mob. The firm of Hanley, Dodge, and Briscoe was as good as gone. Walter Briscoe had already retired. Arlo Dodge was of retirement age and wealthy, so losing his company wouldn't affect him too badly. The forty people the firm employed would be out of a job. They would be left to the nightmare of dealing with the Illinois Department of Employment Security and the agony of applying and interviewing for decent-paying jobs in an employment ecosystem that paid exceedingly little for such an expensive city.

"Things have a way of working out in the end. Maybe this is the start of something better for you."

"Or maybe I'm going to end up in a strip club when I can't pay my rent. I already told you I can't dance."

"You have family."

"No, I don't. My mom is dead. My grandmother is in a care facility. I don't have any cousins."

"You have a stepmother."

Jennifer stopped short. She sat back in her chair. "It would be weird if I waltzed up and asked her for help. I'm not going to do that."

"She would like to meet you," said Abe.

"Why?"

That was a good question. Abe didn't know if he could answer it. "I guess, if your father had found out you existed twenty years ago, she would have been your stepmother for real. She would have helped raise you. You're also a bridge to her husband, whom she just lost. You're both flailing right now. The world seems cruel and surreal, I'm sure. Maybe she can be an anchor for you, and you can be an anchor for her."

Jennifer chewed her lower lip for a moment while she considered this. "Is she nice?"

"I like her."

There was another long period of silence. Jennifer stared up at the fluorescent lights overhead and tried not to cry. "I would like to meet her."

Abe stood. "I'll come get you in a few minutes. We'll head over there."

ABE MELTED BACK into the mass of humanity swirling around the station's lobby. Cops mingled with citizens. People came to pay off traffic tickets or complain about a parking citation. People waited to talk to a detective about stolen property. Somewhere in the building, Abe knew Duff was raiding a vending machine for its last Reese's Peanut Butter Cups.

Abe moved down one of the corridors toward Betts's office. There were small, private waiting rooms down one side of the corridor. They were simple cubicles used to talk to distressed families about missing teens, or they were private waiting rooms for grieving families who had been given terrible news. Each room was soundproofed and had a window with blinds that could be closed for maximum privacy.

In one of the rooms at the end of the hall, Arlo Dodge sat in a chair with his lawyer next to him. The lawyer was doughy and pale with an expensive haircut. They were waiting for someone to take Dodge's statement about his partner's activities. Dodge looked much more rumpled than he had that morning. His tie was loosened, and the top button of his shirt was undone so that it gaped open to reveal a thin patch of gray chest hair at the top of his sternum.

Abe stood and watched the man. The shape of his head, the face, the lack of a chin—all were features Abe saw in the mirror daily. Could that man really be his father?

There was a large part of Abe that wanted to move on and forget Arlo Dodge. His mother never told him about his father for a reason. She never told him that reason, but there had to be a reason, right? She gave him her last name, not the name of his father, whoever that might be. She had her own agenda. She did a wonderful job of raising him. She was the very definition of self-sacrifice for the sake of a child. That part of Abe that wanted to move on felt like he would be betraying his mother if he spoke to Arlo Dodge.

But there was that small part of him that always wanted to know his father. Being a father to Matilda was the most important thing in the world to him, made doubly so because of a lack of a father in his

own life. The odds were slim that Dodge was truly his father, but he needed to be certain.

Abe steeled himself with a deep breath and knocked on the door. He opened it and poked his head into the room. "Mr. Dodge? Could I speak with you for a moment privately?"

Dodge and the lawyer regarded Abe for a beat. The lawyer asked, "Is this about the situation with Mr. Hanley?"

"It is not. It's just a quick personal question. Nothing at all to do with anything about the case."

"Ask it then," said the lawyer.

"Could I do it privately?" asked Abe.

The lawyer looked to Dodge, who gave a brief nod. The lawyer closed his laptop and left it on the table. "I'll get us some coffee."

The lawyer left Abe in the small interview room with Arlo Dodge.

Dodge stared hard at Abe for a minute. "You're that detective fellow, aren't you? Well, what's your question?"

Abe remained standing. If the man said no, he would apologize and bolt from the room. "Did you ever know a woman named Martha Allard? This would have been back in the summer of 1974."

Dodge's brow wrinkled in thought. "Seventy-four, you say? I guess I was in the Army then. Where would she have been?"

"Here. Chicago. Probably the northside. I think she lived near Norwood Park or Rosemount back then."

Dodge crossed his arms and tapped a finger against his lips. "Martha Allard. No, I don't think the name rings a bell. Why do you ask?"

"Martha was my mother. She never told me who my father was, and when I saw you, I couldn't help but think of how much you and I look alike."

Dodge fixed a steely gaze on Abe and took him in from head to toe. "God, you're right. Same build, same face. We could be father and son, couldn't we?"

"I just figured I'd ask. I knew the odds were slim."

"In '74, I was still in the Army. I was down south in Georgia for a time. If I came back to Chicago, it was only for a visit, and I certainly don't remember a woman named Martha Allard. I'm sorry."

"That's all right. I'm glad I asked, though. Thank you for you time."

Abe gave Dodge a slight bow of his head as a sign of parting and stepped into the hall. He had almost closed the door when Dodge called him back into the room. "Wait!"

Abe stepped back into the interview room.

"I had a brother, Horace. We all called him Horse, though. I seem to remember him with a young woman, a redhead, thin and wispy. She had a wonderful smile and a lovely laugh."

Abe felt his heart stop beating. His mother was a redhead, and that's where Tilda got her mane from. And although she did not smile or laugh too often when he was a boy, thanks to their daily struggles, when she did, her smile outshone the sun, and her laugh was like music. "That sounds like my mother."

"They met when he was home on leave. He had been in Vietnam with the Army, part of the evacuation teams. He was in the 324th, if I recall correctly. He was in logistics for them. He came home in the summer of '74 and shipped out to Germany later that year. I remember her coming around the house a few times. She was very nice. I don't think her name was Martha, though. He had a strange nickname for her."

There was a deep pang of longing in Abe's heart. He missed his mom. "Mop. She told me her nickname used to be Mop."

Arlo Dodge's eyes lit up with recognition. "Mop! Yes! We called her Moppy."

Abe felt a stinging sensation at the corner of his eyes. His chest felt heavy. "That was Mom."

Dodge stood, drawing himself to his full, impressive height. He was at least two inches taller than Abe. He grabbed Abe by the shoulders. "Good god. You might be my nephew."

Dodge held him at arm's length for a few moments before he sat down, suddenly weak. "This is…unbelievable."

Abe was at a loss. "Do you think I could speak to your brother?"

Dodge was adrift in his own thoughts. "A nephew. I don't know what to say."

"Could I speak to Horace?" Abe felt calling him *Horse* would show disrespect for some reason.

Dodge came back into his thoughts. His mouth pursed, and he shook his head. "Oh, son. No. I'm sorry. Horse passed away some years back. He was in a car accident. He survived it, but the surgery gave him blood clots, and one went to his brain…and there wasn't much they could do."

"I'm sorry," said Abe.

"Not half as sorry as I am." Dodge reached out and grabbed Abe by the wrist. There was profound wistfulness in his eyes, as if he were seeing his brother again and reliving lost memories. "He would have loved to have a son. He never had any children."

An IRS agent entered the room with Dodge's lawyer. "We'll begin shortly, Mr. Dodge."

Dodge came back from the memory journey he had been taking. He blinked his eyes rapidly several times. "Your name was Allard, right?"

"Yes, sir. Abe Allard."

"Do you have a way I can contact you, Mr. Allard?"

"Please, call me Abe." Abe pulled one of the Allard & Duffy Investigations cards he always carried in his wallet. He held it out to the man who was probably his uncle. It felt strange to think that. More than forty-six years of believing he had no relatives, and suddenly, there was an uncle in front of him. It gave him an inkling of what Jennifer Carthage was feeling. "Available night or day."

Dodge slipped the card into his jacket and patted Abe on the shoulder. "I will be calling. That is a promise."

"I'll look forward to it, sir."

"You call me Arlo." Dodge sat next to his lawyer and straightened his tie. He nodded at the IRS agent. "Ask away."

Abe started to shut the door, but Dodge interrupted the agent and called him back. "Abe, one other thing."

Abe stuck his head into the room. "Yes, sir?"

"Do you have any children?"

"A daughter. Sixteen years old."

Arlo smiled broadly. "Wonderful. Horse would have loved to have been a grandfather, I bet. I should like to meet her sometime."

"I can arrange that."

"I'll look forward to it."

Abe closed the door. Through the window, he saw Dodge compose himself and put on a serious business face. Abe did not know how to feel at the moment. There were parts of him that were elated and parts that were suddenly terrified. Nothing was concrete, of course. For all he knew, maybe Horace Dodge wasn't his father. Maybe his mother had found someone who looked exactly like Horace Dodge after he was out of her life. A DNA test would solidify it, but it felt too right to think he needed one. This had to be his uncle. He had a paternal family now. He hoped, wherever she was at that moment, his mother understood.

18

ABE STOPPED HIS van in front of Vicky Bloch's house. The curbside parking was plentiful as people were not yet returning home from work for the evening. He and Duff exited the front doors, and Duff pulled the sliding door in back so Jennifer could step out.

The heat was still oppressive, a thick, clinging film of dampness coating every surface. The weatherman on the radio said a cold front from the Rockies was pushing southeast through Minnesota and would meet the high-pressure system pushing up from the south later that night. Like any weather change, it would bring some cooling to the metro area, but they would pay with severe storms where the two fronts clashed.

Jennifer exhaled a nervous breath. She shook out her hands to expel the pent-up energy building within her. A meeting of this magnitude was intimidating. She did not look her best. She did not feel her best. She was scared and worried. She saw Abe looking on with concern and tried to smile. "I'm too old to feel like a little kid."

"You say that, but I routinely eat Cinnamon Toast Crunch while watching cartoons," said Duff. "You're never too old to feel like a kid."

"Are you ready?" Abe tried to give her a reassuring smile, but he knew it was a weird grimace instead of something warm and comforting. It was the best he could do.

"I guess I am."

Abe knocked on the door. After a few seconds, Vicky Bloch answered. She was dressed plainly. Her hair was held back by a headband. Her face crinkled like she was about to cry when she saw Jennifer, but she held back. "My god, you do look like your father."

"Jennifer, this is Vicky Bloch, your stepmother." Abe took a step back.

"It's nice to meet you." Jennifer held out a hand.

Vicky pushed her hand to the side and swept her into a hug. Jennifer was rigid for a moment, unsure of how to process this act of grace, compassion, and humanity. Then, the dam broke, and she threw her arms around Vicky. Both women sobbed, leaning against each other for support.

"THINK THEY'LL BE all right?" Abe started *The Bad-Luck Charm*. He watched the two women sitting and talking on the porch of the Bloch home. Vicky had asked Abe and Duff to stay, but they declined. The two women had much to discuss, and they certainly didn't need two middle-aged men dragging down their conversation by sitting at the table with them. Some things needed privacy.

"They'll be fine. Eventually. Grief is a weird critter." Duff pulled on the seat belt and fiddled with his phone. "Check this out." He stuck the phone in front of Abe's face.

It was too close, and Abe had to lean back and squint to see what he was showing him. It was a picture of a kitten with crinkly fur, an angular face, and large ears.

"It's a Devon Rex. They're hypoallergenic, and they don't feel like you're holding a human ass in your hands. We get one, we teach it to solve murders, and we make bank. Hell, I bet we could even find some pathetic dude with no life to write stories about us."

"No detective cats."

"You say that now, but once we franchise him, the money will roll in."

"No franchising." Abe pulled the van from the curb and drifted down the road. He opened the windows to get what his mother used to call *two-fifty-five AC*—you roll down two windows and go fifty-five miles per hour.

The promised cold front from Minnesota was coming, and the heat was scheduled to break any minute. Massive, billowing thunderheads loomed to the northwest as proof. They promised a helluva bout of thunder, lightning, and wind, but it would be a welcome change after the past week's unbearable sauna.

Abe guided the van southward, meandering through the busy traffic, heading back to Chinatown.

Duff did not speak, and Abe knew better than to talk to him. After a case, Duff sometimes fell into a deep funk. The puzzle was solved, and there was only the wait for the next one.

Duff's face was swollen and horribly bruised from meeting the floor at Han Sang-wook's. Both eyes had dark bruises under them. His nose was puffy. His cheek was an abhorrent shade of purple. It looked painful, but he had not complained about it once.

They listened to WDRV on the way back. Stevie Ray Vaughan had just given way to Journey, and Steve Perry was currently imploring them not to stop believing.

Abe's mother had liked Journey. They weren't her favorite band, but she loved Steve Perry's voice. That made him think of Horace Dodge. He wished his mother were still around to confirm Horace's part in his parentage.

"I talked to Arlo Dodge."

Duff said nothing. He continued to look at his phone.

"He's my uncle, I think. My dad was named Horace Dodge. He was in the Army, too."

Duff looked up from his phone. "You said *was*."

"Arlo said Horace died some years ago. Car accident."

Duff went back to his phone. "Shame."

They lapsed into silence while Abe negotiated the city's streets.

"Do you think Larry is dead now?"

Abe looked back at Duff. "Larry?"

"The gangster. The guy who tried to kill us. Think Sammy Han offed him? Or, more accurately: had him offed by someone else?" Men who headed criminal organizations rarely did the dirty work themselves.

Abe didn't want to think about it. "Why do you ask?"

"Larry wasn't all that old, was he? Maybe thirty, at the most."

"And?" Abe was used to Duff being cryptic, but this seemed an odd thing to bring up at that moment.

"If he's dead, then he only lived for so long. Horace Dodge probably didn't expect to die in a car accident the morning he left the house. I'm betting Robert Bloch didn't expect to die Friday night. Jennifer Carthage's mother probably thought she would get more time on this rock, too."

"So did my mom. But life isn't fair. People sometimes die. That's how life works."

Duff set his phone down in the drink holder on the center console. "No, that's how *death* works. Life works the opposite way. Life is what we do when we're alive. We live."

"Why are you being so philosophical right now? This isn't like you."

Duff shrugged and looked out the window at the passing buildings. "Just be a damn shame if you didn't get out and live a little before you died is all I'm saying."

"I live."

"You don't. Neither do I, but that's by choice. You should, though. You should get out and do more."

"This is about Jo Dunbar, isn't it?"

Duff shrugged. "Maybe. Maybe not. I'm just pointing out the fact that you haven't really done any living since your divorce. And you were barely alive before the divorce."

"She's too young for me."

"Not really. Half your age plus seven is thirty. She's past that."

"She might want a family, kids. I'm past that."

"You're making decisions for her, dude. Let her be the one to tell you what she wants. I'm not telling you to get married and have babies. I'm only telling you that you, as a guy, have the autonomous freedom to ask a grown-ass woman to get a burger with you occasionally, have a couple of laughs, and not think that it's going to end in immediate and contractually binding lifelong commitment."

"That's not how I operate, and you know that."

"You have put yourself in a box, my man. It's no way to have a healthy existence."

"You should talk."

"I know. Pot. Kettle. I get it. But I'm not you."

"I'm fine. I will be fine."

"Will you though?" Duff pointed to an open parking spot on the curb. "Let me out. Right there." He pocketed his phone.

"What? Why?"

"Just do it."

Abe pulled over and put the van in park. "Why? What's going on?"

Duff opened his door, got out, and shut it behind him. He walked down the sidewalk without even a glance back at Abe. They were still two miles from their office apartment.

Abe leaned out the van window. "Where are you going?"

Abe watched his partner turn right and disappear behind a building. Duff's methods were inscrutable at times. Abe trusted the man to care for himself, but this was strange, even by Duff's usual standards of strangeness. Abe was confused, but he was used to being confused around Duff. It was part of the territory.

Abe was about to shift the car back into drive when someone called his name.

He leaned out the window again and saw Jo Dunbar, still in uniform, walking down the street with Keith Schrader. The police officers acknowledged him with a wave, and Abe responded in kind.

Abe knew why Duff demanded he pull over. It was a testament to the big man's observational skills that he spotted the police officers while Abe had been completely oblivious to them. Abe would never understand how he did it.

Dunbar jogged up to the van. "You know you're parked illegally, right? Do I need to ticket you?"

"Not parked. Just pulled over to let Duff out."

"Where is he?"

Abe gestured vaguely down the street. "Who knows? He's kind of like a squirrel that way. I let him out, and he just vanishes."

Dunbar looped her thumbs into her duty belt. "What are you doing here?"

Abe explained the events of the day after they were separated at the accounting firm. He told her about taking Jennifer to Vicky Bloch's house.

Dunbar and Schrader had stayed behind to help the IRS agents secure all the electronics when Abe and Duff went to the station with the detectives after Hanley's arrest.

When he finished, Dunbar shook her head in disbelief. "This is such a crazy story. Could you imagine finding out you have an adult child?"

Abe thought about his own potential paternal parentage. "It's an odd twist of fate, for sure."

Dunbar reached out and put a hand on Abe's forearm where it sat on the edge of the open van window. "Thanks for letting me tag along for some of this. It was fun watching you two work."

Abe's skin felt electric under her touch. He had to swallow hard to be able to speak. "Thanks for being willing to help."

"Maybe we can do this again sometime. I like police work, but detective work is far more interesting."

"I'd like that."

Dunbar pulled her hand back from his arm. "You heading home now?"

Abe nodded. What else would he be doing? He had no life.

"Well, you enjoy your rest. You earned it." Dunbar smiled at Abe and turned to head back to her partner.

Abe felt a desperate need not to let her go. He needed to say something, just keep her nearby. He blurted, "You've been in uniform since last night. Isn't it about time for you to call it a day?"

"It's been a long one, no doubt. We were just heading back to clock out."

Abe knew what Duff wanted him to do, why he had been so philosophic. It touched a chord in Abe. Maybe Duff was right. Maybe he did need to start living. After all, Katherine had moved on with her life, Tilda was advancing in hers—only Abe was still stuck in post-divorce limbo. He needed to do something, do *anything*.

What's the worst thing that can happen? She says no? She laughs? People laughed at Abe his whole life, and being married to a closeted lesbian had made him hear *no* more than most men. He should be immune to the word.

Jo Dunbar was out of his league in every way, shape, and form, but that meant he was already at the bottom. He couldn't fall any lower. If she rejected him, it would be a smart move on her part, and Abe would never fault her for it. He didn't bring anything to the table, and he knew it. But it wouldn't hurt to try, would it?

Abe took a deep breath and summoned up a reserve of courage from a place deep within himself, a well of strength he didn't know he still possessed. "Jo, could I buy you dinner sometime?"

Dunbar gave him a sly half-smile. She stepped back and appraised him for a long, terrible moment. Abe waited for the polite rejection.

Dunbar's grin blossomed into a genuine smile. "Only if I can buy you dessert."

Somewhere in the distance, Abe could have sworn he heard the *Hallelujah Chorus*. Miracles did abound.

THE APARTMENT WAS blissfully cold. One of Meyer Himmelman's guys had installed a new AC unit while Abe and Duff were gone, and the little window unit was cranking out the chilly BTUs when Duff arrived.

True to form, the promised storms rolled into Chicago when Duff was still two hundred yards from the apartment. The initial downpour had been aggressive, a painful fall of wind and water in equal measure, drenching him to the skin in seconds, accompanied by violent lightning and deafening thunder.

The cold temperatures in the apartment were not so welcome when one was already wet and freezing from a storm system powered by cold Canadian air. Duff had to traipse across the office to shut off the AC before treating himself to a hot shower.

Duff dried himself off in the apartment's bathroom. He hung his jeans and his t-shirt to dry on the shower curtain bar. The bright side to the downpour was that it extended him another day or two before he would need to do laundry, a task he loathed.

Duff wrapped his towel around his waist out of habit—the longstanding no-nudity-in-the-office rule—and opened the bathroom door. He was instantly aware of two men in the apartment.

Han Sang-wook was sitting in Abe's desk chair, his feet on the desk. He was sipping a Diet Coke gleaned, no doubt, from the apartment's refrigerator. Han was in a black suit and white shirt, no tie. The swift and silent Mr. Pak was standing next to the door. Suit and tie. Very stiff and formal.

Duff was surprised to see them, but didn't show it. "Hey, fellas. Did you come over to play *Settlers of Catan?*"

Han raised his Diet Coke in a toast to Duff. "You guys really aren't drinkers, are you? You didn't even have beer in the fridge. What kind of Chicago men are you if you don't even have a couple of cans of Miller Lite?"

"We're not Chicago men. I'm more of a Wisconsin and Canada man, and by *man* I mean an emotionally stunted boy in a man costume, and Abe's not really a man." Duff walked across the apartment to his bedroom and shut the door. He emerged a second later wearing basketball shorts and a Brewers t-shirt.

"If he's not a man, then what is he?"

"I'm not sure. I'm leaning toward sentient Jell-O in human form." Duff got a Diet Coke for himself and moved to his desk. He sat in his chair and mimicked Han's pose. He held up his can in a toast to Han, and then tilted it toward Mr. Pak.

"Your face looks like hell, brother."

Duff touched his swollen cheek. "It feels like hell. I guess it's a matching set, then."

"Let me apologize for Mr. Pak's zeal."

"Apology accepted." Duff took a long draw from his Diet Coke, belched, and idly scratched at his belly. "I'm guessing you didn't show up because you were looking for a third for three-handed Euchre."

"I came to say thank you." Han took his feet off Abe's desk. He leaned forward, elbows on his knees. "Your call to Archie Vang last night gave us time to move some things around, and the IRS was remarkably disappointed when they raided the warehouse today. You saved me a ton of headaches."

"Not a problem," said Duff.

"As a thank you, I wanted to let you know we didn't kill Larry, just as you asked. He won't ever walk normally again, but he's still alive. He's probably going to have to learn to write with his left hand, too. But...you know, it's better than not living, I guess. You probably won't see him in the city ever again, either. But he is definitely alive. You have my word on that."

"Abe will be thrilled to hear it."

Han stood to leave. "I just wanted to say thank you in person. You didn't have to make the call, but I'm grateful you did."

"The best way to thank me is with cash."

Han reached into the interior pocket of his black suit coat. "I've heard it can be done in other ways." He held out a slim plastic card.

Duff leaned forward and took it from him. "Culver's gift cards are always acceptable in this house."

"Should we need your services, we'll be in touch." Han moved toward the door. Mr. Pak opened it for him.

"Before you go, can I ask one question?"

Han paused. He did not turn back to face Duff. "Go ahead."

"Are you guys the ones moving guns and money right now? Was Pucillo right?"

Han finished the pilfered can of Diet Coke. He crushed it in his hand and tossed it underhanded into the recycling bin near the entry. "Mr. Duffy, it's probably best you don't ask questions about things you don't want to be involved in."

"Just Duff."

"As you say." Han walked out the door without another word.

Mr. Pak stepped out after him, but bowed slightly toward Duff before he shut the door.

The refusal to answer his question told Duff everything he needed to know about who was moving guns. He texted a note to Petey Pucillo's henchman, Dante. No fair saving one crime lord without letting the other crime lords know what they were up to. Neutrality was important.

Duff was left in the silence of the apartment. The stormfront had moved through the area briskly, and a light rain drummed against the apartment windows.

Duff checked his phone. No calls. No messages. Nothing. He plugged the phone into the charger on his desk and debated his evening's plans.

The Pirates were stinking up PNC Park on a terrible pitching day when the Cincinnati Reds were taking every advantage to hit bombs out of the park. It wasn't an appealing game by any stretch.

He had the Brewers deep in their campaign on his PlayStation, but had no desire to log into the machine and battle it out with the Cubs at that moment.

Clive Staples Duffy was bored.

Duff left his desk and went to his bedroom. Beneath his underwear in his bureau, one of the few places he knew Abe would never look for anything, he scrounged a foil-covered plastic tray the size of his palm. He grabbed his keys and left the apartment. He went outside and dodged the rain until he got to the rear of the building in the alley behind El Muro.

Under an awning by the dumpsters was an overturned industrial bucket that once held five gallons of manteca for the taquería's fryers. It was where some of Cesar Salazar's cooks liked to sit while they took a smoke break. As proof, the asphalt and gravel under the awning was littered with cigarette butts and a few empty cans of Modelo Especial.

Duff pulled back the foil from the tray and set it near the rear of the dumpster. He sat on the industrial lard bucket, which, coincidentally, was something his mother used to call him on occasion, and made a clicking noise with his tongue. Then he waited.

The rain fell over the cooling asphalt as night settled in. The sodium lamp in the alley buzzed high overhead and lit the alley with sickly blue light. Duff sat under the awning and watched rivulets of rain move slowly away from him as they ran down the street toward the sewer drain near the road.

After a few minutes, a wet, bedraggled orange cat crawled out from beneath the big restaurant dumpster. It was a large tom, muscled from years of struggle on the city's streets. It was missing half of one ear, was blind in one eye, and had a tail that had been broken years ago, healed poorly, and now had a 75-degree bend to it.

The cat crept to the little tray of cat food Duff had set out. It eyed Duff cautiously, judging the distance between him and it. When the cat was comfortable with the fact that Duff wasn't going to lunge at it and try to grab it, the poor thing began to eat.

Duff had noticed the cat from his window a few weeks ago. It took him seven long nights of putting out cat food and waiting nearby silently to get the animal to eat in his presence. Now, they had achieved a tentative friendship. The cat would bolt if Duff tried to pet it, but it seemed to accept Duff's presence with grudging aplomb.

"I bet you knew who killed Robert Bloch right away, didn't you?" Duff said to the animal.

The cat, of course, said nothing.

Duff watched it wolf down most of the food in the plastic tray. The back door to El Muro burst open, and the cat bolted, a blazing streak of orange disappearing into the darkness beyond the alley light.

Manuel Olvero, a young kid who had worked for Cesar for more than a year, was dragging out two full trash bags to the dumpster. He gave a little start when he saw Duff, but he nodded in greeting. "How you doing, Duff?"

"*Bueno*," said Duff. "*Y tu?*"

"Not too bad, hombre." Manuel tossed the trash into the dumpster. "You want a burrito?"

"Not tonight, but thanks for asking."

Manuel returned to the taquería, the heavy door banging closed behind him.

Duff turned his attention back to the rain. He knew from experience the cat was gone, self-preservation being more important than food. It might be back the next night. Or the next. Or it might never show itself again. The cat had its own agenda, and Duff respected that.

There was always a melancholy emptiness after a case, and Duff was bad at processing it. Instead, he shut down and drifted through life until the next one popped up. It was easier than trying to be a functioning human being.

Duff lost track of time. He might have sat in the alley for ten minutes or ten hours. He wasn't sure. The heat wave was officially extinguished by the storm, and the temperatures dropped into the sixties. The air felt normal again, manageable. The world around him seemed to take a deep breath and exhale, grateful for the respite from the heat.

Duff caught sight of movement out of the corner of his eye, low to the ground. He saw a creature crawling underneath the dumpster. Not the cat. Something else. Something different. It lumbered. It waddled. Duff immediately felt an affinity for it. He also lumbered and waddled.

A dirty gray-white thing crawled out from under the dumpster. It had an angular face and dark, beady black eyes. It approached the tray of cat food Duff had laid out and began to eat what the orange cat had abandoned.

Abe said no cats. He never said no opossums, though.

Duff made a clicking noise with his tongue. The opossum paused to glance at him. Duff gave the creature a little wave. "What's up, brother?"

The opossum ignored him and continued to eat.

Duff began to hum. He stopped long enough to ask the creature, "Do you like John Sebastian?"

Hot town, summer in the city...

Acknowledgments

Stephen King said the acknowledgments section of every novel is always the hardest one to write because it's the only part of the book where you have to tell the truth.

I have usually enjoyed writing this section because it is the last thing I write. The rest of it is done, edited, polished, and beta-read. It's ready to go.

This section...this section is variable.

I never really know what I'm going to write until I start writing it, and even then, it's kind of sketchy.

This is the fifth book in the Abe and Duff Mystery Series. While the sales of this series haven't been overwhelming, the people who have read it and understand my weird sense of humor seem to love it, and for that, I am eternally grateful.

When you write a book, you always set out to write the book you want to read. For me, that meant guys who were the antithesis of characters like Jack Reacher and Mitch Rapp. Nothing against Messrs. Reacher or Rapp *(I love those books!)*, but they're not me. I'm not winning any fistfights. I'm sniping anything from afar. I'm not turning cool phrases in the heat of the moment. And I'm damn sure not having hot shower sexy times with the girl who gets introduced to the hero in chapter two.

I wanted guys who looked like me, acted like me, and lost constantly at life like me. Lower-middle class schlubs without a lot to look forward to—those are my people. Those guys who have to listen to the Brewers game on the radio while they're at work because going to the ballpark is too expensive, those are my people.

Luckily, there are other people out there in this world who understand those guys, as well.

When people ask me what genre I write, I tell them it's soft-boiled, low-octane literature for people who like stupid banter. It's what I know.

Abe and Duff have surpassed my tiny dreams. Two television production companies have been interested in turning these clowns into small-screen detectives, and while nothing came of either of those two opportunities, it was still nice to feel like I'd made some noise for a bit.

The world of publishing is so gatekeeper-heavy, it gets discouraging to be rejected so often, so it's extra rewarding when people actually respond to what you're doing. Literary agents and traditional publishers might not be interested in what I'm putting out into the world, but at least a couple of TV guys have figured out what I'm doing doesn't totally suck, and they tried to make the rest of the world see that, too.

Still, I always hope for more. I'm guilty of the sin of hoping.

And as they say in British football: *It's the hope that kills you.*

But I'll continue to hope.

As usual, I'd like to thank my family: Kaija and Annika, for their support and for letting me get away with spending so much time typing, hiding in the office, and staring off into space. Thanks to my parents, who made me read as a child, even when I didn't feel like it. Thanks to my dad for believing the world was ready for a new Abe and Duff book. A nod of the head to my sister, who doesn't really do much to help this process (*she hasn't read anything I've written*), but enjoys being acknowledged, nonetheless. I'd also like to thank my in-laws, Karl and Tanya, for being fans. It helps to have a support system.

Thanks to Ann and Emily, Jack and Jena, Jordan, Ryan and Dusty, the gang at Primal Cue, Jerry at Culver's, Michelle, David and Mandy, Wendy, and all my other pals and fellow reprobates who believe in this stuff, even when I struggle.

Thanks to all the Madison-area writers who are kind enough to pretend I belong in the same ballpark with them (*even though I don't feel like I do most of the time*): Maggie Ginsberg, Cayce Osborne, Jerry Peterson, Christine DeSmet, Kathleen Ernst, Maddy Hunter, Beth Amos, Laura Anne Bird, Michael Popke, Bill Bodden, Alex Bledsoe, and the dozens of other people I'm forgetting at the moment. Thanks to Michael Allen Mallory, who's a Minnesotan, but still a cool guy despite that fact. And to Dana Storino, who is a friggin' FIB, but I don't hold it against her: thanks for being a cheerleader and talking me out of the imposter syndrome people in this business are so prone to having.

Do me a favor and buy some of their books, too.

Thanks, as well, to the home run hitters I still try to pattern myself after for all these years: Craig Johnson, CJ Box, Karin Slaughter, Carl Hiaasen, Michael Connelly, Matt Goldman, Douglas Preston and Lincoln Child, John Sandford, and the late, great Joseph Wambaugh. These people are the templates. Check out their books if you get a chance.

Thanks as well to the twenty or so true blievers who slum on my social media and tell me they're looking forward to the next adventure. Writing books is a thankless gig, so to get those occasional thank-yous from people who care about what you do is invaluable.

A thousand thank yous to the fine people at Mystery to Me in Madison, Frankie's Gifts in Theinsville, and Inkcap Books in Stoughton. It's difficult for small-timers like me to get books onto shelves, so any assistance is always appreciated. The support of local, independent bookstores is invaluable. I don't sell a ton of hard copies, but when I do, it's usually because someone in one of those stores recommended my work and hand-sold the copy.

I hope this book has lived up to their hype.

Lastly, most of this book was written in my little home office over the course of the last year and a half. My weird little walleyed Heeler-Corgi mix, Eddy, would lie by my side and snooze while I worked for much of my writing time. She was a great dog and enjoyed the simple things in life like walks, treats, and belly rubs.

As I was finishing the writing of the last chapter or two of this book, Eddy developed a serious autoimmune disorder, developed dire complications as a result of that, and we unfortunately had to let her cross the Rainbow Bridge. Her picture now sits on the right corner of my desk, but it's not the same as having her at my feet.

It's always tough to lose those little critters, particularly when not due to old age. She passed only a few months shy of her tenth birthday. She was with us for almost nine years.

While I didn't dedicate this book to her, mostly because her reading habits were terrible, she will forever be an inspiration to me for so many things.

If you read *Bought the Farm*, the fourth book in the Abe & Duff series, you will remember that Duff made friends with a dog in one of the scenes. He wanted that dog to be a detective dog. That moment was directly inspired by Eddy.

Dogs are better than people. Duff knew that.

And Eddy was one of the best dogs.

She is greatly missed.

Thanks for reading.

May 2025
Sun Prairie, Wis.

About the Author

Sean Patrick Little is a writer, speaker, editor, educator, and general literary dude from Sun Prairie, Wisconsin.

He is the author of the best-selling Survivor Journals series and the critically praised Abe & Duff mystery series. He has also authored one book in the Shelby Ree mystery series, a space opera called Strange Angels, and is always at work on the next project.

He holds a BA in Broadcast Journalism from the University of Wisconsin-Whitewater, a BFA in Fiction Writing from Winona State University, and a master's degree in Education from St. Mary's University of Minnesota.

He has been a teacher, a paint salesman, and a pizza delivery guy. He regularly teaches writing and publishing seminars at libraries and book clubs whenever asked.

Little is a member of the Wisconsin Writer's Association, the Authors Guild, the Mystery Writers of America, and Sisters in Crime.

...And if any of them ever find out about it, they're going to be quite upset.

Other Books by Sean Patrick Little

The Abe and Duff Mystery Series
    The Single Twin
    Fouth and Wrong
    Where Art Thou
    Bought the Farm

*The Shelby Ree Mystery Series**
    Welcome to Meskousing

The Survivor Journals
    After Everyone Died
    Long Empty Roads
    All We Have
    We Still Remain**

Project Archangel
    Strange Angels

* *Welcome to Meskousing* is a spin-off series from the Abe & Duff Mystery Series

** *We Still Remain* is set in the same world as The Survivor Journals, but exists as a standalone novel.